Blunder

"If what you say is true, our efforts will have been a total waste," Sanders said slowly.

Gray stared at the DISA director in shock. Wilson's work had shown that DISA's approach to destroying what Orion held had a fatal flaw. Yet Sanders was refusing to admit the truth—that his staff had blundered.

With a fragment of his attention, Gray noticed, as they stepped outside the building, that the demonstrators had disappeared; mainly, he was trying to think of a way to get through Sanders's barrier of egotism. Wilson was the key—his work would have to make Sanders realize—

The shockwave of a blast knocked them to the ground and sent bricks and debris flying.

When Gray recovered, he looked at the lab building and felt a cold tremor of fear. A quarter of the building had been blown apart— Wilson's section!

A Cold Wind from Orion

A NOVEL BY

Scott Asnin

A Del Rey Book

BALLANTINE BOOKS • NEW YORK

A Cold Wind from Orion is a work of fiction, and all opinions, premises, and speculations herein are the author's own and do not represent the view of any corporation or government agency

A Del Rey Book
Published by Ballantine Books

Copyright © 1980 by Scott Asnin

All rights reserved under International and Pan-American Copyright Conventions. Published in the United States by Ballantine Books, a division of Random House, Inc., New York, and simultaneously in Canada by Random House of Canada, Limited, Toronto, Canada.

Library of Congress Catalog Card Number: 80-66167

ISBN 0-345-28498-4

Manufactured in the United States of America

First Edition: September 1980

Cover art by Atila Hega

For Roxanne and Jim,
and the Magnolia valley

The author wishes to acknowledge Tom Garrison and Dr. James Hardy for their respective encouragement and contribution. And Wyatt Underwood, who inspired the title.

Prologue

Inside the third cylinder the temperature variation was entering its 56,586th night cycle, and would quickly drop to the cold-side extreme of −174°C. There would be the usual stresses and strains on the surrounding support structure, and from points further away, but no sounds—not a creak or other audible evidence of contraction—would bear witness to that. In this place, development of the auditory sense would be superfluous.

Adaptation had moved in other directions. There had been no climate control for over ten years, and the intensity of the day-night fluctuation of 360°C produced more useful genetic responses.

Beyond the cylinder were two layers of titanium membrane, then a network of structural trusswork which held the other cylinders firmly in its rectangular pattern. A heavier aluminum shell enclosed it all. The mass within Cylinder Three had years earlier concentrated near a hairline fault at one end of the rounded inner wall, and was now very close to infiltrating the membranes, aided by its well-developed corrosive characteristic.

Outside of the still-glistening compartments there was apparent void. With the exception of the distant point light sources and constantly phasing bright disks, each having its own effect on the mass, it was a deceptively black and empty background.

But this background was alive with a continual flux of cosmic and gamma radiation, the garbled radio waves of other galaxies, plasma streams from solar bursts, and constantly shifting gravitational perturbations, all of which had provided the assembly a highly energetic, dynamic environment. An intensely volatile soup. The contents of Cylinder Three had been required to adjust to these extraordinary conditions. For years there had been stimulus, and response to stimulus. Adaptations through hundreds of thousands of generations. Mendel's law had been first followed precisely, replicated systematically, then broken just as systematically. By now the process had achieved its own peculiar perfection.

Nowhere in proximity was there evident even a spark of rudimentary thought. Nothing to cry out. No possibility of perceiving those laws of physics—conventional, nuclear, or relativistic—which had created the condition, shaped its cycle, and would make deterministic the next phase.

There was instead only a cold, silent wind as the assembly swept an invisible path through even more invisible fields 330 kilometers above the blue planet below.

Chapter One

Michikamau Lake, Newfoundland, seemed an unlikely place to make headline news. No one but a few lonely Labrador trappers had heard of it until that evening in January when Cosmos 1134 spewed chunks of its blackened, radioactive body over the cold northern tundra. A few startled moose felt spacecraft fragments shatter into the icy lakebed. A day later the geological survey team that reported a fiery shower of meteors the night before would stumble over melted craters in the snow to find still another scattered collection of Soviet satellite technology.

Gregory Sanders put down the evening edition of the *Post*, which was already carrying an article featuring the predicted impact ellipse stretching over most of North America. The GODS Effect was becoming more than a nuisance. It seemed that every other month now something was dropping in, and the Russians still didn't appear to give a damn what they let come down. There had been the disastrous impact into Marseilles, with no communications, no prior warning, nothing. Luckily, the others had struck in remote areas. He wondered again why the Soviets hadn't taken better precautions, provided controlled entries, done a neater job of it. Our side had at least managed some spacecraft control—had even brought a couple back via the Shuttle, until Congress clamped the funding lid on tight.

Sanders returned his attention to the *Post* article, and read further. The Russians had apparently tried to guide this vehicle in with its remaining bit of attitude-control gas. But one of their thrusters had stuck in the *on* position. He imagined the condition—one thruster firing continually off the center of gravity until all fuel was gone and the satellite was tumbling out of control like an insect driven mad by a blast of bug spray. The Russians were still, after all their scientific progress, five years behind us in technological sophistication. Sanders resigned himself to the fact that it was necessary to maintain that gap.

He stared unfocused out the multipaned bay window of his Georgetown study. It was a misty, cold evening in Washington. Snow was forecast tomorrow. He thought about the billions that had been diverted from otherwise useful space funding since the decade began, solely to avoid damage and loss from the General Orbit Decay Syndrome. It was something that all space activity of the sixties and seventies had conveniently overlooked, and the debt was now being paid—by the United States, by Russia, by the European agencies, and by forty-seven unfortunate Frenchmen who had been given not a hint that their hospital was at point zero of a Cosmos impact trajectory. Since Skylab had fallen, Sanders' own organization, the Defense Intelligence Space Agency, had lost three surveillance satellites, while USSA, the civilian branch, had seven spacecraft come down. Half of them had been guided to safe impacts; the rest fortunately hit sparsely populated areas, or water. Three of DISA's most sophisticated research satellites had been saved, thanks to reluctant congressional approval to rescue them with the manned Shuttle. Not a comforting record—just a lucky one.

Sanders counted the Russian losses in his mind. As director of DISA, his perceptions were bound by the mathematics of any problem. His thoughts organized themselves into the patterns necessary to transform military and CIA activity into an integrated strategy for operating the U.S. space defense network. He recalled that the Russians' problems began a year before Skylab fell, with the number of Cosmos losses accelerating into the eighties as the GODS Effect reached its peak. They had lost nineteen, as best as he could remember. This Cosmos would make an even twenty. How much their intelligence capability had thus far been affected by the problem the CIA could accurately estimate. Many had already been replaced, but gaps in their network were beginning to show up. He looked again at the paper, searching for a specific reference, and quickly found it. This latest problem spacecraft was reported by the Soviets to be Cosmos 1134—they had even generously provided its original orbital parameters, now that the information no longer mattered. Sanders' orderly thoughts scanned his mental dossier of Soviet satellite missions. There seemed to be something significant about that number, this orbit . . . some important connection was struggling to the surface.

Suddenly he knew.

At the same moment the mental alarms were triggered, a sweeping anxiety started deep in his stomach and washed over his entire body. With some effort he managed to calm himself. The message now was formed in full clarity. Cosmos 1134 was monitoring the Orion Platform. All the grim details were suddenly at hand, even though so many years had passed. After the Skylab mission failed to resolve its problem, DISA managed to lift Orion two hundred kilometers higher to prolong its orbital life, and the Cosmos spy followed it up. They were nearly in the same orbit.

Now Cosmos 1134 was falling. And what was onboard the Orion Platform could never be allowed to reenter Earth's atmosphere.

Sanders lurched out of the study to the hall telephone. He called Chris Brookhaven, director of the U.S. Space Administration. His words were controlled, insistent. A closed meeting with the Congressional Committee on Science and Space must be called immediately. In thirty minutes the two agency directors hastily put together the story that Brookhaven would have to present to an unsympathetic and skeptical group of congressmen.

The following afternoon was the earliest they could pull the meeting together. As the members of the committee began to file in to their places behind the rounded conference table, Sanders found himself already feeling uneasy. The little sleep he had gotten the night before didn't help, but the primary cause of his concern was the man who was assembling his notes at the speaker's podium. Chris Brookhaven was at best an uncertainty in the hectic planning and development that had to be done, and done perfectly, over the next few months. With tension increasing and the pressures he foresaw coming in from all sides, Sanders doubted his colleague had the strength to keep things together for the duration. And Brookhaven's discomfort with their cover story, although it would be carefully suppressed before the committee, was still apparent to the DISA director. Or was he imagining that?

Brookhaven began smoothly and kept the early part of his talk relatively technical and dry. As they had planned. The Committee on Science and Space liked to think itself scientific, but was actually comprised of people whose scientific background was possibly one step above the layman's. The chairman, Duane Clark of California, alone could claim any solid familiarity with astronautics. Clark had been with Aerospace Sciences in Redondo Beach when the space program emerged during the sixties, until he was elected a Republican representative from Orange County. The rest received most of their knowledge from *Aviation Week* or other space journals, supplemented by frequent junkets to the space centers in Houston, Pasadena, Sunnyvale, and Maryland—and publicity engagements with the Shuttle astronauts during election years.

Except for Clark, and Alan Benton of Wisconsin, they were a dull bunch and rarely had anything to contribute. Benton thought he had a mandate from his constituents to protect them from everything, especially from the wild ideas of ivory-tower types who constantly tried to bilk the public with funding requests for such unrewarding projects as a reconnaissance mission to Saturn's sixth moon, Titan.

Sanders observed the proceedings unobtrusively from the back of the room as the USSA director began the briefing. Brookhaven shuffled his notes and cleared his throat.

"Gentlemen," he began, "this meeting concerns the

rescue of another crucial bit of our space hardware, and although I realize we at USSA are under strict orders not to request money for this type of mission, I believe you will see how urgent this particular situation is." Remembering he hadn't bothered to enforce security, he interrupted himself: "Before I get into the details, I'd like the guard to verify credentials of all those present. This needs to be a closed session, and I'd like all unnecessary persons and all press cleared out."

The sergeant-at-arms quickly passed among those in the room, checking clearance levels. Brookhaven gave a nod or shake of the head as each was checked and announced, and all but Sanders and two of the committee's clerical staff, besides the panel, were quickly escorted from the conference room. One Capitol correspondent appealed to Chairman Clark, but was firmly turned down and ushered out.

Satisfied that the hearing could now be held in relative security, Brookhaven continued: "I'd first like to review the status of our orbit decay problem and give you a brief refresher on its history. Some of the members are new to the committee, and may be interested in knowing what we actually mean by the GODS Effect. Do you agree, Mr. Chairman?"

Clark gave him a go-ahead. Two of the ten on the committee had only recently come onboard following their election, and although the effects of the General Orbit Decay Syndrome were well known, the physics of the situation was still something of a mystery to the layman. So Brookhaven began his history lesson:

"As you all know, many of our Earth-orbiting spacecraft have experienced premature orbital decay, and have reentered the atmosphere much earlier than we ever anticipated. This has become a significant problem to the space agencies since the late seventies. We now know there are two primary celestial factors which have contributed to this."

Brookhaven pushed a silent button, the lights dimmed, and an unseen projectionist focused his first slide on the screen to the right of the committeeroom. The image presented a series of graphs, the type of technical data that invariably made the committee cringe, although they went through this with every scientific briefing.

"My first picture shows a history of the solar cycle, or sunspot activity, from 1900 until the present time." The slide presented a series of undulating, roller-coaster curves, showing all the high and low periods of sunspots and solar flares during the century. "Every eleven years or so, solar activity progresses through a complete cycle—that is, it starts on a normal level, decreases to a minimum, then grows to a peak intensity toward the end before it resumes the next wave. During the peak, the sun puts out a heightened flow of energy, actually a flow of radiation, called the solar wind. It's known to scientists as plasma and varies in strength as the cycle varies. As you can see, we are now approaching the end of the peak in the current cycle, which began late in 1979 and has sustained itself longer than usual. This effect causes a number of problems, like interruptions in radio and TV communications, but most specifically it heats up the upper atmosphere. Now, when the atmosphere heats up, it expands and at the same time becomes more dense. And the denser atmosphere slows down any satellite that comes near it. Of course, when a satellite slows down it also loses altitude. Very much like turning on a small retrorocket that works gradually over a long time. That's the first half of the problem."

Brookhaven paused to make sure the point had gotten through. Clark helped him out. "This means, Chris, that all our low orbital satellites are sinking—their orbits slowed down by gradually entering an expanded and thickened atmospheric layer?"

"Yes. Fortunately, most of our spacecraft are up so high, thousands of kilometers, that the effect is insignificant. And another group is small enough that the increased drag is barely felt. If nothing else intervened, our problems would be less severe. That leads to the other half of the syndrome—what the astrophysicists have called the Grand Alignment."

The slide advance was pressed, and the first image with the Sun cycles was replaced by a picture of the solar system, planets circling about the Sun, as found in any eighth-grade science text. But the solar system was strangely unbalanced.

"As you can see by the caption, this illustrates the solar system in 1982. Notice that the four great planets, Jupiter, Saturn, Uranus, and Neptune, which represent 99.4 percent of the mass in the system besides the Sun, are all aligned on one side. They are now slowly leaving that position. But what happened during this rare event, which occurs only once every one hundred and eighty years, is that those planets created an imbalance in gravitational pull on all the smaller planets nearer the Sun—especially Mars and Earth, to a lesser degree on Venus and Mercury. It's similar to the effect the Moon has on the Earth's tides. This lineup of mass had a profound effect on earthquake activity during the last few years, by pulling the great continental shelves, tectonic plates, into one another to an extent we now have recently and dramatically witnessed. What we also know, and can calculate very accurately, is how vulnerable our satellites have been to the phenomenon. Many of their orbits were tugged around by the mass imbalance, and at precisely the worst time—during the peak of the solar cycle. They have literally been pulled down into a significantly denser atmosphere by the gravity imbalance. The combination of these two conditions has become referred to as the General Orbit Decay Syndrome—the GODS Effect."

Representative Benton finished his summary for him: "Which explains why so many of our satellites, along with those of the Europeans and Soviets, have come crashing down over our heads in the last five years."

"Right—it's been a problem for all of us. The question we're left with involves identifying which spacecraft are currently in trouble, and estimating exactly when those will come down. Our prediction methods are much improved today over the limited knowledge available in the late seventies, because we now have calibrated the GODS Effect fairly precisely. There is also the benefit of having thirty—thirty-one with the last Cosmos fall—data points to help us model the phenomenon. My last slide shows what the situation looks like for our set of problem satellites."

A third picture replaced the imbalanced solar system with a scattering of points on a two-dimensional plot, where superimposed contours were labeled by quarters of years. Brookhaven took up his lecture: "This chart represents those satellites, of all U.S. agencies, that are now within the critical decay region. Their various altitudes, inclinations, and shapes determine the range of the scatter. The contour lines you see overlying the array very simply indicate when they are predicted to come down."

Benton broke in again: "You mean we are going to lose that many more? I count twenty or so!"

"There are twenty-four. As you know, we began the task of saving those which were more important, expensive, or irreplaceable. But funding was cut to the point where we were forced to give the program up."

"True, but Jesus, that's a hell of a waste. How many of these are actually expected to impact the Earth?"

"Only a couple. The rest should disintegrate on entry."

Chairman Clark turned to Benton. "I guess we have to live with that, Alan. President Lansing has made the decision, so our hands are tied. We simply have to absorb the losses or replace those that must be replaced." He paused a moment, then continued: "Okay, Chris, we all understand the situation now —what's the point of this urgent, and closed-door, meeting?"

"It relates to one of the points on this chart." Brookhaven located his electronic pointer, and beamed an arrow to the screen. "At this particular orbital condition we have a leftover hardware item from the Skylab project." The pointer fell within the lowest contour line. "Although Skylab came down years ago, this particular piece of equipment has outlasted the station because of its smaller mass and smoother profile. It was a trailed module—deployed from the station and put out at a safe distance of one kilometer. The existence of this experiment has never been made public, for reasons which will soon become obvious." He waited a second.

Clark obliged: "To this committee, I presume?"

"Yes. The secrecy limitation has now officially lapsed, but you'll no doubt agree it should be reestablished. During the mid-seventies, the administration asked us to perform a classified experiment, principally to assure the military we had the same capability as the Soviets." He took a heavy breath before going on with the deceit. "We were directed to carry up and deploy, during the seventy-four Skylab visit, a space prototype nuclear reactor. It was all handled in secret. Only the President, a few at the Pentagon, the Nuclear Regulatory Commission, and the necessary individuals at USSA were aware of the nature of the package. The Skylab astronauts weren't even told. They knew only the details of the deployment sequence—although by the end of their training, and after deployment, they probably could have guessed."

Benton reacted predictably: "You realize this is all, of course, in complete violation of every position we've taken on nuclear material in Earth orbit! For ten years we've complained to the Soviets for doing that, and all the time we had this thing in orbit. I find that incredible!"

"I agree, but we really had no choice but to go along—which brings me to the urgency of this particular USSA request." Brookhaven paused. "The reactor will be coming down within six months. For obvious political reasons, we can't acknowledge the truth. So we must dispose of the reactor, and do so with a minimum of publicity."

Benton was angry. "Jesus Christ. And you have a plan for doing just that, I suppose, that will only cost us ten billion in old currency?"

"I have, and it won't be that much. A few hundred million at most."

Then Clark broke in: "Before we get into this, just what are we facing here, Chris? What are the dangers? Is there any chance the package will disintegrate during entry? And if not, can we guide it into the ocean?"

"No to the last two. It's too massive to burn up.

And there is no control onboard. It is just a large chunk of nuclear material."

"And what happens if we get impact?"

"Its terminal velocity will be eleven hundred kilometers per hour. If we continue to be lucky, as we have been with our other spacecraft, a 98 percent probability exists that the crash point will be in some harmless place. If our luck runs out, it might be another Marseilles incident. Two hundred pounds of Uranium 235 at that velocity crashing into any inhabited area would be devastating."

Clark: "An explosion?"

"Not likely—but possible."

"Damn, this is ugly." Clark reinforced their displeasure. Then silence prevailed for a long moment as a few heads shook in quiet disbelief. "We, of course, have to go to the President with this immediately. Or have you told him?"

"Not yet. We want you to have all the data before he's presented with our solution."

"Wait a minute, goddammit." Benton's face was now flaming red. "First of all, let's make clear that this has all been handled in a totally unethical, immoral manner, and the facts make liars of us all. That this committee has only now been made aware of the affair is unbelievable. We hear of it a few months before a possible disaster! But even worse, didn't your people at USSA think of this potential problem when you put the damned thing up? I'm beginning to wonder what good all the money we pour into your research accomplishes if it comes to this. I know, we've heard the arguments before: You weren't aware of the seriousness of the problem back then. But, Christ, man, if you're putting up stuff this dangerous you should have considered that it might come down someday."

Brookhaven knew he had a rebuttal to that point of view, which applied regardless of the particular issue. "Yes, we were considering the problem of decay, and even recognized that someday we'd have to deal with it. But at the time the someday seemed more like 1990. Now, as to why our predictions were in error: As you know, Mr. Benton, all our studies have been severely constrained by very tight space budgeting. All along we've warned Congress that if you continue to squeeze our research money to nothing and still expect spectacular results, there will be important, sometimes crucial, study areas that fall through a crack and disappear. We've argued this point hundreds of times, with very little success. It always comes down to a matter of what gets the immediate job done, the satellite up, the men on the Moon. A matter of expedience. I guess we have all been moderately lucky—so far we've only lost a space station, ten satellites, and three astronauts."

Benton wasn't buying the argument. "With anything as potentially dangerous as nuclear material in space, you surely could have taken the necessary precautions."

"We took precautions. The only failure was our inability to accurately account for the intensity of this solar cycle, and our neglect of the planetary alignment. If we had had time, we might have gotten closer. Keep in mind that this all occurred during the space crunch of the mid-seventies, a time when we experienced massive layoffs of scientists and engineers. A time when everyone was apparently satiated and bored by space spectaculars. Those were very lean years—"

"All right, Chris, your complaint is noted," Clark interrupted. "So we now are faced with a six-month deadline. What do you offer us?"

Brookhaven nervously shuffled his notes, then glanced briefly toward Sanders. He would have to be very careful with the rest. "First, we will need a special authorization to modify the Space Tug to be compatible with this nuclear package. That shouldn't cost more than one hundred and fifty million—only fifteen million in new dollars. In simple language, our plan is to fly the Tug to the reactor, perform some fashion of hard dock, then, using the Tug propulsion, boost the assembly into an orbit sufficiently high to remove it from the GODS region. We should be able to lift it nine hundred kilometers, which would secure it virtually forever."

"Well, that sounds simple enough. Now, how do we get the Tug up there?" Clark asked.

"That's the second part. We will need to take over the next Shuttle flight—that's the April launch."

"And give up its planned mission?"

"Yes, probably. The orbit we require isn't compatible for a shared venture."

"So let me see, that represents another two hundred million?"

"It's unavoidable."

"What else?" Clark asked.

"We need a specially trained crew. The currently assigned April crew will need to be replaced by our special team—the one assigned to handle military deployment. In connection with that, you need to be aware that there will be some involvement with DISA. Their expertise must be integrated into this particular mission."

Benton looked out into the room and fixed his gaze on Sanders. "So, Mr. Sanders, I suppose this is what brings you here today. You've surely interrupted your busy schedule defending outer space to sit in on a relatively peaceful civilian mission."

The director of DISA had been carefully taking in every word of the presentation and was now feeling a bit more at ease. He felt that his counterpart had presented a fairly tight story. So far Brookhaven had resisted being pushed into difficult corners, and things were holding together well.

His reply to Benton was calm, controlled: "DISA is here on an advisory basis only. We were involved with the original nuclear deployment, so there are technical details that only our agency can supply. We might also share some of our security measures with Chris on this one."

"I'm sure that DISA will enjoy infiltrating even the peaceful side of the space program, given the opportunity."

No response by Sanders was needed, and Benton left it at that, satisfied that he had been able to take at least a small shot at the DISA chief.

The agency had frustrated the committee for years, since its creation in the seventies. The committee had absolutely no control over DISA, a situation that it deeply resented. With USSA they could play God and make all its life and death decisions through their budget recommendations. But Sanders' group was untouchable, like the CIA and Pentagon operations out of which it was born. When DISA needed anything, the request was buried deep behind closed doors. Most of their projects were so secret that the congressmen weren't aware of them until the hardware was already in space accomplishing their clandestine missions. Whenever he had a chance, Benton tried to slip in a dagger between a joint in the armor.

But Sanders knew the game well. He didn't give a damn. As long as his position was protected, he'd let them relieve their petty frustrations. There was always much more at stake, and such was the case now. At this point all he wanted was for Brookhaven to wrap up the matter and to extract himself without further discussion. The committee had bought the cover story, and that was all that was necessary.

Clark was ready to get down to business. He had heard enough.

"How soon do you need the money turned on?"

"Well, the preliminary study funds should be available by next week. We need to get moving toward the hardware design just as soon as possible. There just isn't any time for delay."

"Yes, we have that picture. We'll of course need all the details you've assembled already, and a more comprehensive outline of your plans. Do you have something we can look at now? A package of design information, cost estimates, etc.?"

Brookhaven stumbled. "Uh, not quite ready with that. We have a team working on it today, and you should have it in a day or two."

"Doesn't sound like you guys have it together on this thing. Tell us just exactly when you discovered, or remembered, this urgent problem."

The conversation was becoming tricky. They hadn't worked that issue out the night before. Brookhaven improvised as best he could. "Unfortunately, it was brought to my attention only yesterday. A routine report from satellite tracking. They signal us anytime a space object falls within our final altitude contour—to alert us that it is in jeopardy. Usually we ignore the minor objects—the space junk. When I read their report, I noticed the original orbital position of the object, and—well, something rang a bell. So I got out the files and realized we had a problem."

"You actually mean we were that close to overlooking this entirely?" Benton exclaimed.

"I didn't overlook it."

"It sounds very close to me."

Clark and Benton huddled with the rest in a quiet conference, then Clark spoke: "All right, Chris, we'll talk this over and give you our answer in a couple of days. We don't appreciate the timing, though your case was convincing. I'm sure we'll have some of our own directions to give you after presenting this to Lansing. Make damn sure we have all the background material on our desks by tomorrow."

Brookhaven thanked them, then gathered his notes into a folder. He hurriedly left the chamber. Sanders rose more casually, followed him out to the steps at a discreet distance, then caught him on the walkway outside. It was getting dark, and the day's overcast sky was beginning to drizzle a light, very cold rain.

"Chris, you did well. Very professional. I think they'll buy it."

Brookhaven looked at his accomplice, the dark, graying hair and piercing eyes, almost a stereotype of the typical CIA operative. It made him uneasy to even be around the man. Like dealing with the Gestapo. But it couldn't be avoided. "Thanks for the encouragement."

"You know we have a lot to work out, and soon, don't you?"

He knew. "All right, but not here, not now. After that performance I need to take the pressure off. I'm picking up my secretary in town at six. Let's get together tomorrow."

"No, this can't wait. Stop by my house later tonight," Sanders insisted. "We can't let things start slipping this early."

"Christ, okay. But it will be late."

"I'll stay up. And relax. DISA will cover you completely. Certainly no perjury can be proven."

"You're trying to make it sound so simple. There are ethics involved here, you know. Maybe you don't. I'm misleading the same group that controls the funding of our projects from now till 2001." Brookhaven moved closer to Sanders and whispered, "I'm damned sure not comfortable playing the game your people know so well."

"I guess we operate that way naturally. You can learn."

"Right. Look what it did for us in the seventies. I'm not used to covert activities."

"Usually it's not terminal. Tonight, then, about ten?"

"How about eleven?"

"Ten. I want you with a clear head."

"Jesus, am I really still involved with this mess?"

"If we keep our stories together, there's nothing to worry about. But we have to do that, Chris, without any holes."

"Okay, I'll try for ten. Now I have to go."

Brookhaven went off into a sea of parked automobiles across the street, Sanders toward another parking lot. His turbo-diesel Mercedes was wedged between two older, domestic, gas-powered monsters. He checked the body for scratches and door dents, his usual compulsion. Satisfied everything was still intact, he got inside and pulled out into the evening traffic, headed for Georgetown. The screen was turned on to the Washington news station in reflex action. He tried not to miss anything, but today he was especially interested.

And there it was. The first report on the five o'clock news. Cosmos 1134, a Russian spy satellite carrying a nuclear reactor, had crashed during last night's pass over Canada. Satellite trackers in Colorado followed its descent through the atmosphere and determined that the impact point was most likely in an isolated part of Newfoundland. No reports were coming in from Moscow—they were keeping completely silent. U.S. officials reiterated that although the satellite did carry Uranium 235, it had not been expected to explode either during entry or on impact. There was no immediate cause for alarm. The Russians had assured us of that.

"They hope." Sanders forced a smile and muttered at his dashboard screen. The news continued. A further report from a Canadian geological survey party camped in a remote outpost near Michikamau Lake may have helped pinpoint the exact location. Our Satellite Impact Investigation Team was being flown to Goose Bay, Labrador, to begin search operations. Nothing more could be learned at this time.

The Washington drizzle was turning to snow. It would be a long drive home that evening. Sanders lit his pipe as the Mercedes slowed to a crawl.

Chapter Two

The morning sky was a slate-gray overcast, typical of the country this far north in January. There was nothing much below but frozen ground and still forests. Breaking through the cold silence and flying low over the expanse of spruce and white birch, a sleek military helicopter of the Mikhail Mil 20 class appeared out of the west, skimming not more than three hundred meters above the trees. Inside, the only passenger was preoccupied with the unpleasant business he had been ordered to attend to during the next week. The stark landscape below went by totally unnoticed.

He had seen it before, many times. On less important trips he would watch it streak by, perhaps even daydream a bit. To this man the area was a wasteland, and why the facilities had been built in such a barren place occasionally led him to wish he could transfer to some operation in the south, near the sea. But of course that was never done. If his assignment were ever to change, he would be sent north and east—far east, into even more isolated regions than his destination this morning.

The pilot spoke, pointing to the sprawl of buildings and towers approaching in the distance just outside Novosibirsk, Siberian center of Soviet space operations. A minute later they were on the outskirts, above ramps, runways, blockhouses. The copter banked right, and in an instant was fluttering directly over the central part of the complex, above rows of sterile gray concrete-and-glass structures whose only color came from the flashes of red stars above the entrance to each office building and laboratory. As the pilot located his target—a circular slab in front of one of the dominant buildings—a huge granite wall in the center of the walkway between rows of labs came into view, the enormous portrait of the bearded Lenin etched into its front. This, too, had little effect on the visitor. After all, Anatole Karenov was fifty-five, too old to still be a revolutionary.

He gathered a few papers into his briefcase and tugged the shoulder harness tightly. Quietly and efficiently, the craft hovered above the circle, then settled onto the pavement. Side doors opened on both sides and he stepped out onto the tarmac. Two officers greeted him immediately, both saluting. He returned the greeting from the Soviet Army lieutenants, and the three of them walked stiffly to the entrance of the nearest building, which had engraved in Russian script over the doorway *Peoples' Center for Soviet Spaceflight*. Just inside the doors, a continuous round desk counter blocked further passage. Another uniformed officer behind the desk nodded at Karenov, who, before he was asked, quickly produced an official-looking folder from the briefcase he held. The guard read it carefully, then summoned another uniformed man.

"Please show Comrade General Karenov to the Special Project Control Center. He is cleared for full access." Part of the desk counter slid aside, and Karenov was led through it into the lobby, onto an elevator, up ten levels, and into a foyer protected by two more guards. His escort presented the set of papers, which were not studied as carefully at this checkpoint. The two stepped aside, saluted the general, and a large metal door marked with hammer and sickle moved silently into the wall.

Karenov entered alone and the door closed behind him. The routine was not unusual for any crisis situation, and every Soviet failure was a crisis. The general walked along a dim corridor illuminated only by the green and red lights flashing from rows of consoles deep within the mission control room. He proceeded past the technicians huddled around their screens, headsets on, and glanced up at the display of orbits on the long screen overhead showing the path of Cosmos 1134 over the continents and oceans, with a highlighted ellipse stretching across North America. Then on to the offices perched in a balcony above the control-room pit.

Coming to a door marked *Spaceflight Control— Director M. Scherensky,* he knocked twice and entered. Marya Scherensky, an attractive woman whose hair was a distinguished dark gray though she was fifteen years younger than Karenov, was poring over a desk full of charts and computer printouts spread before her, which included plots of the orbits Karenov had seen on the overhead display in the control room.

Scherensky looked up, startled. She forced a greeting, barely disguising her distaste for the political interference she knew was to come.

"Yes, good morning, General. Please be seated." She pointed to a visitor's chair in front of her desk. "You see, we are all very much involved today. The news is not good, but with luck—"

"Director Scherensky," Karenov interrupted formally, "the Politburo has prepared a statement to be released to the foreign press. Your name will be assigned to the statement." He did not sit down, but instead put his briefcase down on the chair, opened it, and removed a yellow typewritten sheet. "We have known one another for some time now. The relationship has been for the most part satisfactory. But now I must be frank, since I represent the view of the State."

Scherensky cringed. Would she be asked to take all blame personally and resign the directorship? Yes, it would be their chance to brand her incompetent, an enemy, denounce her as a member of the Alternative Party. She knew how it could go. Even since the Emergence, many were still disappearing into obscurity, with much less justification than she had given. And the KGB had been watching her for a long time. Where would they send her? To some menial position on the railroad or to the oil fields in the east? It could be anywhere.

"The statement reads very simply: 'A report from Director Marya Scherensky, of Cosmos Spaceflight Control: "There is no possibility of danger to the surface environment as the result of mechanical problems on board Cosmos 1134. At 2240 GMT, the spacecraft entered the atmosphere above North America and ceased to exist." ' "

Scherensky waited for the rest. Karenov looked up from the copy of the news release. Almost afraid to speak but forced to regardless, Marya meekly asked, "Is that all?"

"Yes, Comrade, that is all for the public. My message to convey to you personally, and to your staff, is that this matter is an unfortunate negative entry on your record with the State. The continued failure of the Space Planning Committee under your direction to dispose of the nuclear material safely, and quietly, has been regarded as a serious error. You must understand that your performance will be on trial for the foreseeable future. Any continuation of this problem will of course not be tolerated. There will be a formal inquiry, for which I am responsible. Your complete and detailed plan to avoid such failures in the future will be prepared for me to return to the Kremlin by week's end. The plans must be uncontestable."

Scherensky muttered, "Yes, General. My people are already at work . . ."

Again Karenov was not interested in the reply. "You of course realize the embarrassment. We are again forced into cooperation with the Americans and Canadians. That is bad enough. But as you know, since the Marseilles business the Kremlin has agreed to pay reparations and the costs of any land search. And, of course, there are again likely to be fragments large enough to provide U.S. intelligence with the information to develop the design and purpose of our satellite." His voice was now raised to the level of an angry reprimand. "What disturbs us most, Comrade, is that 1134 was involved with monitoring an extremely important American military craft. Continual surveillance of that vehicle was considered the highest priority. Now that is lost. Frankly, we fully expected your replacement of former Chief Duryanov after his Marseilles disgrace would have eliminated all such problems. This was no time to allow such an error."

Scherensky nodded blankly. She was at their mercy. So far this verbal punishment was relatively mild. She knew there would be more. Things would happen, perhaps gradually. Her summer cottage on the Black Sea would be given to another. And with it her base of contact, her refuge away from the watchful eyes of the KGB. What hadn't been said, merely implied, would hurt deeply.

"You will have the report to me on time, Comrade." It was an order. "I will not be back to see you until then. There are other details of this situation which I must attend to in other laboratories." He was ready to leave, closing the briefcase.

Glancing down, Karenov said, "The press statement will be made within the hour. At least the timing is good. It will come after the evening television news in the West, when most are involved with other matters." Finally, he looked directly at Scherensky. "You must hope the debris does not cause great damage."

Karenov turned and left the room, closing the great door behind with a solid *clunk*. Scherensky slumped in her chair, then reached around to the bookshelves behind her, shelves filled with hundreds of notebooks and technical documents and with framed citations from the Party honoring her many contributions to the State. Opening a drawer below, she fumbled inside until her hand closed on a cold bottle she saved for these times when her nerves were stretched to the breaking point. She poured herself two ounces of strong Ukrainian vodka and emptied the glass in one long swallow.

As the alcohol took its effect, her mind began to slowly unclench. She couldn't allow herself to dwell on the immediate puzzling threat. Instead, something Karenov had said was puzzing—something she had heard only peripherally drifted back now. Scherensky wondered just what was so important about this particular Cosmos. She would have to look up the intelligence dossier on the monitored American spacecraft. Surely the Kremlin was again overreacting.

Chapter Three

The Toyota campervan twisted along California 92, the narrow mountain road that eventually found its way to the Pacific. Daren Gray was heading toward the seaside village of Moss Beach, over the gentle Montara foothills, away from the crush of Palo Alto and Stanford University. This evening was to be a needed release from the flurry of activity that had been his life during the past months. The endless speaking tour, the TV talk shows, publicity functions of all sorts, promotionals for his last book, and the increasingly rare attempts to keep in touch with his research at the Genetics Department had all combined to thoroughly exhaust his energies.

And yet he had to admit everything had gone beautifully. Even beyond his usual high expectations for himself. Six months ago he was the newly appointed head of Genetic Biochemistry at Stanford, author of a few technical essays and short books on the relationships among biology, genetics, and DNA research, and on the awesome potential for this field during the century's final decade and a half. At thirty-six he had accomplished enough to gain the respect of both the scientific and the academic communities. But these achievements were now overshadowed. His last book had been acclaimed by important literary and science reviews. *Time* was calling him the "prophet of the architecture of life," and "the guiding force for charting man's potential destiny on Earth." *Controlled Evolution* had become a rallying point for everyone within and on the fringes of genetic engineering, or, using the milder label, recombinant DNA research.

Gray's stand as the leading advocate of its continued study, so controversial among a segment of scientific conservatives, had propelled him into national prominence. And that exposure, even ' for such a strong personality as his, was almost overwhelming. Daren had become, practically overnight, a sensation. Certainly he was now a literary sensation, in addition to his acceptance into the avant-garde of modern science. In his more egotistical moments he envisioned himself in that collection of historical greats who had come before, the revolutionaries—Da Vinci, Copernicus, Darwin, Freud.

Yet most of the time he operated on more solid ground. His research at Stanford was unfinished, and that always brought back his balance. Then, too, there was the lab conversion. Much still lay ahead. The new theories on human genetic restructuring were on their way to reaching the breakthrough predicted by his book. Difficult problems still had to be worked out, but he knew he was on the verge of providing mankind the key to shape its own evolution. He rarely lost track of that profound notion.

Since Watson and Crick and the double helix, DNA work had proceeded, as always in the pursuit of scientific advance, slowly, deliberately, and quietly in the laboratories around the world. Nothing of apparent importance had been uncovered for years—just the steady accumulation of knowledge and technique that, at just the right moment, could converge to propel civilization into a new dimension. There were, of course, the bacterial hybrids of the Delphi Labs. But Daren Gray knew he was the catalyst that would produce the real transcendence, just as Einstein had seventy years earlier.

He drove out of the hills to the eight-lane beach highway and turned north. The sea haze was beginning to form offshore, gathering strength for the evening onslaught against the coastal towns. Daren's thoughts drifted to what had been given up to reach this point. All the fame and attention had not been without some personal cost. Terri had been too overcome by his consuming research and writing involvements to stay. The separation had hurt, but given all his current preoccupations, there simply hadn't been time to deal with her emotional needs. Her discomfort with their new life style was a problem for which he found no solution. When she returned to Wisconsin and the simple life of her family's estate outside Ashland, he knew no other conclusion was possible. Daren's life was now very distant from the relatively relaxed pace of their college years together—the slow advance from graduate assistant to full research professor and finally to Dean of Genetics.

The other sacrifices, he had to admit, were much costlier. Not so much to his career, but to the search for the critical links in the solution that had to be found. He simply no longer had enough time, and this had to change. Since he had become a scientific success, the financial problems he faced in the past were no longer an obstacle. Royalties from his book and the foundation grants coming to Stanford and his department would support his studies for many years. Now the constraining factor would be time.

Daren Gray's only scientific flaw was the obsession to do everything himself. His brilliance was, he felt, something that couldn't be distributed among colleagues. He refused to allow his primary research to be run by proxy. Some of the more mundane operations were delegated to assistants, but the force and spark of it all could be sustained only by being in direct control. His book title, and the thread reinforced in nearly every chapter, implicitly proclaimed his own intellectual force as the key to unlocking the genetic puzzle.

But this would come only if he had the time and energy to devote to it. And this was the major sacrifice. He had resolved after last week's promotional gambit in New York that this evening would be a prelude to a renewed dedication, a determined focus on the next phase of his work. His publisher had been warned that early resumption of his research was crucial and had reluctantly agreed to lift the pressure.

It was now dusk, and the mist of the Pacific was

rolling onto the shore, resting against the first range of coastal foothills. Daren turned on the van's headlights just as a group of motorcyclists passed by on their way south for the weekend. To L.A., he guessed. Or Hussong's, in the Baja.

There were times when he and his circle of friends and the associates who reflected the brightest minds at Stanford contrasted seriously with the other, more familiar elements of California culture. He was on the threshold of sponsoring a brave new world where everything could be ordered to near perfection. And yet he wondered about the direction his work might take. The genus that had driven by him on its Harley-Davidsons would perhaps have to become extinct. The color, the variety, all the eccentricities of the human condition—would they all disappear into a pool of standardized competence and ordinary intellectualism? How could the new world make a place for the character of life—something he had always valued, and still did value, nearly as much as his theories on the engineering of man. The problem often haunted him.

The philosophical justification of his work could break down and leave the species without the creative expression that had, after all, led directly to its current state of knowledge. To continue might well be a devastating error for civilization. And yet . . . it was a gamble that was going to be taken. These speculations consistently brought him back to the same conclusion. If life could really be engineered and evolution controlled precisely to fit some ideal, the process would be discovered by someone someday. He was convinced that any discovery, any truth, which was within reach, would be found out ultimately. Any denial or suppression of a scientific truth could only be temporary. Better the truth arise in an open environment, subjected to whatever criticism and controversy were necessary to shape the knowledge into a positive direction for man on the planet.

If the concepts he had pursued were developed behind the closed doors of government laboratories, or within any closed society immune from public inspection, their application would become, without question, the guarantor of totalitarianism and Orwellian prophesies. People were particularly sensitive to that possibility this year. No, genetic engineering had to be born into an environment that would incorporate the knowledge with a human sensitivity, treat the idea to a very close scrutiny, and use it for the improvement of life without distorting the knowledge into a political solution, into a method for ensuring the smooth operation of a state.

These reflections only reinforced his determination to get on with the next stage of the research. The preparations for that had been left in a precarious and confused condition three months before when his publisher began transforming him into a celebrity and Terri began thinking about the tranquillity of the Wisconsin woods.

Daren was now into the strip of shops, restaurants, and bars that comprised the business end of Moss Beach, clustered tightly along the ocean frontage. He was looking for the hillside road just north of the strip, which would carry him one hundred meters above the coast highway. The lights of the campervan sought out the sign to Sandia Road. Finding it, he turned right in first gear, pushing the van up the narrow dirt access to the Granada subdivision, where somewhere among the scattered rustic Spanish ranchettes he would find Laine Jeremy's cabin, the good company and release he hoped would reawaken his energies.

It would be more than therapeutic to see Laine again. She was one of the most delightful stars in the friendly group that had almost spontaneously condensed together. Daren had neglected nearly all social contact with them for too long—and especially felt the absence of her company during the past hectic months. She had been there before to supply the right perspectives he so frequently lost track of, and had been a real comfort during his troubled period with Terri.

Laine and Mark Wilson, his primary fellow researcher at Stanford, had lived together for two years in the small rustic beach house provided by Henry Jeremy. The influential Stanford trustee had given it to his daughter on her graduation, partly as a reward for her nomination as *magna cum laude* in Computer Science, partly as a tax shelter. It was intended to be a retreat for her to use during graduate studies, and it served that purpose well. Now that she was managing computer operations for Coast Research Labs in Palo Alto, the cabin had become a convenient gathering place for the Stanford group—a liberated zone where they could come together for nearly any reason. Some, like Daren, came for the chance to find good company and stimulating conversation. Some came to activate the creative spirit away from academic pressures. Others used the place as a haven for pure escape, to indulge their fantasies with the legalized marijuana varieties. That group was now experimenting with a Colombian hybrid. The more adventurous were staying with still-outlawed cocaine.

Daren would rarely partake of these diversions—would usually pass them up for the good selection of California wines that were always in ample supply, thanks to Henry Jeremy's friends in Napa Valley. This particular evening he wanted his head mellow but clear. The rest of his weekend was free, the first in a long while, and he needed his mind intact to plan the studies he had resolved would begin Monday.

He eased the van into a space alongside the row of cars parked down the hill from the house, its lights twinkling in the hazy California dusk. He locked the door and followed the winding steps up to the wood deck in front of the picture windows that looked west over the ocean. As he went in through the open front doorway, he was greeted by an ebullient Mark Wilson.

"Well, come in. Our star has blessed us with his honored presence."

"Now, Mark, let's not be excessive. I'm still the modest person you've known and loved all these years, and expect to be treated that way. Fame has hopefully left my humility untouched."

"Ah, Daren, you know we love you in spite of your success," Laine Jeremy insisted as she emerged from their study to welcome him. "But you are so much more loved now that you're famous. You'd better be careful . . . we've assembled a collection of very attractive admirers here tonight."

"Now, he may not be ready for that," Mark smiled.

"On the contrary . . . I must accept some of the spoils of victory. As you know, moderation in all things has never been my style."

"In that case, old fellow, come over to the fire and share some excellent South American organic delight that we're trying especially for this occasion. We're all here to help you celebrate your success, so you may as well get in touch with your status as the current guru of Stanford's finest."

"I accept the honor, but I think I'll be more comfortable with the usual. Do you have a bottle or two of Henry's late-harvest Reisling, and a proper glass? I do have to watch my image."

"Ah, my friend, such concessions we must make for the young nobles of our age. But of course we've stocked your favorite. Sit and I'll provide you with the soft stuff." Mark went off to their wine pantry.

Laine took Daren by the arm and led him into the circle of people who filled the spaces around the massive rock fireplace in the center of the living room. Sofas and cushions were occupied by lounging friends he'd known for years at the university. As he approached, the group, which had only casually acknowledged his entrance, turned quiet for a moment . . . then burst forth with a hearty round of applause and friendly shouts, in the best tradition of an English club. It might have been a put-on, but he knew their style, and this was a genuine show of respect and approval for his newly found success. Congratulations on the book followed, and Daren acknowledged that he probably deserved it. They moved aside enough to make a spot for him beside the warm blaze so he could rest against one of the scattered large cushions. Mark brought in the wine, and they all settled into comfortable positions, some returning to earlier conversations, some ready to make Daren the center of attraction and inspiration.

A pipe of the Colombian was passed first to Daren as guest of honor, and to be sociable he accepted, taking in his one obligatory inhalation of the evening. After the pipe moved on, an attractive blond art instructor began an irreverent chant of "This is the body, the blood, of our only begotten son . . . take, eat, and enjoy."

"Such ritualism among the allegedly worldly people of Stanford," Daren observed.

"Yes, we must treat our gods with due respect," Laine countered. Daren poured from the wine bottle and filled his glass.

"Anyone else wish to moderate?" he asked.

There were a couple of takers, including Laine and Shelly, a bearded parapsych professor. Mark and the rest preferred the smoke. They drifted into small talk for a relaxing hour. The System, Laine's home computer, was programmed to produce a soothing audio-visual display of the recent Marin County jazz festival. It was exactly what Daren needed. He went through half a bottle of wine before the talk drifted back to his status as a celebrity.

"So tell us, Dr. Gray—we would like to hear your views on the current set of world controversies," said Mark.

"Ah, yes, let's see—where should I begin? It's true that I've now become an expert on all subjects in all fields, especially since I'm a TV personality, interviewed by the talk-show greats. There are probably no limits to the extent of my knowledge of all things."

"It's refreshing to see your humility has indeed remained untouched by all the notoriety," Laine taunted.

"Yes, but it's all a façade. I've been taught to be a salable commodity. Very useful when I'm doing the morning show and talking to the ladies from Philadelphia. But really, folks, it's not the true Daren Gray."

"That we don't believe, of course." Laine attempted to turn serious. "But since you are a recognized authority, have you any opinions on the Russians' new Alternative Party? And is there any way we can help it survive? I've been staying in touch with Marya Scherensky of the Soviet space program, and it all sounds very exciting. With the support of nearly the entire

Soviet scientific community, the Party might become a permanent part of their system."

"Too controversial for me," he jested. "But really, you know my feelings on that. I try to keep in touch with some of those people, but lately the censorship's been severe. I did hear your friend Scherensky's been busy trying to save their satellites, so the KGB has left her alone. And no, there is precious little any of us can do to help. Best we can do is keep track of any new suppressions. Actually, I must confess I haven't followed recent events that closely. Just been too busy."

"All right, we don't want to push you. How about Torson's last book on cloning? Surely that is something you've kept up with, and near to your heart. I think the title was something like *Duplicate Man*. Have you read it?"

This subject did interest Daren, especially since it elaborated on the writer's earlier distortions, the misuse of a limited understanding of scientific fact. He knew that if the group could stand it, he could go on about the subject indefinitely. The book's theme, although presented by an amateur, came close to the direction of his own work.

"You people know how to get me started, don't you?"

"We know . . . we're ready to be entertained," said Mark. "When you get too boring or go on too long, we'll let you know. Or tune you out. In either case it'll be obvious. Tonight the old Daren Gray ego should be strong enough to absorb that. By the way, we've been receiving quite a few inquiries at Stanford about all of this. So far no one's been able to confirm his credentials as a scientist."

"That, my friend, is a terrible understatement. The guy is a complete novice, who happened to be on the fringe of some very important studies in England. He does write well, though, almost as well as I, and his story is certainly entertaining. But technically there are so many flaws that it was a chore for my scientific sensitivities to allow me to finish the book. And I have to admit, I only got through the first part of it before I recoiled in horror."

"So you missed the best part," Laine noted.

"No, I read the last chapter—skipped the middle."

"But yet what he proposes is now close to plausible . . . the perfect clone."

"We're still not there, and certainly not using his fantasized technology. It just can't be done that way. If anyone were really close, it would be our team. And I can assure you, there are simply too many complications for such a thing to happen just yet, complications that can't be eliminated in any laboratory . . . that now exists."

"You aren't just showing some professional bias and making a case for our own superior theory and technique?" Mark speculated.

"Perhaps . . . but let me give you an analogy. To duplicate anything as infinitely complex as human DNA, you theoretically need to do this in a perfectly isolated, perfectly clean environment. Any infinitesimal interference, any atom out of place, would alter the entire process. You all have the *Star Trek* tapes, right? When the heroes are beamed through the space surrounding some obscure planet, they step into a force field that can dematerialize their bodies—clothing, phasers, and all—into separate individual atoms, breaking the atomic bonds and transporting the collection of a thousand billion subatomic particles through space, through the walls of the *Enterprise,* and onto the planet surface below. There the same force field has the power to reassemble everything into its original form.

"It's a great theory, and personally I think it will ultimately happen. Perhaps early in the 2000's. But recall your high school science. You approximate this reassembly process when you try to grow a crystal. To obtain a perfect amplification of a primary seed. You put the seed into a supersaturated solution, and it should grow into an exact duplicate of the structure you started with.

"But what actually happens when you try the experiment? Although you don't notice it at first, at the seed level a single molecule, just one, gets stuck slightly out of place in the pattern, and as the crystal grows it forms an appendage, an offshoot crystal, so that as the entire structure is built up, or reassembled, it becomes something much different than the perfect seed that started it all. The new crystal is flawed from the start because there is simply no way to keep the conditions perfect. The diamond growers come close but never completely succeed. Heisenberg's uncertainty principle enters into the picture."

Laine was right with him. "Heisenberg, eh? I think I vaguely remember something about the fellow. He postulated that there is always some basic uncertainty, some random motion, when you're dealing with subatomic interactions . . . so that in the very basic sense, nothing can ever be absolutely deterministic. It gets wrapped up in philosophy too, doesn't it?"

"Ah yes, your undergraduate years weren't a total waste of time, woman. Good to know that you can follow my reasoning."

"You're not dealing with epsilons here, you know," Mark added.

"You're both such a welcome pleasure to chat with . . . and it does make my points easier to get across. Thanks, folks. But on with my analogy. Each particle has an uncertainty associated with it, so that you simply cannot control things perfectly on the atomic level. That is the theory. So, going back to *Star Trek,* if you tried to reassemble Spock, he might come out looking like a blend of himself and Uhura."

"That might be more interesting than what you wanted," Laine noted. There followed a round of laughter and some imaginative speculations on bisexuality themes. It was the parapsych professor, Shelly, who brought up the question which naturally followed this line of reasoning.

"If this is the case, and Heisenberg's principle applies to the reassembly of anything at these levels, then how do you support your theory on controlled evolution? The perfect engineering of the DNA structure?"

"Shelly, I'm surprised. If you had read my book carefully, you would have known that the theory doesn't pretend to duplicate exactly the entire structure of DNA."

"I confess, I haven't read it all for comprehension."

"My God, an illiterate metaphysician."

"Now, now, be kind. I deal in the possibilities of the mind. And mine doesn't have time to pore over such technical matters as your treatise."

"If *Time* magazine can grasp it, it should be within your powers."

"All right, I'll read it for content next chance I get. But I still deserve an answer. You at least suggested that you could restructure DNA and control genetics in a deterministic manner. Somehow you sidestep Heisenberg."

"Yes, that is true. We can suppress or enhance physical characteristics by mechanically switching the molecular patterns of the gene. But, and this is the important limit, we're still working on the first level of molecules—we shuffle molecule x to molecule y's place and move y to z. And that might strengthen the heart valve or correct a bone deformation. It's all a first-order process. Fairly easy to do with modern techniques—laser surgery, ionizing radiation, and enzyme reaction. And on this level, we carry the whole package of Heisenbergian uncertainties and randomness along with the transfers. So they become no more of a factor than if one were to remove an appendix or replace a cornea. It's when we try to go beyond, into the level below molecular rearrangement, that the process becomes touchy. And that's what Torson claims has been done by the group in England. He alleges that the entire DNA blueprint has been replicated, synthetically and perfectly, without jarring the original, let's say. There is no input of any extraneous energy. His hybrid presumably succeeds with the entire organism reproduced cell for cell, neuron for neuron, in every exact detail as found in the original. Now, imagine that happening without adding an iota of random energy to the particles involved."

"I think I'm beginning to see," said Shelly.

"And yet"—Daren wanted to keep the door open—"it is still, theoretically, possible. And there will ultimately be a way to approach the perfection that Torson reports—to do the exact clone." He paused awhile and took a long drink of the Reisling, warming his toes before the fire, waiting for them to ask more, preparing to avoid telling them of his actual breakthrough.

"Well, do *you* have the way? Is that going to come in your next million-dollar bestseller?" Laine asked.

"Perhaps. Mark knows the drift of my research lately."

"Yes, and it is just that, a drift. It's stalled in the lab and has been since you became famous. Does the answer have something to do with benign neglect?" Mark needled.

"Well, I accept the harrassment. We will begin to correct that situation next week. I hope you're ready to work again."

"C'mon, you know I'm bored when we aren't making a breakthrough every month. If you'd just let me in on your secret, I could start the experimental setups immediately. But you'll have to give me some idea of where it's going and the authority to do something myself, instead of dominating everything as usual."

"What do you know about it already?" Daren ignored the legitimate complaint.

Mark thought back to two months ago, when the studies were put in mothballs. "The paper on sealed vacuum recombination?"

"That's part of it."

"The laser stimulation?"

"You're on the right track already."

"Still, that doesn't tell me much. You haven't disclosed any details."

"It will be clear in time. Let's save further discussion for next week, after I've had a chance to put my thoughts together better."

"I think I'll refill the pipe. This conversation is taxing my feeble brain," said Mark.

"Good idea—your best inspiration seems to come under the influence."

"Like all great thinkers."

The pipe was filled and passed around again. Three

or four of the group had drifted into a comatose state and left them, so Daren felt obliged to take the offering.

Laine took a couple of intakes this time. The drug seemed to stimulate remote portions of her memory.

"Daren, what, if anything, does all this have to do with that unpleasant business back in the seventies? The disappearance of those two on your staff, with a bundle of your experimental results? Could they have taken it all to England and begun the work that Torson has reported? They really dropped completely out of sight, didn't they?"

This was a sensitive point with Daren. He knew little enough about the affair. But what he did know or had eventually been able to piece together could not be shared with them. Walters and Dankin, his colleagues at the time, had not only dropped out of sight, but had abruptly vanished without a word from the university, his lab, their apartments, one warm Friday in March of 1973. With them had gone a full year's worth of data from hundreds of critical experiments. The loss was a profound setback to his early genetic studies.

"I don't know, Laine. I doubt they went to England. There was just so much behind-the-scenes intrigue back then that I've never been able to sort it all out."

"Weren't you under some pressure not to make any noise over it? And I recall strained meetings between you and the dean. Sounded to me like the government was involved. Especially since no one would talk about the thing."

"I guess it would look that way. You've touched on a very sore spot." Gray took another long swallow of wine.

He had a damned good idea where Walters and Dankin were. For some reason, back then the government had needed DNA researchers desperately for highly classified work. He himself had been contacted a week before his colleagues disappeared and was given one of the most persuasive and tempting recruitment offers he had ever encountered. But hearing that the assignment was with the DOD, he declined. On principle.

Gray had waited only two days for some sign, some word from his missing staff. Then he went directly to the Dean of Science and expressed his concerns. Gray was ready to call in the police, possibly even the FBI. The dean turned off all such suggestions. In his files were two letters of resignation. The university had been notified this would happen, that special circumstances were involved. There had been no coercion and nothing more could be done. Loss of Gray's research data would have to be absorbed by the department.

Not satisfied with that explanation, Gray sought legal help but received total noncooperation from everyone involved. The dean, the local officials, the government agencies—all ignored his appeals. His attorney continued to push until finally contact was made and a compromise reached with a representative from the legal side of the Defense Intelligence Agency. Gray would be allowed access to the raw experimental data that had been taken—but no contact with his lost experimenters. There was also the promise of no additional interference in his Stanford research. In return Gray was to drop the issue and remain silent. He was advised by his counsel that it would be futile to pursue the matter any further. Nothing more would be acknowledged by the government. Ever.

Reluctantly he accepted their conditions. That was to be the end of it. The government honored its part. And he had honored his, grudgingly at first; then as his research made up for the loss and the important breakthroughs began to come, the intrusion gradually faded away—an ugly remnant of a forgotten era. His preoccupation with his studies displaced the distaste he had felt, and only now and then, as on this evening, when he was reminded of the tactics so commonly employed during those times, was he tempted to reveal what he knew.

Perhaps at some point in the future he would. But not yet. He had to trust that if his part of the agreement was kept, his work would continue. He couldn't risk any more interference. And he had to push ahead until his theories could become public domain. Once a part of the knowledge bank of science, there would no longer be any possibility of their being absorbed into the "black shop" of the military. This was the path to take. He could not give them any excuse for moving in on him again. Certainly not now.

Mark had drifted away into more superficial conversation, as had most of the others who were still conscious. Laine sensed that Daren was immersed in some distant musing, and she suggested a break.

"Let's take a beach walk, Daren . . . I think you've lost nearly everyone. It looks as if they're all going under for the evening, and I need to feel the salt air."

"As usual, you come up with an excellent idea at a perfect time. I think I'd like to do that."

Laine found a shawl and pulled it around her. The two walked out of the cabin onto the veranda and down their private trail to the beach, along a path that wound by the inlet of a cove, under the concrete bridge that put the coast highway far above them, up into the foggy night. Along the shore the waves were breaking noisily, and the feeling was especially intoxicating to Daren after the intellectualism of the early conversations. His troubled memories of the resurrected episode needed to be pounded away by the surf. He let himself feel the air; they both drank it in deeply, and then walked in silence for a long while.

Daren was the first to break their quiet mood. "Laine, how are you and Mark doing? Last time I left Stanford things were pretty tense—but you seemed okay tonight. Are things better?"

Laine quietly shook her head. "You know, we get along beautifully most of the time, but . . . oh, it's just not there anymore. The last months we've tried to work out a lot, but . . . we're really at the classical end-of-relationship. And Mark knows it too. Jesus, it's just that we both find it so damned hard to make a break after so long. And for me, two years is long. I'm fairly well set up to handle things . . . with Daddy's cabin to keep me sheltered from the storm. And Coast Research is keeping me very busy. But Mark, I think, is afraid of being cut loose. He'd do all right eventually. But, hell, he doesn't have anything else except his work and a lot of insecurities. It's going to be rough on him." She paused a moment, then added, "But why am I boring you with all of this?"

"Because I asked, and care about you both."

"Daren, you do, and I know that. Thanks for being such a friend."

"Hey, I'll always be that . . . at least. You expected the rush of my life the last half year to neutralize all my feelings?"

"Well, to be honest, Terri did have a few complaints. And one was definitely that you had forgotten how to feel compassion for your fellow-man . . . or woman."

"I don't doubt that. But with you, especially, I am trying to get back in touch. There's still a little human left under this shell."

"I think maybe some of that was trying to slip through tonight. You need to let it."

"Good. And with you two, whatever happens, I've always felt special things for you both. If you need someone to talk to, a male insight, whatever that's worth in this era, let me know. Okay?"

"You're on. I may need that."

They walked on a bit more, past a group of college kids camped out on the beach, sitting around the last flames of a campfire, who waved and invited them to join. The two smiled and waved back, moving on into the deserted sand.

This time Laine interrupted their quiet. "Tell me, Daren, what do you do now?"

"Not sure I understand the question."

"Well, now that you're an unqualified success, what's next? What I really mean is . . . what do you do for an encore?"

"Do I need one?"

"Maybe not, but . . . doesn't it bother you just a little that this may be the high point of your scientific life? With the publication of your book, the important concepts, the discoveries, are all set out and established for others to follow. All that seems to be left is for the technicians to carry out your orders."

Daren smiled at her, warming to the sensitive and

intelligent curiosity that had always been part of her personality.

"But there, my good friend, you are very wrong. Only the first steps have been taken. True, I have defined a rather well-marked path—but there are some important forks in the road ahead. And . . . and this you must certainly know . . . any good scientist, or even any good writer, always holds something back, something not yet fully illuminated, only suspected. We always must retain a certain aura of mystery. Einstein set forth his many theories on relativity—yet held out his entire life for the quest of the unified-field theory. He may have found it. But we never knew. He could have discovered the key and held back waiting for some further proof . . . or simply out of perversity. In any case, he died with the puzzle pieces still locked firmly in his head.

"In my case I've built the foundation and drawn up the blueprints. Now the challenge is to erect the building. My designs on how to rearrange DNA are just that. Designs. The problem now is how to go about it."

"But your book is very specific about how to proceed. It seemed to me that the technical obstacles were nearly overcome already."

"It had to seem that way. My publisher insisted on a strong ending. And for the most part, the techniques I proposed are sufficient. But . . . and this is the key point . . . there is one more breakthrough that has yet to come. And this is what I'm going to be getting into heavily, starting this next week."

"Well, it certainly sounds mysterious enough, but you've surrounded your explanation in a bunch of generalities. Are you trying to be evasive with me?"

"Probably. I can't tell you the details . . . without having you take a vow of secrecy, at least until the break comes and I can report the next round of results and the final conclusion."

"You know me—I've been surrounded by egotistical scientists long enough to know your ideas are sacred and very jealously guarded until you publish. You can trust me. I respect the situation."

"That's very important, for a number of reasons.

And I do trust you." He put an arm around her and gave her a warm hug. She accepted the show of affection and his acknowledgment that she was an ally.

"Remember our earlier talk about the flawed crystal?"

"Yes. I thought it was a good analogy. It helped make your point."

"Well, everything that is proposed in my book is qualified by that problem. We can only make genetic changes on a gross scale. I said we could switch molecule x for molecule y to correct a bone deformity. That, unfortunately, is only partially true. We can do it, and we'll be successful maybe 95% of the time, but the more delicate or complicated the switch we attempt, the more considerably the odds lessen."

"So controlled evolution isn't really controllable? Regardless of what your book claims? You fraud!"

"Wait a minute. Before you turn me over to the consumer-protection agency, let me go on."

"I guess I'll give you a chance."

"Why was the crystal flawed?"

"Because of Heisenberg. The randomness."

"Right. And the uncertainties exist because of a very specific reason. The environment is not perfectly controllable, and that contaminates all our operations. We can only come close with existing laboratory methods."

"But your book suggests we should be able to approach the perfect conditions."

"Correct again. But I don't really say how. Where do we find an environment that is so pure that the contaminants, the randomness, are reduced to the point of being invisible to the atomic particles we are operating on?"

"I'm beginning to see the solution you're looking for . . . but where on Earth do you find such a perfect condition when we're constantly feeding more and more pollutants into the atmosphere and moving away from just those perfect conditions you need?"

"That's the answer."

"What is?"

"Not on Earth."

"In space. Of course."

"You've got it. We must leave the contaminants behind. Space offers nearly the complete absence of impurity and random activity. It still exists, of course, but well below the levels needed for genetic operations."

"I'm impressed."

"But there's more. The few studies I've done on this theme suggest that not only do we get the advantage of a pure environment in space, but there is a strong possibility that the 'contaminants' that do exist out there, the cosmic particles and gamma radiation coming in from the galaxy, may actually promote the molecular recombinations I've proposed. With a little assist from laser technology."

"Well, Dr. Gray, it all certainly seems plausible. Do you have any results to prove this brainstorm?"

"No results yet. The theory is about to be tested. But no existing concepts or physical laws run counter to the idea. It even fits in nicely with relativity. If we reduce the contaminants to near zero, with cosmic radiation as a catalyst and a laser as the surgeon's knife, the era of the true clone may be much closer than I let on earlier. It's possible that even the Heisenbergian uncertainties can be forced to near zero."

"So, I suppose all you need is for someone to build you a recombination lab in space. And up you'll go, with your team of assistants."

"Of course. Do you think I could get Papa Jeremy to loan me two billion?"

"Sure. I'll propose your idea to him at our next lunch in San Francisco."

"Fortunately, there is a halfway step that can be taken now."

"And that is . . ."

"Another secret."

"C'mon, I thought we were allies."

"All right. But seriously, not a word about this part to anyone. What I'm about to tell you is controversial, and if word leaked out prematurely it could put a lot of pressure on us at probably the worst time."

"I'll swear on your last book review."

"Well, we'll be moving in on you within two weeks,

so you are probably clever enough to figure the plan out on your own."

"Huh?"

"The space physics lab at Coast Research. I think it's across the complex from your computer offices."

"Oh yes, we use it for satellite testing. It simulates space-vacuum conditions. Now your plan becomes clear."

"Thought it would. We're going to convert it into a sealed lab for genetic research. The fences should go up in a week."

"Who knows about this? Does Henry?"

"No, some things are out of even his hands. So far only myself, Mark, the Dean of Science at Stanford, the Governor, the President's Science Adviser. And now you, who won't breathe a word to anyone."

"Why is this all such a damned secret?"

"For two reasons, both obvious. The first is avoidance of publicity."

"The second must be you don't want details of your theory to get out."

"We're afraid that what we operate on could get out. The whole area around that lab will be in quarantine. Our experimentation is potentially dangerous."

"I don't want to know any more."

"Too bad. I was about to ask if you would like to have the computer side of the operations."

"I'll think about it."

Daren smiled and pulled her close. He met no resistance. The two paused . . . for a moment looking out over the Pacific, then up at the night sky, where the mist had parted enough to give them a view of the winter constellation Orion. They turned after a few minutes and walked along the sand, following their tracks back to the beach house.

Chapter Four

It was eleven-thirty before Sanders finally saw the car lights poking their way through the falling snow and scattered trees, whose branches drooped under the cold weight now covering his secluded retreat. As he watched the gray Seville inch its way along his winding driveway, he felt it moved more slowly, less deliberately than he would have wanted. Sanders, at this late hour, did not look forward to coaxing Brookhaven back into the world of coherent thought.

Eventually the car reached a widened, uncleared parking area in front of the arched entranceway to his Tudor mansion. Its engine was killed, lights turned off, and a bundled figure struggled out, then pushed its way up the snow-covered path to a lamp-lighted entry. Reaching the great oak door, the man clanged an iron knocker solidly against the engraved plate beneath.

Sanders was waiting—he opened a second after the knock. "Hello, Chris. Glad you could make it through this lovely Washington weather."

Brookhaven stomped inside, shaking the snow off his shoulders and shoes. "You picked a terrific night for this, Sanders. I could have been somewhere warm and friendly, in front of a cozy fire, with a very agreeable lady . . . all damn evening."

His speech was sufficiently clear to allay Sanders' earlier concern. Although his breath signaled he had obviously been drinking, he didn't seem near the point of being a problem. No doubt the drive had helped, the treacherous parkways demanding a quick sobering up. It would be easier for Sanders to be sociable.

"Well, I can provide you with nearly all you had to leave behind in the city. There's a fire going in the study and the place is certainly warm, even friendly, I think. Only problem I see is that the gender of that friendliness isn't what you had in mind."

"You're right there. Now, where can I hang this coat? It's a bit soggy."

"Here." Sanders took the tweed overcoat and carefully placed it over two wooden hangers on the side of the large hall.

"Your butler gone for the night? Along with the slave who shovels the sidewalks?"

"Don't own any of those. You know I couldn't trust servants in my business."

"Yeah, they would probably be keeping video tapes of all your secret activities. By the way . . . I want none of that funny business between us. I mean it. Actually, I think I'd feel more comfortable at some neutral zone."

"Now, you don't want to go out into that weather again. Just relax, Chris, you've nothing to worry about from me. I'd only be incriminating myself, anyway." He gave the idea time to register. "But more important, everything from here has to be based on mutual trust. And there's absolutely no reason why it shouldn't be. Our involvement in this was equally shared and only in the role of accessories . . . we were both forced to follow orders from the White House. If anything, my responsibility is greater than yours, and if this mess ever opens up I'll willingly admit that. No tricks on my part. That's a promise."

"Can I really trust a former CIA agent?"

"Trust me. Now, let's go into the study. We'll talk first, then have a few rounds of pool later. Had the billiard room remodeled over the holiday."

"I could sure use a hot drink. Irish coffee, if you can do it. After that drive, my blood has solidified."

"Got it. I'll brew my strongest coffee. You need that more. Go on in and thaw out by the fire. I'll join you in a few minutes with the drinks."

Brookhaven walked in under the heavy wood archway that opened into a den, a classic library that seemed to have been stolen from an English mystery. Its walls alternated seventeenth-century castle paneling with floor-to-ceiling bookshelves. On the outer wall, two ceiling-high, mullioned bay windows surrounded an elaborately honeycombed roll-top desk. To his right stood the key to the warm feeling that was starting to reach through his cold clothes, an old stone fireplace that could only have been designed by a European artisan who appreciated large fires and lots of heat. Brookhaven glanced out one of the bay windows, barely spotting lights from the road a hundred meters away through the snow and woods that were transforming Sanders' estate into a wintry beauty. He had to admit some envy. His own luxurious home in Nassau Bay, Texas, couldn't compare with the old-world character Sanders had found in Georgetown. It was a damned comfortable feeling. He collapsed into a large, soft chair by the fire and let it warm him thoroughly.

Sanders returned with two mugs and a cigar box. "Couldn't find any whipping cream, real or otherwise. Other than that, I've made these from Ireland's finest . . . John Jameson. Care for a cigar? Of course they're Havanas."

Brookhaven accepted both drink and smoke. As he produced a lighter and put fire to the cigar, he expressed his approval. "Excellent. It's great to have these available again. Wish I could afford them."

"Hell, I'll get you a box," Sanders offered.

"Appreciate that. But couldn't take 'em back to Texas. The wife would throw me out." Taking a sip of the Irish, he added, "Jesus, this drink's a bit short on whiskey."

"I went a little light. You got a good ounce, but coffee will do more for you at this point."

"Do I look like I need a mother? Next round I make." He took a deep drag on the cigar. "By the way, what is it really you think we need to coordinate? To me, all you and DISA need do is sit back and hope this rescue plan succeeds. And give us some technical input here and there on the details of the Platform. I think we already have the old system designs in our files."

Sanders set his mug down on the low oak table in

front of Brookhaven and walked toward the fireplace. He pulled a log from a well-made stack on the right and poked it onto the heap of burning, glowing coals, pushing the contents into just the right place with an iron of the same vintage as the castle panels. Satisfied with the arrangement, he turned to a nearby shelf that held a collection of pipes and tobacco tins and drew out a carefully selected choice of each, which he carried back to a chair opposite his guest.

"Actually, Chris, there are a number of things we need to resolve before you and your people get so involved there is no time for talking to DISA." Sanders packed an English blend into his Sasieni, tamping it solidly. "As I see it, tonight you and I must cover three basic issues. One involves the general status of the Orion Platform. The others concern secrecy and the contingency plans we have to agree on soon . . . preferably now."

He lit his pipe, puffed heavily five or six times, let the smoke cloud dissolve into the room, then tamped charred tobacco back down into its bowl.

Brookhaven took a large gulp of his Irish, reflecting a moment. "Greg, if there's any way possible, I'd like to concentrate on just the mechanics of this damned mission. The less I have to do with the classified side, the better."

"No trouble. We can keep it that way if we get a few loose ends tied up early. I'll be glad to work the details you'd rather avoid. That's what I'm paid to do, anyway."

"Then I hope we understand each other on this. I wanted nothing to do with the original affair, as you well know. There just wasn't any choice. I suppose it's the same way now. I'll tell you, if DISA had any way of solving this problem on its own, I wouldn't even be talking to you."

"But we don't, Chris. We don't have the Shuttle. Our version is still a year from being operational. And you have the Space Tug, which makes USSA the natural, and only, solution. You know that."

"Yeah. I realize it's up to our side to bail everyone out." Brookhaven had another hearty drink.

"Let's get on with business. What did you find out this morning on Orion's lifetime?"

"Our staff received the tracking data from NORAD in Colorado. They filtered all the orbit histories available, fed those results into our GODS prediction program, and reported their conclusion to me about an hour after the committee meeting. With a 99% confidence factor, Orion should move into Earth's atmosphere by about mid-May. That gives us only four months or so, shorter than what I told them. To say it'll be extremely close is one hell of an understatement. A lot has to get done in a hurry."

"But you do at least have the Space Tug operational, and it has the performance to boost our problem into deep space?"

"Potentially it has that capability. But keep in mind that the Tug has flown only one mission out of the Shuttle so far. There still is a lot of testing to be done before we can guarantee success with what you've proposed. And there's the problem of modifying it to operate near the Platform. And the adaptor redesign for handling your special package."

"I know, I know. There are uncertainties, tests, the usual. But we do have one big step up on the operation. All the basic space hardware has been built and flown, at least once. We're now only talking mods, right?"

"Mostly. But we did have some bugs with the Space Tug's first flight. The electronics supporting the propulsion system were balky—there were two misfires. Some guidance errors crept in that caused us to miss our desired orbit by ten kilometers. And making all the electronics compatible with the Platform's inertial gyros won't be straightforward. A whole lot of design work and testing still has to be done. It's just not as simple as you would like."

"But your people can do it. And in time." It wasn't a question.

"I suppose we have to."

"Yes, you have to." Sanders frowned. "All right, let's pursue a related matter that I need your opinion on." He took a deep pull of his pipe. "How did we both lose track of something this critical? It seemed to me there was a directive giving USSA the responsibility to keep a Priority One monitor on the Platform indefinitely—and to advise DISA of any trajectory difficulties."

"Jesus, those orders lapsed years ago. I'm sure we sent your people a warning that all monitoring would be transferred over to your shop. True, we were watching the orbital condition and recording a slug of telemetry. But when the Skylab support funds were cut— that's where we had the operation hidden—our cover was gone, so we had to stop all our efforts. At that point the responsibility and accumulated data were shifted, or were supposed to be, over to your side."

"And you're certain we were notified?"

"You had to be. Priority One business isn't easily overlooked."

"Yet somehow it was."

"I vaguely remember a name—the liaison between our agencies. Paul Creighton, I think."

"Yes, that's right." Remembering the connection, Sanders thought aloud. "He was handling all our interfaces. This was all in his department back then. And about that time . . . when was the transfer made?"

"Our funds terminated early in seventy-seven. It would have been soon after."

"He was moving into a special operation for the Europeans. Crap! So that's when it dropped out of sight."

"I guess so. After all, Orion was your baby. Doesn't DISA follow up on its own satellites?"

"Of course we do. But I'm beginning to put together the picture. The problem was the original nature of the Orion mission. Before the White House stepped in, the Orion Platform was set up to be a test bed for classified research, and all of those experiments were supposed to be over by seventy-six. Although the most important operation failed, we were still able to perform the basic research. Had to do with some rather potent space weaponry that you don't need to know about. It's all obsolete, anyway. But the problem was that very few besides ourselves knew what was really going on. It's the way we had to operate. Each engineer was given only a small piece of the puzzle to work out so that no one was aware of the potential crisis we had, or would have, with a reentry. And I have to admit that in those days reentry was nothing I seriously worried about. My guess is that when we finally deactivated Orion in seventy-six after all the standard data had been gathered, the vehicle was assigned to the category of inert spacecraft. When Creighton got your transfer of Priority One, he no doubt assumed that since Orion was considered dormant, the priority no longer applied." Sanders sank into his chair. "That's not much of an excuse. Basically, we blew it." The DISA director glowered at his admission.

"Chris, about the data collected by Skylab on the condition of the package—you're certain that it was all turned over?"

"Yes. That went directly to one of your research labs."

"Did you handle the transfer personally?"

"Those were the orders. It all was coded, and delivered to Fort Gabriel. A Department ZW74, best as I can recall."

Sanders remembered, and flagged it within his mind's filing system. "That's correct. So I can assume that we have everything generated during the original operation?"

"Everything from the early readings right through the rocket module's failure, the astronauts' attempts to fix it, and at least two weeks of your payload's activity. Plus about two years of tracking and attitude information. You have it all somewhere. We weren't allowed to keep a thing. As far as we're concerned, the file was closed years ago. If your people have lost it, there's nothing left."

"I doubt we've lost it. But I'm also sure it's all buried very deeply. We had two research scientists working the data, looking at the readings from the package—they've probably been assigned twenty other jobs since then. Retrieving it will be a major problem."

"Again, that's your worry." Brookhaven finished his drink. "Any chance I can make myself a refill?"

"In a minute. One more thing before we leave the

Orion Platform. What exactly do you know about the package? How much did we actually disclose to you?"

"Well, we—that is, I—could never find out much. The President described only a few basics. I was made aware of a problem with something the military had generated, something that had to be disposed of quickly. We knew the general shape of the payload container, or 'package,' as your people insisted it be called. And all its interfaces with the Orion Platform and communication links with Skylab. We were aware it had been a last-minute addition to Orion—very urgent. But essentially USSA was given only the technical details needed for launching the thing into outer space from Orion's pad, and everything we'd need to guide it along that path. Of course, we got all the propulsion details when the damned rocket wouldn't ignite. Your people were so frantic there wasn't much of the design that was kept secret."

"We couldn't allow it to fire itself back to Earth. But on the package itself, you were never told any specifics?" Sanders didn't seem surprised.

"No, we obviously couldn't be trusted with that. It was all kept quiet. The President impressed on me the importance of cooperating with you all and persistently suggested the dangers of a possible failure. We knew only that whatever was contained in that payload they wanted it sent into space, or at the very least to stay in orbit for a long, long time. From the data stream we collected before the launch attempt, I could assume that whatever dreadful thing the military had produced was very active. The sensor readings showed beyond any question that something inside was growing in energy. We didn't know what was growing, but the readouts convinced me this was serious business. God knows what the thing's become by now. And I suppose if your people haven't been watching closely, 'he' is the only one who does."

"We'll hopefully find out soon. For one thing, our 'blue team' needs to know before they're sent up there."

"You realize those four have been training over a year for an entirely different mission," Brookhaven noted.

"I know. But they're flexible. They'll be put immediately through an intensive retraining program. We can't trust this to anyone less dedicated or competent. There just can't be a failure this time. This crew all comes from a tradition of test-pilot stock. A mission with overtones of real danger will only motivate them more."

"Do you really expect this to be dangerous?"

"Yes. Given the timing of it all, they'll be operating with the whole system on the edge of the Earth's atmosphere. That can get rough. Operations can be very tricky in that region. And then, of course, there's the questionable condition of the package."

"You expect contamination?"

"We have to consider that possibility. Ten years in orbit will have produced some unknowns."

"Christ, the crew will be told of these risks, I assume."

"Yes, they will know the necessary details. My immediate problem is to reconstruct all the available data so I can give them an accurate idea of what they'll be facing. Which affects how we go about transferring the payload capsule to the Tug. This all has to be done with manual EVA operations. So let's hope the info we want still exists."

Sanders reflected again on the current situation: "It's just damned unfortunate that the final Skylab visit was canceled. We could have wrapped it all up then, replaced propulsion components, and been done with the whole matter. Thanks to Congress and their stinginess, that chance disappeared."

"Maybe DISA and the White House should have come clean with Congress back then. Their decision might well have been different."

"You know better. Same reason we still can't. The problem has to remain secret. If it leaked to the press there would be international repercussions. There would be mass panic."

Sanders relit his pipe, stared brooding at the snow peacefully falling past his window. "The obvious conclusion I come to, even before digging up any of the old data, and based on the critical time element here, is that our current plan can leave no possibility of error. The Shuttle has to get up there on time, and the Space Tug has to boost this thing the hell out of Earth orbit." Sanders pointed at Brookhaven with the stem of his Sasieni. "There simply can't be the slightest chance of letting Orion, or its cargo, reenter."

"You're giving USSA one hell of a responsibility."

"We both have the responsibility. But you definitely have the hard work. At least we know your people can accomplish miracles when the pressure's really on. They've shown us that. You simply have got to make sure the pressure's applied." Sanders suppressed his doubts convincingly.

"Let's have that refill now. I need more than fire to warm me."

Sanders nodded. "All right, hand me your mug—I'll fill you with another shot. Do me a favor and poke the fire while I'm in the kitchen."

He left, and Brookhaven found the poker, then absently pushed around the glowing embers, not really knowing what he was supposed to accomplish. Putting the iron rod back in its place, he grabbed two split logs and dropped them into the stirred coals. By the time he returned to his chair, the newly added wood erupted into a warming blaze. Brookhaven was drawn to it, hypnotized by the primal feeling. Then his mind drifted back to the discomfort he felt for the whole affair. Why were they still covering up? The incident occurred years ago. Why not just acknowledge the thing as a mistake? The past had clearly shown the result of hiding any unpleasantness that would eventually come out of the closet. They could just go to Lansing, explain the matter, and begin to prepare the public . . . for what? Christ, thought Brookhaven, after he again reached the dead end. Prepare them for the unknown. A package of unspecified military origin that could be spreading itself all over the atmosphere, scattering the "whatever" about the four winds.

Sanders returned with the drinks, having again skimped on the whiskey in the mug that was handed to his guest. His own was a double.

"Good job with the fire, Chris. It's certainly come back to life," Sanders noted.

Brookhaven ignored the compliment. "Greg, what the hell is up there?"

Sanders seriously considered giving him a straight answer. He would, after all, be carrying the primary burden of resolving the problem and holding the story together. But the rules were very strict. Perhaps in time.

"It's Top Secret Code Seven. I can't, Chris. What you know already about the matter is sufficient."

"Then refresh my memory on that. It was never very clear why we were brought in. Why couldn't they have taken care of the thing in a less complicated way?"

Sanders knew Brookhaven should at least be given a partial explanation. He carefully filtered out those portions of the affair which were the most sensitive.

"Basically the military had no choice but to carry this out in space. A surface solution was impossible. And we were both convenient. It was a question of timing. Our group was about to launch the Orion Platform, a huge research station intended to demonstrate a number of those classified experiments I mentioned before. We were sending it up on the last Saturn V Moon rocket, reserved for DISA's use. The highest levels became involved, and saw us as a natural. At that time Orion was the only spacecraft large enough to be configured as an orbital launch pad for a secondary payload insertion into deep space. The nature of the payload prohibited its direct launch from the Cape. It had to fly out of Vandenberg, where all risks could be minimized. And we were already set up there.

"Everyone felt safe with Orion, and Saturn V had proven its reliability. So we stripped half of our proposed experiments off the structure, and added a space propulsion stage that could accommodate the military's package. The idea was to get it into orbit, observe its reaction to the space environment, then propel it onto a collision course with the Sun.

"The only problem which that presented was the targeting precision required for a remote orbital launch. We needed a control center at close range, capable of taking over manual guidance if there were any complications. And that's where your agency came into the picture. Skylab had all the basic computer and navigation power to handle that end. It was already up, and was a proven manned laboratory. Orion's orbital destination was changed to match Skylab's. Your astronauts would execute the rest of the operation, and the military's problem would disappear. Now the outcome is history. You know the rest."

Brookhaven recalled the conclusion: "Yes, Orion went up successfully a month before the fourth crew reached the lab. You apparently monitored the package and concluded its contents hadn't been diminished by space exposure, so the decision to launch was *go* from the start of our activity. Then everything seemed to go wrong. The oxygen leak in the cabin. The thermal fluctuations. The guidance loss. When they finally settled into a condition where the launch from Orion could be attempted, it was your turn to go sour. Your secondary stage failed to ignite. We risked three EVA's to check and repair faulty circuitry, all of which got us nowhere. None of the manual overrides worked. After four days of hectic and futile attempts, it was decided to put off the operation until the next crew was sent up and your ground personnel could isolate the failures. There was no other solution."

Sanders continued from there: "We could have worked it all out if Congress hadn't put an abrupt end to future visits and literally abandoned Skylab, which is now only a dim memory. So we activated all the thrusters Orion carried, and using all its fuel, lifted it into as high an orbit as possible. That bought us an extra two hundred kilometers, which of course we then thought would mean twenty to thirty years of life. Which has now proven to be a tragic error, since we find ourselves only a few months away from . . . a descent."

Brookhaven interrupted: "You mean from a disaster."

Sanders could only stare outside into the darkness.

Brookhaven went on: "This whole situation is preposterous. I simply cannot believe the loose way you people operate. Placing anything potentially dangerous into Earth orbit must be patently illegal according to international treaty, ignoring the question of morality."

"Illegality is an irrelevant term when the situation is perceived as desperate. Those were desperate years, which is exactly what led the military into the original problem."

"It still stinks, no matter what rationalization you choose. Greg, how far back does this go? And what's become of the early effort that found its way into the package?"

"Well, the whole thing began under Johnson's administration and was carried through the Republican terms, so those executive circles were aware, along with the CIA, perhaps a few at the FBI, and of course the military's own people. It's all been kept securely in the closet. I doubt Lansing knows anything. The entire affair faded into benign neglect as the political climate calmed down. I suppose all that remains now are our dust-covered studies lying around a basement vault at the Fort Gabriel lab." He knew the last statement was far from true.

Brookhaven was having none of it. "All that remains, you mean, is a huge military spacecraft on the verge of bringing a probably lethal payload back to Earth." They both sat in silence for a long minute.

Realizing his own concern had been successfully transferred, Sanders decided to press on to more practical matters. "Chris, we have to get into the problem of secrecy." Both men took lengthy drinks of the Irish, then Sanders continued: "We have to keep the truth strictly to ourselves, with our staff aware of only parts of this. It has to stay that way, unless disclosure becomes unavoidable. Our cover mission should be approved based on the committee's reaction. The Shuttle crew will have to know certain details of the payload, and of course of the dangers. But that should be it. Not Clark's committee, not Lansing, not his staff or cabinet, no one else needs the knowledge. My belief is that only in the event of presidential decision against funding—which seems unlikely—or congressional delay would Lansing need to be given the details. But if that should happen, we would lay it all out. At that point, he couldn't very well say no."

"I think he should be told now. The responsibility

we're talking about is far greater than you or I should take on our own. After all, it was the executive branch that brought us in. It rests with them."

"No, this isn't the time. Christ, Lansing might decide to bring it all out, and open up a Pandora's box of public scrutiny. The spillover would have to affect the performance of your agency. Imagine yourself trying to carry out the mission subject to that exposure. Not wise, Chris. If and when he is told, it must be as a last resort . . . our trump card. We have to agree on this point."

Brookhaven let himself be transfixed by the fire for a long minute. Sanders was right. The task would absorb all his energy, without the complications that could arise if he were burdened with congressional investigations and endless cross-examination by the press. To succeed at all, they would have to keep their profile very low.

"All right, agreed. But we'll have to play it by ear along the way, and be sensitive to whatever leaks out."

"We certainly can't let that happen. The crew will have to be sequestered throughout and a convincing cover kept intact. Given that, we should sail smoothly through the next months.

"And now we get to my final point . . . contingencies. I think you must realize we need a guarantee. How do you plan to guarantee that our proposed space operation will work, assuming all other hurdles are negotiated?" He let the question hang in the air with his pipe smoke, and settled deeply into the stuffed chair. Trying to disguise the acuteness of his concern about depending solely on an agency not under his control, he fiddled with the pipe, knocking out the final ashes from his first bowl, carefully refilling a second.

"Well, what we have to do is go with our standard philosophy of redundancy. For every piece of hardware, there will be a backup. We design against single-point failures—that is, we avoid any one link that, if it goes, takes the entire system with it. All this is nominal practice with any spacecraft, and is amplified for a manned mission."

Sanders thought about that for a minute. "To me,

that's not enough. Considering the stakes involved, I personally would feel better if we could send up two Space Tugs, and back up the entire operation with a second vehicle. You do this with planetary missions."

"The problem with that is the Tug's size. We can pack only one of these things into the Shuttle. And using two Shuttle launches is unthinkable. We'll be pushing to have the April version modified and fully checked out."

"It has to be ready, Chris."

"I know . . . it will be. If we have to, we'll direct all of USSA's manpower and money into it."

"Back to my point. You've certainly had spacecraft with redundant designs fail in flight."

"True, but usually it's only a partial failure. We can usually salvage at least part of the mission."

"Suppose you lose the Tug's main boost engines? You mentioned the first flight had its problems."

"Well, I guess it's true, if you go to the extreme, that since this machine has only one basic function, propulsion, if the engines go, we fail. But that's strictly a very remote situation. There are four engines on the Tug, and if one goes we still have the others. We might not make it to the Sun, but we would get an orbit a couple thousand kilometers higher. I may have sounded too pessimistic earlier. We did get a 95% success first time out."

"You haven't convinced me yet."

"Okay, let me finish. First, redundancy means every system that supports the engines will be backed up by a secondary. Second, the Tug will be modified to correct the problems of its initial flight. Third, all the engines will have been test-fired in the lab before the Space Tug goes back up."

"In the lab? Not in a space environment?"

"In a simulated space environment. Very close to perfect."

"Could you send up spare engines on the Shuttle?"

"Hell, they can't carry up a parts store of replacements. Besides, it's too much to ask the crew to rebuild the damned thing in space. Our technology isn't quite ready for that. Look, Greg, we already have a good design. And it's too late in the game to be thinking about using anything else."

Sanders' worried mind searched for alternatives. "I understand the constraints . . . and your philosophy. You're approaching this as you would any other mission, an approach that has worked in the past. Okay. But I think this requires one more degree of insurance. The danger warrants something extraordinary. Don't you agree?"

"Of course I agree. But what you want just isn't available."

"What if DISA were to fly up another Space Tug using our own launch vehicle? We could provide the standby."

"Good idea, except for two things. One, the thing's too bulky to sit on top of one of your Titans. It only fits one launch system—the Shuttle's. Secondly, we only have one Tug that can be made ready by April. The others are way behind in development. Perhaps if we could wait a year your idea would make more sense."

Sanders sank even deeper into his chair, and into the thoughts that would push him to a decision he was beginning to see as unavoidable.

"If anything goes wrong with this plan, how soon could you recycle for a second try?"

"One month, absolute minimum. Orion will be down by then."

"And we can't get to it a month early—say in March?"

"It will take all our energies to make it by late April."

Sanders gazed up into the smoke cloud that was forming horizontal layers between his head and the ceiling, now filling nearly the whole room.

"So in fact, Chris, we have just this one chance."

"I can't argue with that summary. All I can offer in consolation is that I'll be personally in charge of the whole project, beginning to end, and I know what failure will mean. I guess you have to have that much confidence in me, and in the people at USSA."

"I do, Chris. I really do. It's just that on our side of this business, DISA is always conditioned to prepare for every possibility—we think in terms of what might happen to our mission if one of our spacecraft is lost . . . in our case, to enemy activity."

"Well, we shouldn't have to worry about hostile attack. Certainly the Russians won't give a shit about a quiet USSA Shuttle mission. And, when you come right down to it, we are our own enemy on this one."

"That's very comforting. I'll use that line next time I go before the Joint Chiefs."

Both men laughed at the suggestion, eagerly grabbing any comic relief offered to break the tension filling the room. Brookhaven was ready to maintain the mood change . . . Sanders was nearly there.

"Chris, you have a lot of work ahead. There will be many potential holes to fall into, and you'll have to stay alert to those. But keep in mind, between the two of us, if you get boxed in anywhere, financially or technically, I can, and will, turn the full energy of DISA into supporting the program. Understood? Just come to me before anything gets out of control."

"Appreciate the offer. It helps relieve some of the pressure. But, with the blessings of Clark's committee and the President, we should work the money problem quickly, and the technical problems at this point look manageable."

Sanders put down his pipe and, with mug in hand, rose from his chair and offered a handshake, which was accepted. "We'll stay close on this. Now, let's leave the war room. If you're ready for a few strategic games of eight ball, I'll get you another Irish . . . this time with some whiskey."

"You bastard. Isn't this a contrary espionage technique?"

"I'm out of practice," he chuckled. "Down the hall, two doors to the right, you'll find my new playroom. If you need it, the head's on your way, to your left. I'll be along in a few minutes. And you'd better practice, since we're talking big stakes. I want a dollar a game, in new currency."

Sanders turned toward the kitchen. As Brookhaven started down the hall, he noted, "This place looks like

a Clue board. Appropriate for a man in your profession."

"Don't take any secret passages."

"We already have."

The director of DISA smiled. He liked Brookhaven.
The man would have the technical ability to solve
their problem, no question of that. And yet . . . could
he perform under the pressures that would be building?
Never before had a USSA mission faced a deadline
this real. As much as Sanders wanted to believe, and
relinquish his own personal role in the adventure, he
simply could not. The senses that had been cultivated
over years in the delicate game of intelligence had set
off an uneasiness that refused to lift.

There simply was no backup. Unless Sanders created
his own. Tomorrow he would locate the ZW74 study
team to determine more precisely how dangerous their
problem had grown. The day after, at DISA headquarters, he would have to redirect the SCEPTER
activity.

Chapter Five

Once his options were clearly understood, Gregory Sanders wasted no time in developing the most efficient path to follow. With the cool efficiency that had led him to the directorship of DISA, and the compulsion for exactness instilled by his earlier CIA experience, he began the journey down that optimal route—a route that would bring the space technologies of the superpowers into direct confrontation.

Early the next morning he was in his office at DISA, making a series of local calls. His first reached Fort Gabriel's Department for Special Studies. He asked for code ZW74. There was a long pause. His clearance was being checked. Then Walters was on the line, with the video left off, per security regulations.

"This is Don Walters."

"Greg Sanders, DISA. I want a review of the work you did on Zone Wind. Can you be ready by ten o'clock?"

"That's going pretty far back."

"Yes, I know. Can you have it?"

"Uh . . . do you want a formal pitch?"

"No. Very informal. Only to myself. I'm particularly interested in the conclusions you reached on that study. Clear it with your department chief."

"I'll have to call in Mel Dankin. He's working in another lab. You do want to see us both, I assume."

"Yes. I'll want to review everything."

"All right. We'll get busy. Bye."

The next call was to Paul Creighton, in his own building.

"Hello, Paul, this is Greg Sanders."

"Yes, sir, what can I do for you this morning?"

"Do you remember Zone Wind?"

"Vaguely."

"Bring your file on it, and see me in my office."

"Right now?"

"Right now."

Sanders signaled his secretary, asking her to retrieve his own file on the project from their vault. She returned with the folder in minutes. He was reviewing the collection of Top Secret material as Creighton was announced and asked to step inside. He automatically closed the door behind him.

"What's up, Greg?"

"Look through your file. See if you can locate the last communication you received from the USSA people."

Creighton sat down in front of Sanders' desk, and began leafing through the paperwork. "The last seems to be a data transmittal form, dated eighth February, 1977. They note that the set concludes their data monitoring. The coded data was relayed to ZW74."

"Find the next memo dated prior to that. And read it."

He shuffled the papers. "This might be it." Creighton read silently, slowly beginning to realize its message, that it probably meant trouble. Showing obvious uneasiness, he mumbled, "H'm . . . it indicates USSA's intention to terminate monitoring of the Orion Platform."

"Does it ask for a DISA response?"

"Uh, yes, I think so."

"Read that part, aloud."

"Well, they say . . . 'It is requested that DISA formally direct USSA on continuation of the monitoring, if so desired. Without such direction, and indication of support funding, all monitoring will cease by February one, 1977. Reply expected ASAP.' "

Creighton sheepishly stared at the document.

"Well, Paul, what was the disposition?"

The man looked up into the cold eyes, his face reddened. "I don't recall receiving this memo, Greg.

And if I did, I probably assumed Orion was a dead issue." Then, after a pause, "I guess they were given no direction."

"I guess not. What were you working that winter?"

"Let's see . . . it was the European satellite network, I believe. Yes, we were all fairly heavily engrossed in that one."

"Understand. But this was critically important. Priority One. Were you ignoring everything besides your own project?"

"No. Well . . . not exactly. I had my secretary flag what seemed important. We both may have missed this."

"There's no excuse for that. Do you know where Zone Wind is now?"

The project details were slowly re-forming themselves in Creighton's mind. "Let me remember. That was the special military package. That's right. We were doing a deep-space disposal, with the Skylab cooperating. The attempt failed, and we planned to repair the propulsion stage later."

Sanders continued for him, wanting to move on to his point: "USSA's fifth Skylab visit was to do that. It never happened. Congress cut out future visits. Zone Wind is still onboard Orion."

The realization took firm hold of Creighton. "Do we have a serious problem with Orion, and GODS?"

"Critically serious. Orion is coming down within months." Silence followed. Sanders concluded: "In the future, Paul, I don't want anything missed that goes by your desk. Certainly not Priority One. I want you to appoint a deputy to go through everything received by your office. Is that clear?"

"Yes, sir. I'll see to it today. I guess the only excuse I have is my preoccupation with the Europeans—which I know isn't much of an explanation. Sorry."

"Just see that the correction is made. Now, I've got some other business to settle. That's all today." He buzzed again, the door was opened, letting Creighton quickly disappear into the hallway.

"Sharon, put this back into the vault, under a new category. Mark it SCEPTER."

"Okay, Mr. Sanders. Will do."

"And bring me the personal file on Paul Creighton."

She hurried off while Sanders formulated the entry he would have to make in Creighton's record. It would be necessary. That type of lapse was intolerable.

By ten o'clock he was inside Fort Gabriel's basement laboratories, after an hour's drive in his Mercedes down I95 through the sprawling Virginia suburbs. He was in Special Studies, and an escort had been required. After being led through a labyrinth of dark hallways, passing by scores of closed, combination-locked doors, he was standing before a nondescript entrance, labeled only 104B. Sanders' escort picked up the wall phone in the hallway and dialed.

A moment later the door opened, the fluorescent lights from inside nearly blinding Sanders. A light-brown-haired, slightly balding man in his late thirties appeared, dressed as drearily as any government engineer would be expected to. His lip wore a sparse blond moustache. From his belt dangled a calculator case.

"Hi, I'm Don Walters. You're Director Sanders," he said as he determined that by inspecting the blue badge his visitor displayed on his jacket lapel. "Come in, please." The escort left, and Sanders entered a windowless office, made dismally small by the floor-to-ceiling stack of thousands of computer printouts and magnetic tape files.

"We have our final results all documented. You can look them over first. Sorry, but Dankin couldn't get over this morning. Said he was tied up at the bio lab."

"Get him over here, Don. If necessary, we'll call his supervisor. I'll talk to him."

"Okay, sir, you'll probably need to do that."

The call was made. In five minutes Dankin appeared —a thin, eye-glassed, nervous scientist about Walters' age. The wait had given Sanders time to go through their last summary document on Zone Wind.

"Sit down, both of you. Now that I've seen this, I think there are only a few questions to ask."

The two seated themselves at the desk around

Sanders, who then went directly to the heart of his concern. "These conclusions are derived from all the data received through February 1977?" He needed to make sure nothing had been overlooked.

"That's correct, every scrap of data was considered."

"You indicate that three compartments of the package were giving readings that followed a normal growth pattern, a geometric progression. The other was showing unusual behavior."

"Well, it's been a while, but as I recall, that was what we found," Walters confirmed. "The three with normal patterns included both control samples and the one which was exposed to direct gamma radiation. The other, which had received laser excitation, was oscillating between periods of flat, or no, growth and exponential periods. All groups, at that time, were still well within the container's capacity limit."

"Have you made any long-term predictions?"

"No, we were only allowed to study and document the processed data received. Actually, this was all supposed to be turned off."

"Do you have programs set up to extrapolate from the existing data?"

Walters responded: "Yes, I suppose we do. But that would be fairly expensive. Takes hours of computer time on the IBM. We're modeling a very complex system, you realize."

"I know. I need to know the predicted state of each compartment projected to the current date. Can you have that . . . by this afternoon? I'll authorize the money."

"No, I doubt it. We'd be tying up 80% of our entire lab computing facility for those hours. That would take one hell of a priority level."

"I'll clear it. Go ahead with your input setup. This all retains its original top secret classification, by the way. Dankin, how much do you remember about Zone Wind? And what are you working on now?"

"Well, sir, I'm doing a bio survey of Chinese agriculture. It's been years since I was in touch with this project. I remember we looked at an enormous amount of telemetry data, but the funding went away and we didn't have the people or the time needed to make much out of it. We were pushing even to come up with the conclusions Walters gave you."

"Funding will soon cease to be a problem. I would like you to write up a few summaries on all this and what directions you wanted to pursue . . . every study, every theory you might have tested given the resources. We have a real problem here. The Orion Platform is coming down." He studied their reaction to that. "You're going to have a team again, and they will need a solid reference to start from. There's a lot of work to do, and we only have a few months."

He stood up, thanked them both for their time, asked to take copies of the data summaries back to DISA. He was told to check them out at the basement clearing desk.

Sanders added, "Again, you must treat this conversation, and everything related to it, Code Seven business. Zone Wind, especially. Do you both understand?"

Both engineers indicated they did. Walters escorted the DISA director with his bundle of reports to the clearing desk, then up to the front lobby.

By three he had fully digested the Fort Gabriel summaries, and having carefully studied the payload activity data, he was eagerly awaiting the report that came from ZW74. It came in over his office screen.

Their computer program had run successfully, with a 99.8% confidence factor in the predictions. Extrapolated to present date, the laser-stimulated group which showed erratic growth periods would now be into an exponential cycle, pushing close to its compartment limits. The three with normal growth patterns would be nearly filled to design capacity. Whether any compartments had ruptured would depend on the nature of the internal changes which had occurred, on factors too complex to estimate accurately. The actual effect of the laser excitation was still a major unknown. There were ambiguous indications of both control and enhancement of growth. No conclusions could be drawn. The observed, and predicted, oscillations had been too wildly irregular to make sense.

ZW74 had gone one step further. Their results had been fed into another program simulating satellite descent and the heat load on the Orion Platform and its package. Preliminary estimates led to the conclusion that 60% of the known payload content could survive entry. No speculations were made for the unknowns. All compartments would be shattered, and their contents released, during the atmospheric breakup.

Sanders read the last lines over twice. There was no longer even the slightest remnant of a question. He called in Sharon.

"Get me Simpson, Manning, and Du Priest from the SCEPTER program. I need them all for an eight o'clock meeting, tomorrow, in this office."

Before he could call it a day, there was one more action to take. He called Special Studies Director Bridges at the Pentagon. In a voice and expression that could not be misinterpreted as other than urgent, Sanders asked who, besides Walters and Dankin, could be assembled into a crash study group, whose research would combine the disciplines of biological warfare, general microbiology, and DNA manipulation. He was told there was virtually no one available. So many of the projects had been turned off years ago, most of the researchers had left for private industry, or the universities.

"I want your people to begin an immediate, intense, and persuasive recruiting campaign. Get back as many of our former scientists as possible. Tap all available sources, industry, universities, medical research, especially the DNA research centers—they've collected most of our brightest people."

Bridges wanted to know how many were needed, what specific disciplines, how much to offer, and who would provide the money.

"Send me the names of everyone who worked a project called Zone Wind. And their specialties. We'll start there. As for offers, make them so outrageous it will be impossible to refuse. Probably we'll need fifteen to twenty people now . . . so let's try to get them for seven to eight thousand a year, new dollars. But be flexible and convincing. Don't worry about the source of the money. DISA will have it transferred to your department by the week's end. Can you start on two million, new?"

A surprised and convinced Special Studies director could do nothing but promise to have it all in motion in a week. He apologized for the time delay, but said it would take the recruiters that long to reach contact points and set up interviews. Sanders understood.

The following day was devoted entirely to internal DISA business. Simpson, Manning, and Du Priest— the military liaison, program director, and technical manager of SCEPTER—were in Sanders' office promptly at eight, to discuss what they assumed would be the status of their project. All were supplied with enough strong coffee to assure their director they would be sufficiently awake for what was going to be an important realignment of their thinking.

Before he was asked, Manning offered casually, "If you want to hear that we're on schedule, Greg, you may be disappointed." He paused just long enough. "We're ahead of it." They grinned, as did Sanders. Theirs was the best team he had ever assembled on a defense project. They consistently overperformed on anything they were assigned.

"Gentlemen, what can I say? You know you're good. Problem is, when you're that good, you are soon expected to perform miracles. At least, expected to stay impossibly flexible. Which leads to the point of this morning's meeting. We've had some major redirection on SCEPTER. Or, I should say, for our second SCEPTER spacecraft. Fortunately the flexibility you worked so hard to build into the system will make its conversion much less difficult than it could have been. Still, the conversion will be radical. All of the sophisticated surveillance sensors of SCEPTER I will be stripped from the second version. All onboard telephoto equipment will go. All special communications. All long-range anti-satellite sensors. All anti-jamming devices. Everything related to protection and evasion. SCEPTER II will not be threatened . . . in the conventional sense."

Du Priest's curiosity wouldn't let him wait. "What are we sending up instead . . . a carton of anti-Soviet propaganda leaflets and some Hershey bars?"

Sanders laughed. "No. On the contrary. SCEPTER II will be a bit more aggressive than anything we've seen authorized on this side of the world. Perhaps even on theirs." He pressed a switch that closed an inner sound-proofed door. A few throats were softly cleared.

"All of SCEPTER's surveillance and defensive modules will be replaced by a neutron laser system . . . weapons class. It's not definite yet, but the particular unit will most likely be a model named HIMNL-9. I believe that stands for High-Intensity Multipath Neutron Laser. It's very large. I'll have the 'dark shop' people at Land Technics send you the physical dimensions and specs on the supporting modules that will be required. Sorry, chaps, but I can't go any further into the details behind all of this yet. You'll have to wait until we get into the mission design. Now, there will be two other systems to be given room onboard, and support connections. Both much smaller than HIMNL-9. We'll need a very high quality, medium-range zoom television camera, relaying real time. Capable of good closeups from, let's say, about five hundred meters. Next comes the only real unknown. We will have a yet-to-be-developed molecular biology sensor. The work on that hasn't even begun, but think about what you may need to support one. Enough of a challenge? I'll try to design a size and power envelope, to give you a hint."

Manning jumped in. "How about a small hint at the target?"

"I can't. Not yet. You'll all know in time. Right now we work the design. Du Priest, that's your problem. Come to me with any questions that I might be able to answer. Manning, you need to start the stripping process on SCEPTER II . . . it's in the vertical clean room now, isn't it, nearing final assembly. That will be another challenge. Don't take out anything Du

Priest may need. Hope you two remain friends through this."

Sanders knew they would. They only argued over the most efficient way to solve a problem, which merely served to enhance the mutual respect shared not only by those two gifted men, but among all in the room.

"Now for you, Simpson. Your role in all of this will be to get the Army to let us test HIMNL-9 at White Sands. You're to be in charge of all the testing, once they agree. You'll need to let them know we'll be testing against both inert material, mostly titanium and aluminum, and organic matter. For the organic tests we'll need an environmentally closed compound —specially sealed blockhouse, remote operations on the laser, close-in observation system for special sensors, that sort of thing. Along with this, it should be obvious you'll be spending more time in the 'dark shop' at Land. I'll arrange the clearance."

The DISA director opened his desk drawer, searching for a tobacco pouch. "I know there are questions, gentlemen. But just let them simmer awhile. Go back to your offices, think this over, let your minds roam around what will be needed to do your job. Brainstorm among yourselves. Keep what I told Simpson about the test targets confined to this room only, and the general nature of the change limited only to those who must know. And your schedule is this. We need to put SCEPTER II up, fully operational, four months from now."

The tobacco pouch was located, and he began to stuff a pipe. "Now, thank you for your time. I'll let you get to work."

As they left the room, Sanders was thinking about his decision. Brookhaven had really left him no choice —DISA had to supply the guarantee that the Orion monster would not return to its creators. He had quickly ruled out all orbital nuclear detonations. They would be useless against the contents of the package. HIMNL-9 was a natural. A quiet stream of dual neutron-photon beams, already developed for the intended purpose of disabling satellites, was the perfect solution. At this point it was of little consequence that its deployment was forbidden by SALT III. Greg Sanders had no intention of ever letting the White House, or the Russians, in on his decision.

Chapter Six

A full month had passed since the initial meeting between the directors of America's space agencies. Five thousand kilometers west of their activities, on the Pacific side of the continent, isolated from such hostile business as HIMNL-9, Daren Gray was supervising the conversion of the Coast space-physics facility into his Recombination Lab. He had just finished writing up, in elaborate detail, a preliminary series of experiments to demonstrate his proposed techniques. They would first run through test sequences to verify the biosecurity of the vacuum chamber and the smooth mechanical operations of the sophisticated microsurgery apparatus which would allow him to rearrange rungs on the DNA ladder.

Responsibility for the development and management of computer support for the research had been taken over by Laine Jeremy. Gray had made the recommendation—he could think of no one more competent, and Coast Research was delighted to have a woman in charge of such a prestigious study. It helped them appease the government auditors who still kept close watch over the minority mix of their management staffing. Neither had Coast been insensitive to the political power held by Henry Jeremy—his position as Stanford trustee, which supplied Coast a large part of its work, had certainly helped in securing Laine's appointment.

Daren was having a lunch date with Laine that day and had driven over from Stanford to take advantage of an unusually warm February weather system settling over Silicon Valley. He also wanted to share with her a disturbing letter just received from some colleagues on the East Coast.

They met in the center's crowded cafeteria. Laine suggested they pick up sandwiches and fruit, then find a sunny place in the grassy common of their campus-like complex. Locating a secluded spot surrounded by a group of small coastal cedar, with a faint view of hills in the distance peaking between the uninspired glassed office buildings, they collapsed into the grass, opened and passed around their lunch, and quietly enjoyed their momentary escape from the technical world.

Finishing a cafeteria-polished apple, Laine asked, with an underlying tone of self-confidence, "Well, Daren, are you satisfied with our progress so far?"

"I guess for a woman you've done all right." He tried to look serious.

"Mm . . . you couldn't be more left-handed."

"Of course I'm satisfied. You've become the perfect complement to our Stanford team. And you know how pleased I am that you're a part of all this. Hell, what Mark and I have done has been mostly dog work—setting up procedures, making sure the lab's physical system was built properly, necessary but routine stuff. Your part demanded much more creativity, and you've done that beautifully. Henry should be proud. You're a credit to your race."

"Thanks again."

"I just hope we have a chance to go through with it."

"What?"

"The letter I mentioned this morning. From Maryland."

"Your rivals at Fort Derrick?"

"Yes. They've got serious problems with an East Coast pressure group you may have heard of. Called People Against Genetic Tampering—PAGENT for short. Their spokesman's a fanatic named Joshua Wilkens. We've had a few letters and petitions sent us over the last year by them. Their chief complaint is the obvious—that we're altering the tapestry of life, toying with what should be sacred, stripping away the mystery of nature. So far it's all been pretty mild . . .

here. But they're based in New York, and Maryland is close enough to get a bit more direct attention. Fort Derrick reopened their lab a month ago, after it had been through another remodeling ordered by the National Institute of Health—following its last biology leak. Since then, the place has apparently been treated to a growing number of demonstrations from PAGENT, and it's lately turned ugly, according to Miles Severinson, the lab chief. People harassed on their way in and out . . . that sort of thing."

"Sounds like something we could be facing. I see why you're concerned. Sometimes it's hard to work under those conditions . . . if it becomes too vocal, you can't ignore it."

"Especially when you can sympathize, to a degree." He let his mind drift momentarily into the classical arguments. Then, absently, he continued: "Severinson wants me to fly out there next week. He's trying to arrange some televised debates between notable scientists on our side and PAGENT. That means, I would guess, he and I against Wilkens. Some of their local congressmen are getting involved, too. Arguing against the lab's proximity to major metropolitan areas. It should be challenging."

"Are you going?"

"I'm not sure. I suppose I should, but we're so close to our program start here, I can't see just leaving our work hanging. I could be tied up there a week. What do you think?"

"I think you should go. If they succeed in closing the shop in Maryland, it's fairly obvious we'll be their next target. You can afford to delay a week. Actually, Mark and I can take care of the final readiness tests, then by the time you're back, we'll be all set to begin the experiments."

"Can you and Mark work together . . . I mean, without friction?"

"Sure. Professionally we get along fine. Since he moved out, there have been a few touchy moments when we've tried to talk over the relationship, looking back, that sort of dead-ended conversation. But he's really doing better than I'd expected, and on a working

level everything has been very smooth. Although . . .
I think he's slightly astounded at how well I'm manag-
ing the Coast side. He never did accept the fact that
I possessed a mind that could function technically
perhaps as well as his. But I must be convincing him.
Certainly I have convinced you."

"I can't disagree with that. If you think you both
can handle it on a day-to-day basis, I'll talk to Mark
this afternoon. Guess you'd be working together starting Monday, while I'll be sharpening my debate skills
against the loyal opposition. You have all the test
details you need?"

"Yes, of course. Had our programmers set it all up
a week ago. Now relax. Make the trip. Without any
fear of sacrificing your scientific reputation. It's in good
hands."

"H'm . . . the best I've seen in quite a while."

"Careful."

By Friday all arrangements had been made for
placing the Recombination Lab into a week-long test
sequence, to culminate in an official blessing of its
performance, and a final go-ahead to begin the exhaustive
testing of Gray's theories. Daren observed with some
relief Laine's correct estimate of how well she and Mark
Wilson could work together. And Mark had been delighted to take the responsibility of chief scientist.

A Saturday morning phone call to Maryland helped
Daren assemble the reference material he would need
to back himself up in the proposed debate, and the
rest of the day was consumed by pulling together
the necessities of any trip. Sunday Laine drove him to
the airport, where he caught a noon flight out of S.F.
International that put him into Dulles at 7 P.M., re-
senting the loss of half a day. But Miles Severinson
met him at the arrival gate, which improved his mood
by letting him escape the problem of finding the fastest
way through the maze of towns up to Frederick, near
the Army base containing their lab.

On the drive to Severinson's home where he was to
be put up for the week, they talked of their respective
research, communicating openly as friendly scientists,

without the barrier of secrecy usually erected between rivals. The two were moving along different lanes of the same track—Severinson growing hybrid strains of *E. coli*, Gray playing with human DNA. Both fell into an easy sharing of ideas and techniques.

The same conversation continued through a late dinner at a seafood restaurant near Hood College, with Miles and wife, who tolerated their esoterica by enjoying being out for the evening. Gray sensed her unavoidable boredom, and tried more than a few times to change their subject, but Miles insisted on returning to the matter that was preoccupying him so thoroughly. During the after-dinner drinking, Severinson turned to the debate that had now been officially set up for Wednesday at the local television studio. Both of them were to sit on a panel with Wilkens of PAGENT, Armstrong of the state legislature, and Monroe, congressional representative for their district. It was to be an hour of confrontation moderated by a local newsman. Severinson then let slip, appearing to be casual, that there had been some contact made with *Face the Nation*, who indicated interest in negotiating a Daren Gray interview. It would be strictly standby status, competing with the President's budget advisor. Miles asked Daren if he minded the liberty taken in extending the offer . . . and Gray tried to disguise the delight he took at having been quietly elevated to such an esteemed place in the world of science. He said he would welcome the opportunity.

It was eleven-thirty before they returned to Severinson's place. Daren was shown to a guest room, thanked his hosts for the good dinner and conversation, then went immediately to bed.

That Monday morning began quietly enough, with breakfast provided by Miles, whose wife was sleeping in, and a leisurely drive out to Fort Derrick. But as they approached the front gates of the base, Miles noted with obvious apprehension that the size of the demonstration had doubled since the previous week. The street in front was in fact clogged with placard carriers, preventing any vehicle movement. Miles parked half a block away, and the two walked slowly toward the assembled protest groups marching in a roughly circular style directly in front of the gates, chanting what seemed to be repetitions of *"Don't play God . . . no gene freaks."*

Severinson appeared to be used to this form of activity, as he led Daren into the street among the demonstrators, looking over heads and between signs for the entrance to the compound. He spotted a group of uniformed Army guards about six meters beyond a forest of protestors locked arm-in-arm, forming an effective barricade to the site.

"We'll try to slide around this. I can't believe the Army hasn't broken it up yet."

"I don't think the military is allowed to use force against civilians anymore. But I'd expect to see the state police called in."

They pushed around to one side. Severinson spotted a small opening in the crush of protestors, and tried to step through it, with Daren following closely behind. Within sight of the gate they were stopped—confronted by a burly, intense young man with a bright red beard, wearing a stocking cap with a *"Stop Genetic Atrocity"* button pinned to it, and a black armband that displayed the white letters PAGENT.

"You can't go in," he boomed. "The people won't allow it. This lab is closed."

Severinson, in no mood to be bullied, responded by trying to push around him. He was shoved back firmly into Gray, who nearly lost his footing. Miles was angry now, and lunged forward—this time two more demonstrators had joined the red beard, locked arms, and held fast against Severinson's assault. The hole was now completely closed, and their mood was becoming even more defiant.

Gray grabbed his colleague, sensing his obvious anger would only lead to more trouble. "Miles, let's get out of here. The police will have to deal with this. I'm not into a fistfight with these people." He pulled him away from the human wall, and Severinson reluctantly let himself be drawn out of the group, shouting insults as he retreated from the protest that was now much louder, more densely packed than when they began their attempted penetration.

Once they were beyond the commotion, Miles fumed. "Jesus Christ, this pisses me off. They just don't understand. We're not monsters. We're simple scientists, trying to do something for their own goddamned good."

"Maybe it's the association with the old germ-warfare center you chose for your Lab's location. That surely doesn't help the image."

"Christ, it's only a coincidence. Look, we're not the goddamned military establishment. You'd think Hitler was personally in charge of the research—trying to eliminate the genes of Jewry. They're just not rational."

Trying to calm him down, Gray offered, "You're right about the irrationality behind this. Miles, can we find a quiet bar somewhere near, where we can pull ourselves together?"

"Yeah, but let's find a phone on our way. I need to make a few calls."

They drove a few miles, without spotting a phone, to a lounge Severinson knew near the college where the base officers and many of his staff met for "afternoon club." A rustic place, with mellow Virginia country atmosphere. Miles found a phone in the lobby. He called the state police. They had been notified earlier, and were already sending twenty squad cars full of troopers in riot gear to disperse the demonstration. He then called his office on the base. There was no answer. Apparently no one got in. A call to the base commander confirmed that. Only those in before 7 A.M. had missed the blockade—that meant only Army personnel. The commander had been instructed to take no action unless the state police were unable to break things up and asked for help."

"Nothing we can do but have a drink. I could use a double Scotch." They found a booth in a corner, under a shaggy deer head that looked out over the warm, but nearly deserted, lounge. Both ordered doubles, and as the alcohol gradually took hold of Severinson, his anger turned to a more controlled state of concern.

"This isn't good, Daren. The whole thing bothers

me. This type of overreaction is what cripples science. You realize we could all be turned off, shut down by those empty-headed alarmists. We're back to Galileo and the Inquisition. Already their actions have set us back years."

"It'll pass. We can make some good points this week, in a more reasonable forum, and reverse some of the negative publicity. The *Face the Nation* spot, if we get it, should do a lot in that direction . . . the public needs to hear some sober, reassuring justification for our research. You've done the right thing by asking me out. I feel I can help. But it's important we both stay cool and rational in the face of all the irrationality we'll be facing. You have to control that Viking urge to fight back."

He muttered, finishing his double, "What you don't know yet is the other half of the problem." Severinson lit a synthetic cigarette.

"There's more than what happened today? Like . . . sabotage?"

"Oh, no. The lab's pretty safe from that, being inside an armed military camp. Though, in a sense, in my more paranoid moments, I think it could be considered a form of that. Certainly it's a dilution of our effort, our ability to do the research. What's happened, Daren, is that we're losing our key researchers. Four of my most critical experimental scientists and seven technicians have resigned in the last month . . . just after we were finally set up. And this is the real mystery . . . do you know where they've gone?" He took a deep drag. "Into government, no less. Public service, for Christ's sake. All I could determine for sure was somewhere in the Pentagon. Could be CIA, NSA, could be any branch. Each of them mentioned salary offers that they couldn't resist. I asked the four scientists to give me an idea how much so we could try to work a matching raise. They were offered eighty thousand a year in old currency! My boss barely makes that, and he's in Washington. Now, only the military has that kind of money. So it must be for something hot."

Gray didn't need to have the situation spelled out any further. Something in the DNA field had been resurrected, and when the military needed scientists, they always got them. He flashed to the loss of his own colleagues, under much less rewarding conditions. But what did the Pentagon need with a carefully selected group of microbiologists and recombinant DNA technicians . . . now? Biological warfare didn't seem a reasonable answer. We weren't at war. Not even close to one. Besides, all that business was supposedly forbidden by the Geneva Treaty. There had been no catastrophic plagues, or epidemics. No serious new biological threat since legionnaire's disease, years ago. Gray wondered if it might be in response to suspected new forms of terrorist activity.

Miles interrupted his chain of speculation. "There may even be more. I've gotten an indication that—and I know this does sound paranoid, but it comes from a respected source—that some of the demonstrations and harassment, especially that from PAGENT, may have been encouraged by government agents."

"Now, wait a minute. What purpose would that serve?"

"It's not all that outlandish. Some of the people I lost expressed quite a lot of discomfort with working under the pressure of the demonstrations. Many, in fact, had received threatening phone calls, that sort of thing. I've gotten them myself, so I know it's not been pleasant. They told me the government promised them, along with a lot of money, obscurity and anonymity, if they wanted. And, if needed, protection. Of course, we could offer none of that."

"That doesn't prove a connection. Who's your source?"

"A captain, at the base. You don't need his name. He recognized a face in the crowd of PAGENT people a few weeks ago. Someone from FBI he had met at a briefing on counterespionage training for base agents. He thought it very curious . . . told me about it over drinks one afternoon. I asked if he was certain. He was."

"They are that determined." It was a statement. Daren wondered why his lab hadn't felt the same pressures. "Why have they picked you, Miles?"

"All I can figure is that most of our people used to work in government. In fact, most for the military. Guess they wanted the old team back. It's almost poetic retaliation. We picked up this group during our own hiring campaign in seventy-five, when recombinant research was becoming a growth industry and they were being let go, victims of funding cutbacks. We got them all pretty cheap."

"This doesn't solve your problem, and sounds a bit selfish . . . but I hope to God that's all they want."

The situation Miles described that morning haunted Daren's thoughts the next few weeks. During his *Face the Nation* interview he publicly speculated on the military's renewed interest in biological research. Whatever they were up to, whatever it might mean to his own research, this time he wasn't going to let the government involvement go unnoticed.

Chapter Seven

Anatole Karenov was looking forward to his return to Moscow. The last month at Novosibirsk had been extremely frustrating. This particular Russian winter had relentlessly maintained a blanket of oppressive cold, and the fierce wind off the steppes persisted for the entire period of his stay. His continual wrestling with Scherensky and the planning staff over remodeling the Cosmos flight sequence had been a grueling contest of wills, resolved only the last week through Marya's bitter concession to postpone future Cosmos flights until a critical propulsion component was redesigned and available. The entire effort had been agonizing.

Yet it was the unsettling business emanating from the Kremlin that caused Karenov the most concern, and that had become a serious distraction. The show trials of the Alternative Party were clearly outrageous. He could no longer rationalize them, could no longer accept the premise that such a lesson was needed for the good of the State. And while he knew their theory well—suppress all deviations from the true course—this time the extent of the action would prove counterproductive, of that he was certain. Although the creation of a climate of fear would accomplish its near-term objective internally, there were too many outside the bloc who would be frightened away for good. At just the time communism could make its long-awaited play in an energy-weakened Europe, Russia again was showing its thin veneer of socialist idealism to be floating over the still-simmering molten core of Stalinism. Would the Gulag never vanish?

Karenov was far from considering himself a trouble-maker. In fact, his allegiance to the Central Party had been a model of what the system attempted to cultivate. There had never been in his mind the slightest question about the direction Soviet society had to follow. At least, not before 1968. Then Dubcek had arisen in Czechoslovakia as a fresh example for many Russians, a figure who seemed right for their time, who might lead communist society into its next stage of evolution, one of enlightenment and a more humanistic ideal. When that light was so ruthlessly crushed out, Karenov began to have his first serious doubts about the vision emanating from the collective wisdom of the Politburo.

As the years passed by the gloomy aftermath of Dubcek and the Prague Spring, another hope emerged as détente slowly grew into the Soviet system, a flower cultivated by the strange American President Nixon and grasped by his own government. He had therefore been encouraged in the feeling that perhaps once the spark had been lit, it might again proceed, though more slowly and less brashly consistent with the Russian style, in the direction of a more humanitarian climate. Thus Karenov had supported détente enthusiastically.

And then his country had signed the Helsinki Accords, opening the doors ever so slightly. But conditions everywhere seemed to be improving. The technical exchanges, the cultural contacts, even the sophisticated goods that would be coming in from the West were secondary to the possibility that the Kremlin would loosen, was loosening, its iron grip on the Soviet people. They had even begun to tolerate a certain level of dissent. A mood of cautious optimism was once again beginning to push aside the melancholy Russian soul.

But, as always, it lasted far too briefly. The pendulum had begun swinging with a vengeance. First came the intrigues in the African continent, in Latin America and the Middle East, with the Cubans enlisted as their proxy warriors. Next the Persian adventure, which had outraged nearly the entire world. Karenov, of course, understood his leadership's cynical motives in this too, knew it was deemed necessary to encourage revolution everywhere except within or too near the motherland. Then came the collapse of SALT II and the Sino-American alliance, which again brought the great powers to the brink, followed by the hasty patchwork of SALT III. And now, incredibly, there was the unexpectedly strong internal reaction—the human-rights movement, the Russian Emergence, and finally the new Alternative Party, which was being supported by large segments of the arts, sciences, and professions.

The pushing match which resulted could only further entrench the Kremlin. So he had anticipated some tightening up, some show of determination that would silence the dissident cause, show them the futility of believing they could change Soviet internal policy.

So now, too, came another succession of trials. A few would have sufficed. But the show was again going too far. Members of the Alternative Party, whose only crime was to express desire for a more humanistic communism, were being sentenced to fifteen years hard labor. Even the communist parties of Europe were denouncing the show of intolerance. The State had as usual countered from a position of anger. It was an emotional response. Not well reasoned. Certainly not at all well calibrated to provoke the appropriate end result.

It was this failure of judgment that bothered Karenov most acutely. More so than the retreat from a positive direction for the people. The Politburo was acting irrationally. If one applied logic to the matter, the whole thing was nonsensical. Communism was poised to make inroads within an economically declining West. At the same time, the Kremlin was showing Russia at its authoritarian worst. The same nonproductive cycle was being repeated.

The action was, to Karenov, logically inconsistent. And his realization of this was leading him to believe that perhaps it was time for a change in their high command. The Politburo had reached senility, had probably become too far out of touch with the world to operate wisely. He had therefore decided that on his return to Moscow, he would test the waters. Very carefully, and discreetly, he would pursue those secret avenues that were traditionally followed whenever a major change in the Soviet power structure seemed necessary to save the State from self-destruction. He was even prepared to contact leaders of the Alternative Party.

So it was this mood of anticipated adventure that contributed most importantly to his eager desire to leave Novosibirsk, and reenter the world of Moscow politics. He was feeling this strongly when the official courier delivered the sealed package sent him from the Kremlin.

The wind was particularly strong that day, audible through the thick walls of his barracks apartment on the border of the space complex. He was taking great satisfaction from his completion of the final report on the disposition of the Cosmos incident, the last chapter necessary to free himself from his current exile. The message he read brought all his plans to an abrupt halt. As if the Soviet command possessed a sixth sense, one which could somehow detect whenever an official was entertaining a drift in thought or action that could be considered mischief. The message neutralized any possibility of Karenov soon pursuing his ideas on political realignment.

Intelligence reports had come into the KGB, which had collected the information, analyzed the material, and then passed on their suspicions to the Kremlin. Two items had been noted as possibly correlated, both involving U.S. military activity. First, there appeared to be definite reason to believe the Pentagon was engaged in an accelerated study of biological engineering, possibly biological warfare. Secondly, a tight curtain of secrecy had simultaneously closed around a USSA Shuttle flight and the defense space agency's surveillance program known as SCEPTER—so tight, in fact, that a special personnel screening had abruptly and totally cut all information flow from contacts in that area. Since the situation had potential implications for Soviet space activity, and Karenov was already located at the center containing all space-related reference material and the data base which could support research on the problem, he was ordered to spend the next weeks carefully studying the KGB reports, which had been included in the delivered package. He was to evaluate the suspected connection, and fold into his analysis all additional KGB input from their continuing effort. The Kremlin had canceled his return trip to Moscow. Any business he had anticipated accomplishing there would be handled for him by his staff.

Karenov's initial reaction was complete disgust. At the Kremlin, for once again interfering in his own plans. At the KGB, for fabricating what was probably another preposterous story to hurl back at the Americans and to continue the policy of insults. At the Americans, who he knew were developing for SCEPTER sophisticated surveillance sensors and anti-satellite capabilities that bordered on a breach of the SALT III accords. Also, at their stupidity for giving the KGB enough information to proceed on this witch hunt. And now he was to decide if the reports had any validity. Given his current inclination toward the lack of rationality in the Soviet command, the allegations of the KGB could easily be pure fantasy spun from the propagandist machine that constantly tried to keep the international climate off balance. Could he take this matter seriously? He doubted it. And the doubts were becoming a debilitating influence on his capability to function in a productive manner. It was increasingly difficult to maintain any serious interest in these matters.

In a state of motivational impotence, he did the only logical thing he could. He read the KGB summaries in their entirety. Then he read the supporting material that had detailed certain suspicious activities of the U.S. military during the years 1971 through 1974. He completed the reading within an hour, and the sum of all he chose to absorb from the pages of sketchy information and grossly stretched associations was clear. It was all the most outrageous, most preposterous fabrication.

One half-hour later Anatole Karenov was in the

communications branch of the central administrative building of Novosibirsk. His reply to the leadership of the Kremlin was brief and to the point. Karenov stated his view that the proposed study was an incredible waste of his time, that he had other, many other, more important matters to accomplish in other parts of his agency. He respectfully requested permission to return immediately, as planned, to Moscow. Analysts of lesser importance could be assigned to study the KGB's latest concern. He was needed elsewhere.

Chapter Eight

The explosion sent shreds of titanium shattering off or plunging through every object around the test site for a distance of two kilometers. A blinding ruby fireball blossomed where moments earlier the one-and-a-quarter-ton HIMNL-9 had rested, humming louder and louder, steadily glowing an ominous red. Anyone viewing the event would have been awed by its beauty—a dazzling display of magentas, oranges, and yellows in the blast nucleus, with flecks of silver and white glinting in the sunlight as the shrapnel mushroomed into a lethal starburst.

But there had been no observers—at a safe distance. So there was no one left at the site to appreciate this drama of light and sound. The bodies of six weapons technicians had been blown into atoms an instant after the laser reached critical energy. The four observers were swept hundreds of meters from their observation shield, mutilated beyond recognition. A minute later all the airborne debris clattered to the ground, and it was over. Nothing remained but a blackened crater and a still-glowing puddle of liquid metal at its center . . . and fragments of human flesh, metal, and rock scattered over the charred desert sand.

The lone monitor at White Sands' central complex sixteen kilometers away was on the phone to the base commander, Stevens. But the report he made was superfluous. The entire complex felt the shock waves of the blast. Everyone knew there had been a catastrophe.

Four hours later Gregory Sanders and two investigators from Land Technics arrived in a specially chartered jet, having left Washington immediately after the grim report was relayed via satellite by Stevens. An extensive area around the blast point had been quarantined, with no one allowed in to investigate until the Washington team was given its chance. Sanders and the two Land scientists went directly to the only direct witness. Lieutenant Conroy had been at the complex's monitoring station watching test data stream into his console, numbers flashing across the screen, until all the needles went to their pegs and his lights turned bright red.

Everyone else in the control room was ordered to leave, and the module doors were then locked securely. Four nervous men stood in a tight circle around the still-glowing display panel. Then Sanders asked the obvious questions:

"Conroy, hasn't there been any response from their underground bunkers?"

"None whatsoever, sir. And the phone lines are still intact. We've tested the link."

"Then was there no warning, no hint of an imminent explosion?"

"I . . . I'm really not sure. My readings were looking normal until just before the end. The laser had been on for about nine minutes, with its energy powered up to the expected level. It stayed there for most of the test. Now, please remember that I'm no expert in this, it's all new technology to me. But at about the nine-minute mark, a strange thing happened. There was a rapid energy surge. As if the main control had been turned down fast, and then turned up full right after. A huge swing . . . happened in a second. It was all so fast. After that, I watched the screen for maybe another thirty seconds, observing the data increase faster than any rate I'd seen before. I tried to call Simpson at the site. Couldn't reach him. During that time my eyes were glued to the console, and the energy buildup just kept increasing. My board started lighting up. I'd estimate this continued for a full three minutes. I was still on the phone to the observation post when . . ."

He turned silent.

"And then?"

"Then my console went red, and a second later I felt the shock."

Sanders thought a long minute. "Were you in voice contact with anyone before the blast?"

"Not during the test. Last verbal contact was about fifteen minutes before they turned on the laser. Simpson told me they'd all be too busy to stay on the line. We verified that my monitors were picking up test signals all right, and that was it."

"Okay, Conroy, we'll need printed copies of all the data that came in during the test. Everything . . . energies, stress loads, temperature readings, whatever is available. It *is* all recorded, I hope?"

"Sure. Can have everything for you in five minutes."

"And, Conroy, this is national-security business. You're not to speak of this matter to anyone but the people standing here."

"Yes, sir."

An hour later Sanders was staring into another set of consoles and screens. An unmanned drone aircraft had been sent up and was being flown over the test site by remote control. Sanders was watching its photo survey in real time. Onboard were a dozen sensors designed to pick up any indication of residual contamination, any toxic gases, chemicals, or radiation that could possibly be dangerous. Also onboard was a collection of caged lab animals which were being exposed to the air directly over point zero.

The plane circled the area for half an hour. Two objects were spotted, at three hundred fifty and six hundred meters, tentatively identified as human bodies. All readings from the sensor group were, however, coming in completely normal, except for some expected high temperatures at the blast point. The test animals remained healthy.

Major Donovan, who was remotely flying the plane, looked over at Sanders, asked if he should deploy. Sanders nodded a go-ahead, and the Major took the craft to a preselected point, pulled a lever, and released an instrumented module which parachuted gently to a landing just beyond the crater rim. The package contained a second group of test animals—two white rats and a small monkey. Electrodes fastened to their bodies recorded moderate alarm at the surface impact, then signaled all subjects had quickly resumed a normal response.

Sanders focused on those signals, waiting for something to show itself. But everything remained nominal. For five minutes. Then ten. Then twenty. Donovan, still circling his drone, announced he had picked out another body, at nine hundred meters. He would continue to spiral out from the center, photographing everything on the surface. Sanders again nodded approval, got up from the console, and walked over to the corner of the room where the men from Land Technics were quietly studying copies of the recorded test data.

He sat down next to them, silent and intense. He tried desperately to focus his attention on what they were discussing—the dry details of actual versus design performance for the HIMNL-class laser systems—but he drifted.

Even before, as he had watched the aerial survey, forcing himself to concentrate on the sensor readings, a sense of uneasiness was sifting into his consciousness. Now the thoughts formed themselves too clearly to ignore. His private plan was responsible for the loss of ten men. And among the ten was Abe Simpson. More than a DISA manager, Abe had been a close and trusted friend. In either role, Simpson was irreplaceable. And it had all been Sanders' doing. Had he moved too quickly? Was he pushing too hard? And the more basic question hung in the air: Given the grief his unauthorized venture had already produced, could he justify its continuation? But there was still no alternative.

One of the Land men pulled Sanders out of this indulgence in self-doubt by giving him something else to wrestle with.

"Greg, I think we've concluded something very important from the preexplosion data. And very strange. We're going to have to factor this in, but we really don't know yet what it implies."

"And that is?"

"After the sudden swing in the laser energy, which was either a mechanical failure or some frantic input actually controlled by the chief engineer, three minutes of steady energy increase took place before the laser reached criticality. Now comes the mystery. During that buildup, a total of five separate sound and light alarms were designed to be set off as increasing energy levels were reached and exceeded. Our data shows that each round of alarms was triggered."

He paused to let the information register.

Sanders realized the obvious. "So that means the alarms were ignored. Otherwise we would have found the men in their bunkers, probably alive."

"That's the real problem. The bunkers were within easy reach of each group. All were trained to go under at the first hint of trouble. The possible scenarios were rehearsed thoroughly. No gallant heroics to save the laser were allowed."

Sanders puzzled over the facts, looking for the key. "Perhaps the energy surge produced some transient radiation burst that killed them all at that point, leaving HIMNL-9 unattended."

"You could speculate that . . . but no, that solution's really not plausible. The mechanical structure was intact until the very end, and no amount of beam or laser energy could escape in any direction other than along the line of pointing. The beam is too precisely focused, and the shield too overdesigned. Besides, any escaped radiation would have shown in the test data record. There's nothing."

"And yet the alarms did go off, you're sure of that? And no apparent attempt was made to shut things down? And no one got to the bunkers."

"That's right. A real puzzle."

Sanders thought over his own summary. "The power gyration, turning the energy down, then up full—could this have been a hurried attempt at shutdown that was botched?"

"H'm . . . might have been, except turning it back up just doesn't make any sense. It isn't a logical human input. It happened before any alarms were sounded."

"A lot of this doesn't make sense."

The Major broke into their conversation. "Mr. Sanders, it's been thirty minutes on the ground for the test animals, and everything still shows normal. The aerial map is complete out to two kilometers, which appears to be the end of the debris pattern. Should I continue?"

"Did you locate any more . . . bodies?"

"I think so. Something showed at eleven hundred meters, which could have been part of a corpse. It's hard to say for sure."

Sanders shuddered. Deep inside, his earlier anxiety was returning.

A heavily equipped Nuclear Regulatory Commission van crawled along the narrow dirt road that led from well-guarded barricades to the test site. Sensors inside and out took continuous measurements of the atmosphere. All readings were within normal range. The truck seemed completely out of place—its yellow body striped with bright Day-Glo-orange warning signs from the NRC contrasted dramatically with the flat, off-white barrenness of the landscape. Dark glass portholes provided its passengers a good view of the desolation passing by, a scene as dull and uninspired as they were tense and questioning. The men inside approached their destination with a mixture of feelings. They concentrated on the technical challenge ahead—to suppress the reality of what they would have to examine.

Sanders, the Land men, and a medical examiner from the base were to spend the morning poking through the remains of the blast, looking for any clue to its cause. Late into the previous evening all available data had been studied in excruciating detail, and nothing was found to hint at a possible solution. The recorded data from this HIMNL-9 test had been compared bit for bit against previous successful tests, and found to match exactly. Everything pointed to a perfectly routine operation of the laser before the mysterious energy swing. And, in fact, even after. Since HIMNL-9 had never been allowed to build up to such high energy levels in the past, a computer simulation was run at Land

Technics which took an imaginary laser to that same failure point. The simulated data followed the actual White Sands experience precisely. Given the same sudden decrease and increase of the control, the simulated laser at Land experienced a regular energy buildup, sounding hypothetical alarms along the way, until seconds past the three-minute mark, the computer quietly signaled its operators to end the simulation. The fictional HIMNL-9 had just blown itself to bits.

They confirmed there had been no possibility of leakage before criticality. And they had verified and re-verified that the real laser's alarm system had indeed functioned perfectly. Both sound and light pulses could be seen in the data stream recorded by the monitoring instruments.

So they were forced to conclude that nothing in the test of HIMNL-9 was anything but ordinary. Nothing in the data pointed to the slightest failure, either mechanical, electrical, or human—with the singular exception of that one puzzling power reversal. It was as if some maniac had suddenly grabbed the controls away from the chief engineer, and slammed the lever full on.

Their van stopped just outside the rim of the shallow crater, where the package of test animals had landed. The driver spoke over his intercom: "This where you want to stop?"

"Yes, this is fine. We'll deploy our gear, and you can activate the sensors. Give the base our exact location. And give me another reading on the air," Sanders requested.

"Okay, I'll get that." The driver studied his meters, looked over the screens of his console, jotted down important numbers. "Seems to be all right. No contaminants, no radiation."

Sanders carefully considered that report. The van had been equipped with NRC contamination suits flown in from Los Alamos.

"I see no need to bother with the suits. They would only slow us down, and the area appears clean enough."

Then, to the driver, "But you're to stay in the truck, watching the monitors."

"You bet. I wouldn't consider anything else. I've gone through these before."

The four discussed their plan for the day as they checked their cameras, video tape equipment, and recorders.

Sanders summarized: "Dr. Weston and I will make a quick inspection of the test animals, then proceed to the first body in sector D15. You two will begin sampling from the crater center, then move out radially. If you can, dig into the test-stand bunker and check it for survivors. We'll do the same as we pass the observation post. All photos and samples are to be logged and voice-recorded. We want complete descriptions. Understood?"

They all did. It was standard procedure for any air-crash reconstruction. Checklists were gone over one last time. Then the van's side doors were opened and the four passed through, stepping down awkwardly with their gear strapped in place on pack frames, until the group stood outside in the eerie silence, feeling a certain kinship with Armstrong's walk on the moon— the uncertainty of what would be discovered.

Sanders and Weston went to the animals, found them normal and active. They radioed the other two who were heading for point zero. "Test subjects all healthy. Proceed as planned."

"Acknowledged."

The Land team was already photographing and collecting surface samples as Sanders walked toward the observation post, where Simpson had spent the last minutes of his life recording the performance of a laser that now would never see the inside of SCEPTER II. The post was easy to find—they quickly located the single object left protruding from the sand, the tragically unused concrete bunker. Both men stumbled through the sandy soil to the top of its round form. Sanders studied it carefully, noted the pockmarks left by the titanium shrapnel, and observed it was otherwise intact.

He bent over and swept away the sand that had been blown over the top hatch since the blast. He tried the handle release, and the circular hatch door swung open easily. Nothing was jammed. Another piece of the mystery refused to disappear.

Sanders looked inside, probing with his flashlight under benches and tables, hoping for some hint of a curled-up, partially hidden body. But there was nothing. The small pillbox-shaped room contained no secrets. He rose, slowly shook his head at a concerned Dr. Weston, and gently resealed the hatch door.

They walked over to the first body.

At eleven-thirty all four men returned to the van to review their findings. The Land men discussed details of the fragment types they had picked up, of the cooled titanium blob that remained in the crater center, and of the diminishing probability anything useful could be determined by continuing their survey. They would do so for completeness, but weren't encouraged that this could help solve the problem. They confirmed that the second bunker had also gone unused.

Weston put in a call for an NRC medevac vehicle to return the bodies to the base. It was decided he and Sanders would both return so the DISA director could be on hand during the autopsies. The Land men asked Weston in what condition they had been found.

"Well, as suspected, the four bodies still intact were the observers. We could tell that from their clothes. No sign of the others, except for some random shreds of clothing and a few bone fragments." He sighed. "Simpson was the second one we found. They're all torn up badly, perforated by metal shards. Positive identification will be difficult. We were able to find Simpson's badge still on him. We'll need dental records for the others. The last one . . ." he swallowed hard. "It's messy. Only half the body left. Probably was much closer to the blast. Carried the farthest. The other two will have to be identified first."

All the group became quiet again. Then Sanders asked the driver to put him on the radio. He checked with the medevac team. They were on their way.

By three, all recoverable bodies had been sealed, labeled, and carried with Sanders and Weston back to a specially prepared examination room at White Sands' medical building. Sanders paced in a lobby outside as Weston performed the necessary, unpleasant task of inspecting what was left of the mutilated corpses. He was going over the details again in his mind.

The facts still didn't fit into a logical pattern. The smooth, perfect operation of the laser. The sudden, unexplainable energy reversal, followed by five sets of noisy alarms that gave the team three full minutes to reach safety. The failure of anyone to reach that safety. HIMNL-9 was obviously self-destructing, and no one had done a goddamned thing about it.

He was at this impasse when a uniformed man approached, cleared his throat, and nervously asked if he was Gregory Sanders of DISA. Sanders grunted a yes, and then was asked if they could speak a minute, in private. They moved to a quiet corner of the lobby.

"Mr. Sanders, I'm Roger Clinton from the Target Range Section. I've been working on the preparation of test packages for your experiments with the laser, and, well, we found something that may have some bearing on your investigation. I didn't know for sure, but thought it best to report it."

Impatiently Sanders hurried him along. "Okay, what is it?"

"Well, we were doing a routine check, going over the target selection for both test series that were planned—the inorganic compounds and the biology modules that were to be tested at the sealed target range. Your Mr. Simpson had requested the five inorganic targets for testing yesterday . . . the four biology units were to be kept in storage until the second round of testing. On checking that last group, it appears one is missing. Best we can determine is that it was delivered to the firing range by mistake, along with the other five."

Sanders straightened, and turned pale. "Jesus Christ. The targets!" The force of his reaction startled the man from the Target Range Section. Sanders bounded out of the lobby.

On his way back to the blast site he studied the aerial photographs hastily grabbed from the office used the night before in their futile attempt to locate clues in the debris. He quickly found the one sector that had amazingly gone unnoticed. The target setup. And there it was. He looked closely, using a magnifying lens to bring out more detail. Four blackened objects sat in a sandy trench. Two other objects appeared in the same line, to the right, unblackened, untouched. The total number was six!

Sanders looked even more closely. Very faint, but still visible, surrounding the target stand, he picked out a perfectly shaped concentric ring, or crust, light blue in color, lying on the sand at about a seven-meter radius.

He ordered his driver to hurry. As the van raced by the Land pair still in the field, they looked up from their sampling and tried to wave him down. Sanders ignored them, continuing along the road in a trail of dust.

The van was ordered to halt almost two hundred meters away from the target area. This time Sanders took the precaution of sealing up within one of the contamination suits. He reviewed the sensor readings of the outside environment more carefully than before. Still nothing unusual there.

Sanders activated the airlock system, then opened the van's rear hatch, emerging from the protection of the NRC vehicle. Carrying only a group of sample bags, a small aluminum shovel, and his Hasselblad, he made his way across the white sand.

Approaching the target trench, he took a series of photos, then rushed immediately to the targets themselves, stepping cautiously over the encircling blue crust. He looked closely at the fourth target in line, the last one blackened or shattered by the force of the weapon. Unlike the first three, it had not been reduced to rubble by the energy stream, but merely melted into an unrecognizable heap. With his shovel, he pushed it over. The metal plate on the bottom of this unit was rippled and charred, so he could barely read the letters stenciled beneath. But there was really no doubt. They formed the words, *"Biology Test Unit 1—*HIMNL *Testing Program."*

Back at the base complex Sanders dropped off the exposed roll of film he took of the target stand and the area around it at photo processing. Next he deposited the group of sample bags, every one filled to capacity with crusty blue sand, in a refrigerated isolation vault of the medical building. He then hurried up two floors to Weston's lab, pressed a buzzer by the door that sealed the doctor's autopsy examination from the rest of the world, and waited for a reply.

Weston answered over an intercom: "Yes, what is it?"

Sanders spoke into the transmitter mike beside the buzzer: "Greg Sanders here. I need to talk to you. It's important."

"Not now, I'm in the middle of a delicate process. Trying to understand some peculiar results from the autopsies."

"I think I know."

"Oh, you do? Just a minute."

In thirty seconds Weston appeared at the door, dressed in a stained white lab coat, smelling very unpleasant. He pulled down the surgical mask hiding his face.

"And just what do you think I've found?" Weston asked.

"Give me your conclusion first. I need the independent check."

Weston sensed the man's urgency in the gravity of his expression. "These men were dead before the blast."

"And you found no trace of radiation or heat as the lethal agent."

Weston looked at him intently, returning his cold stare. "No, it appears death was caused by a viral or chemical source that caused direct paralysis of the nervous system. Very sudden. Looking at the blood coagulation, I'd put time of death three or four minutes before they were hit by any shrapnel."

Everything finally fit together. HIMNL-9's fourth target was not a block of harmless aluminum. Its fourth test firing had transformed and released the contents of Biological Test Unit 1, which contained a mild sample of what was in Orion's package. That had spread immediately, carrying a fatal wind to everyone at the test site; to the four observers, who must have collapsed in seconds; to the technicians positioned around the laser; to the chief engineer, whose hand was on the control, whose hand twitched erratically as the man trembled while his central nervous system was breaking apart.

For some reason the lethal cloud had died away before reaching the base. There was still a lot to be understood.

Among the many reports and security procedures Sanders organized that evening while closing down the test program, a call was placed to Special Studies Director Bridges at the Pentagon. Bridges was ordered to double the staffing and laboratory space of ZW74 within the week. His recruiters were to identify every biogenetic researcher who had been considered before and who either had not been approached or had resisted their offers. Twenty of the best of that group were to be recontacted and offered bonuses of 10,000 new dollars to begin a special research study for the government. The project was now to consider their funding unlimited.

Chapter Nine

Only the tightest security measures taken since the Manhattan Project kept the White Sands disaster out of the headlines. And yet even without knowledge of that incident, McAndrews of the *Post,* after pursuing a curious assortment of leads, was able to piece together a story that brought the directors of both space agencies to their first critical confrontation. The story gave their projects exactly the exposure they had hoped to avoid. McAndrews' column also reached Daren Gray, who, after puzzling over the strange events occurring within the science community, came a step closer to understanding the relationships among those forces suddenly bearing down on recombinant DNA research.

Chris Brookhaven read the article on Thursday morning, six days following the HIMNL-9 debacle, in his USSA office at Houston. A project scientist working on the April Shuttle handed him their satellite copy of the *Post*'s early edition, pointing out the piece and noting the sensationalism the Eastern press constantly tried to make out of the most harmless activities. Brookhaven tried to appear amused, but as he studied the words and the suggestions of this popular journalist, he could feel the heavy weight of their deception. The plan was already beginning to come apart. His head began to shake unconsciously from side to side. He could sense his hands trembling.

The article was titled *"Secret Shuttles—Danger in Space?"*

It seems that what has been offered to us as a relatively boring operation by the United States Space Administration's Shuttle flight this April may actually be a bit more important and dangerous than advertised. Although USSA would have us believe they are simply performing routine space business that just happens to require the use of Space Tug, my sources have suggested there's more than routine business going on, and possibly a lot to worry about.

Let me share with you some curious activities surrounding this project which have come to light during the past month. The first hint of mystery comes from the secrecy surrounding USSA's training sessions for a new Shuttle crew, who, we discover, have replaced the originally scheduled crew of astronauts in a last-minute switch. As far as I can tell, never in USSA's twenty-year history has any major part of their activity been deliberately closed to the press. Their charter is, of course, to engage in peaceful and open space ventures. And as far as I know, they've lived up to that promise. But now we find an intense and accelerated training program which requires the removal of all newsmen while sessions are in progress. All of these sessions have something to do with EVA operations near Shuttle—and delicate maneuvering of Space Tug. They're going to do something tricky up there that USSA doesn't want us to know about.

That's strange enough, but to make things spookier, we find these training sessions have been attended by observers and technicians from, of all places, our own Defense Intelligence Space Agency. The secret-satellite guys. And you can guess what comment they've had on being approached by reporters after the closed tests. Right. No comment. Nor could we find any USSA official who would shed light on the connection.

So the picture that begins to emerge in this columnist's mind is one of some dubious intrigue involved with their April mission. Now, what could they be up to? We know they're carrying the Space Tug up with them. First thought would be that this robot rocketship will be doing some things with the astronauts' help that are potentially damned useful to the military side. Our imagination can easily envision a crewman flying this robot over to, let's say, a Soviet spy satellite, and . . . sending it careening into the ocean?

Second thought that comes to mind is a little scarier. Now, although I'm usually not the paranoid type—a rather trusting soul, as my readers will attest—I have this nagging worry that there just might be something in space that the military, namely DISA, is damned interested in. Something that's been floating around up there for years. Something they either want to take a closer look at or move into some other orbit. Or—and this is the part I really worry about—something they don't want to come back to Earth at all. Especially if it gets scattered over New York City.

If I recall my dates correctly, the big switch in this Shuttle mission occurred just after the Soviets lost still another Cosmos spy satellite—Number 1134, which showered down bits and pieces of its nuclear reactor, this time over some remote lake in Labrador. We heard the Russians apologize plenty again, and assure us there could never be another Marseilles disaster. And of course USSA officials told the world one more time that our side would never put up anything that dangerous—at least not into a low Earth orbit, vulnerable to the dreaded GODS Effect.

A coincidence in timing? I wouldn't know. But the possibility that something might be up there that they just remembered could be dangerous bothers me a lot. We've repeatedly asked USSA about this, and as you might expect, they laugh it off as a case of overactive imagination. Now, if we *could* accept their point, that would be the end of it. If there were explanations why the DISA people are involved, we'd let it go.

But nothing is explained, and our suspicions are dismissed on foolish speculation. We've been through this before, haven't we? We used to think the Executive branch had the copyrights on that type of obfuscation. Now lesser agencies seem to have learned the technique. Nearly as well.

One more thing before we leave this case of the mysterious Shuttle mission. From another source I hear that DISA is getting involved with some pretty sophisticated studies into some rather disturbing areas. These have something to do with biogenetic research, perhaps biological-warfare research. We've recently heard that an incredibly intense recruiting drive is under way to lure research scientists into military labs. And these scientists are all involved with recombinant DNA and related fields. I spoke with one of those who had just been courted into the service of government. (We talked before he had been assigned anything specific, so nothing here is classified.) When I heard the size of the bonus he was paid to join up, I choked. So did he. That's why he went over. When I asked who was putting up that kind of money, he hesitantly admitted it was a DISA-sponsored study. His recruiter had let that slip.

Now, I must admit, if there is any connection between this and our mystery Shuttle, so far it can't be confirmed. But I will tell you this—if the reason DISA is involved has anything at all to do with there being either nuclear material or funny biological experiments onboard, then I'm worried as hell, and think the public, and the world, needs to be told about it.

The paper was now visibly shaking in Chris Brookhaven's cold hands. He stared at it with a blank expression, then put it down. A full minute passed before his project scientist softly asked if he was all right. The response came out brokenly, carelessly.

"Yes . . . yes, it's okay. Just that this comes at a bad time, that's all. Uh, if you'll excuse me, I guess I'd better check into this story with some people. Thanks for bringing it by."

He was left alone in his office. The thoughts were swirling around in his head. He'd better call Sanders in Washington. Sanders would know how to handle the situation.

Chapter Ten

Greg Sanders could not be reached that Thursday to help allay Brookhaven's anxieties. He was trying desperately to keep another damaging story from surfacing.

The leak had come from one of the lieutenants on the medevac team assigned to recover bodies from HIMNL-9's annihilation. He had told his wife, who passed the story along, quickly reaching a friend's friend, who was with local television news. The man phoned Base Commander Stevens on Wednesday and asked for some official confirmation of the incident. He wanted specific details, and wondered whether the Army had any good reason to withhold the matter from the public. Stevens' response was neither to confirm nor to deny. Instead, the newsman was asked to join the commander the next morning for a closed session with other involved parties. He was promised accurate information in trade for temporary silence. He agreed to the conditions.

Inside a small barracks office on the edge of the base, Sanders, Commander Stevens, and a determined reporter argued two hours about their differing viewpoints, matching national security against First Amendment rights. The newsman made it known he had already prepared a short piece and the story was about to be given to AP—he had even managed a videotaped session with the medevac officer, which would be aired that evening. His intention was to proceed with or without approval from the Army.

Sanders was intent on squashing the story completely. Insisting the affair was national-security business, he threatened any disclosure would bring prosecution by the government, following court orders to stop it. The newsman wasn't buying the intimidation. Commander Stevens realized a compromise would have to be worked out. Reluctantly he was forced into the role of mediator between the other two and decided some official announcement could no longer be avoided.

So Stevens drafted a short news release to be given the press, in which the base acknowledged the deaths of ten experimenters resulting from a small explosion during one of their routine weapons-test procedures. He supplied a list of names of those who had been lost. Specifics of the test itself were to remain classified. Anything the newsman had put together on that would have to be cut—although he would be allowed to report whatever else he felt appropriate to the story. It was made clear that any reference to the type of testing would be a disclosure of military secrets.

The compromise was finally accepted by all three, although Sanders consented grudgingly, and only after Stevens insisted that he really had no other choice. The newsman returned to town carrying the official statement and trying to decide what his story should really include. A worried Greg Sanders collected his assortment of samples, photos, and hastily written reports from the now-terminated HIMNL-9 testing, ignored a message to call base communications, and left White Sands by jet for Washington.

When he arrived that evening, he didn't bother checking in with his office at DISA headquarters, where on his desk lay scattered four urgent phone messages from Chris Brookhaven to contact the USSA director immediately in Houston. Instead, Sanders drove directly to Fort Gabriel and delivered his briefcase filled with the carefully labeled samples and photos to a vault in ZW74's basement lab. There he stayed, alone, until very late, sorting and indexing everything into logical order, preparing an extensive list of instructions and examinations for the study team to pursue that week.

On his way back to Georgetown around one-thirty, Sanders discovered the wire services had already picked up the story out of White Sands. Their report went beyond what they had all agreed to. Not only were the deaths reported, but also that the failed testing program had involved a sophisticated laser-weapons system which had blown itself to pieces. A local state representative was already demanding that a full inquiry be held.

Sanders muttered a low *"Goddamn,"* pressed down hard on the Mercedes accelerator, and hurried through the Washington night.

Early the next morning at DISA Sanders found messages from Chris Brookhaven covering his desk; they also covered the McAndrews column, which Project Manager Manning had left the day before. He closed his office door and placed a call to USSA, Houston. A secretary answered, told Sanders to hold while she located her boss. It took only half a minute. When the connection was made and the video locked in, Sanders could see the tension on the man's face.

"Greg, are you alone there?"

"Yes, Chris, what's up?"

"Where in hell have you been?"

"We had a problem at Sands. I've been tied up."

"Well, if you had called yesterday, all we would have had to worry about was McAndrews. You did see the article?"

"Wait a minute. What article? The *Post* couldn't have gotten the Sands story yesterday!"

"What are you talking about, man? I don't know what the hell is going on at White Sands. I'm talking about McAndrews' column on the DISA connection with our Shuttle mission. That story came out yesterday morning. Jesus, you don't know, do you?"

Sanders glanced down at his desk, pushed papers aside until he located newsprint, then moved the clipped-out editorial page close enough to read the title. "I guess I've got it now, in front of me." He started reading.

"You can read the damned thing later. Right now you'd better start thinking about a full disclosure. Think that over on your way to pick me up at Dulles, United Flight 806."

"What?"

"We have an eleven o'clock appointment at the White House. Today."

"What the hell?"

"You heard right. I got a call late yesterday afternoon. President's man asked us both to meet Lansing to discuss the story in the *Post*. Seems they're being asked questions they can't answer. For some strange reason, Lansing thinks we could offer him some help. Will you meet me at the airport?"

"I'll be there. Don't panic, Chris. We'll work it out."

"I hope so."

Sanders recognized they were close to having it all out. Lansing wasn't stupid. If he had been prompted by the *Post* article to call them in, the matter of the nuclear-reactor rescue would be pursued in detail, and problems with that story would surely surface. And Sanders was certain to be questioned about the report of increased military biogenetic research McAndrews had tagged to DISA sponsorship. As he observed Brookhaven's state of nervous agitation during their drive back from Dulles, he guessed the man could never hold together during a serious executive confrontation. Sanders resigned himself to the inevitable outcome. It would unravel. He began mentally preparing himself to avoid any further descent into the deceit they had spun. If he remained silent, Brookhaven would carry the show. His advice to his colleague was to play it by ear.

But an important decision would then be required. To disclose DISA's SCEPTER plan was another matter. He felt much less secure about bringing that up. Yet Lansing could precipitate that too, if he had made the connection with the White Sands incident. Chances were he hadn't yet. The news was still too fresh, and Lansing must have other things to keep track of. But if he were asked, Sanders could easily concoct some reasonable cover story there—although it was a definite risk. Eventually that truth would also be brought out. And for DISA to continue their plan hidden from executive view was probably not advisable, or practical. There was even the possibility that with the complete picture of what they faced placed before him, Lansing might agree to cooperate with their venture.

Yet things could easily go the other way, with a decision to veto the SCEPTER plan. Concerns about adding more danger upon an existing danger. And joining the conspiracy. Lansing was still overly sensitive to covering anything up. With international tensions what they were, and SALT IV in the final stages of negotiation, he would be reluctant to do anything that might provoke the Soviets.

Sanders found logic failing him. It wouldn't be a clear choice. He decided to postpone that decision until he could gauge the reactions from the man they would soon be facing.

The drive to the White House produced little in the way of rational dialogue between the two directors. Brookhaven was literally a bundle of nerves, and Sanders spent most of the time trying to calm him down, assuring him they would not be held personally responsible regardless of what happened. They attempted with little success to go over some details of their nuclear-reactor story, in case it still held together. But what soon became apparent as the principal factor behind Brookhaven's fragile state was the disturbing revelation that the USSA Shuttle mission was already running a full month behind schedule. Technical problems that hadn't been foreseen were slowing down the modification activity. The race to reach Orion before it reached Earth was becoming perilously tight. And Brookhaven noted that whichever story they followed that day, he would have to report to the President the now-decreased probability of a mission success.

This news pushed Sanders a step closer to making his own decision. As both men sat in the lobby outside the Oval Office, each quietly went over the responses they would give President Lansing. Then huge doors leading into the office were parted, and an aide stepped out announcing that the President was ready to see them. They rose together and walked into the executive sanctuary.

Lansing wasted no time in getting the truth out. After the *Post* article, the White House had been flooded with calls. Some quick checking by Science Adviser Ken Abrams with the Nuclear Regulatory Commission disclosed that there had never been a nuclear reactor built for or sent up with Skylab. CIA and military sources confirmed it. Lansing demanded to know what really was going on with their mission.

With Sanders remaining silent, Brookhaven willingly obliged, ready to be out from under his responsibility and share of the deception. It all flowed out freely. Everything he knew of the problem's history, nearly everything Sanders had told him. The President sat through fifteen minutes of explanation, both he and his two advisers motionless in stony disbelief.

When Brookhaven finished his description of the details of their plan to rescue the military's package from Orion and boost it into deep space, the attention turned immediately to Sanders. The President looked directly at him.

"What is the exact nature of the biology onboard Orion?"

"Military researchers named it anthrax-r. Radiation-resistant and highly toxic. To nearly all life forms. The details should be contained in the archives of the National Security Council. Under the code name Zone Wind."

"We would appreciate your personal account. Please brief us on the background history. We are all very interested. And you can consider all classification restraints waived."

"Including Code Seven?"

Lansing turned to the two men who had been quietly witnessing the disclosure from one side of his office—Abrams and National Security Adviser Stan Berringer. Both gave him an affirmative nod. He returned to Sanders.

"Code Seven, and higher."

Sanders went back to the beginning. It was a story he wished now he did not have to remember.

"In the late sixties, Army research was heavily involved with various forms of biological-warfare agents.

The Pentagon had apparently found itself at a standoff with the Soviets on nuclear-deterrent capability. Neither side could produce a clear advantage. Our big concern was that the Russians had thoroughly prepared themselves, people, industry, and institutions, for survival following an all-out nuclear exchange. Given the turmoil our country was going through, we were totally unable to provide anything close to that. In effect, that situation tipped the nuclear balance in their favor. We were therefore left without an adequate threat. They could survive doomsday, and we couldn't; so the military was directed to find a solution, and all previously enforced constraints were lifted. That naturally opened the door to biochemical warfare."

Lansing winced, then nodded at Sanders. "Continue, please."

"The research was turned on full, and the military succeeded beyond their own expectations. Using all the advances in biochemistry, they successfully evolved a strain of anthrax bacilli, terribly toxic of course, but also with an important new twist. The organism was biologically 'case-hardened.' Something to do with a shell membrane which made the bacilli resistant even to most forms of nuclear radiation. It very nicely provided the ideal solution. With just one missile-equipped sub or underground silo left after the holocaust, we would still have the ability to deploy the strain over the heart of Russia, and destroy all remaining life, reaching down even into the deepest bunkers.

"The whole concept seemed perfect. But as you might imagine, the degree of their success led the Army into an extremely difficult problem finding safe storage for the organisms. Containment had to be absolute. We all caught a glimpse of their problem in sixty-eight, when a tiny sample escaped into the air around Dugway, Utah, and a thousand sheep were killed within minutes. That single incident turned the project around. It was enough to alarm everyone involved. The White House became worried, and redirected all effort toward some means of safe storage or, failing that, some method of detoxification. Development of the strain was abruptly halted. The effort to find that storage never achieved more than partial, short-term success. But worse, during that activity the military researchers discovered that their anthrax-r was indestructible by all available means. They had no control, and no antitoxin. The search continued under complete secrecy for many years, without success

"Then in seventy-four, under orders directly from the President, DISA was asked to solve the problem. We were to develop the final solution for the disposal of anthrax-r. That's the point where the space agencies entered into this. Chris has given you the relevant events from there."

Lansing's expression had turned grave.

"Do you know the current condition of the strain? Whether it has managed to survive to the present? Given ten years in space, what can we expect to find onboard Orion now?"

There was no longer any reason to hide the connection. "We're currently studying that matter in our own research labs. Briefly, it's a unknown factor, although we've been able to make some reasonable guesses."

"Let's have them."

"We expect there might have been some uncontrolled growth early in the original deployment. Predictions suggest the possibility of some leakage from one of the compartments within the larger package. Whether that means a problem with contamination of the entire Platform, we don't know for sure. The original organisms may have evolved into different forms. Could be they are now even more toxic, or they could have long since mutated into benign forms. We're forced to rely on computer simulations, since there is no way to monitor what's going on now inside the payload."

"What we obviously need to know, Mr. Sanders, is just how dangerous a problem we could have if the stuff comes back to Earth."

"We should be conservative and expect that it would be extremely dangerous. If we somehow avoid breakup in the atmosphere, which would produce a worldwide spread, the package would release its contents on hard impact. It would spread rapidly from that point, with the winds."

"So we are in fact talking about a potential biological catastrophe."

"We have to assume that possibility."

"Jesus!" The President stared out a window, then turned back to Sanders. "How many understand the full nature of this problem?"

"Very few. The former Presidents and their advisers. The military and DISA personnel in charge of the original operation. A small group of researchers at Fort Gabriel. Everyone knows it's national-security classified. Control has been complete."

"I guess so, if this office was in the dark." Lansing was beginning to realize the box they were in.

National Security Adviser Stan Berringer picked up the President's concern. "Sir, I think I know what you're considering. But I believe it's impossible to make this public. Not yet, anyway. The effect of a release now could be devastating. On the public, the SALT negotiations. It has international ramifications. My advice would be to let USSA proceed and solve this problem as they plan, before it does anyone any harm."

"Your advice is that we cover up a blunder made ten years ago?"

"It appears the lesser of many evils."

Lansing flinched, seeing the inevitability of that course. "If that's the case, it's obvious that we can't settle for anything less than complete success with this mission. How do you assess your chances, Chris?"

Brookhaven grew uneasy, looked down at the floor. "Well, to be honest, we have had some problems—delays, that is—with the modification of the Shuttle to hold the Space Tug—but I'm hoping to get that back on schedule soon. If we can get to the Orion Platform in time, our probability of success is very high."

"If we get there in time? That can't be an option."

"I agree. But what we face are very real Shuttle constraints. All other systems are on track. But the Shuttle has had to undergo extensive changes from its original setup for this launch. We're using procedures that are being pushed to the limit. The program was never intended to work toward such a critical deadline."

"Delay is unacceptable, if I know anything about the GODS Effect and your predictions on when this station called Orion may be coming down. It won't wait for us, will it? What does it take to guarantee the Shuttle will be ready in time?"

"More money and manpower, and some good luck."

"If we push extra appropriations through Congress, will that give us a guarantee?"

"It will help tremendously. We could pull resources off other projects onto this, and then let those restaff later."

"Ken, see to it that the Science Committees of both houses agree to appropriate whatever figure Mr. Brookhaven comes up with." He thought over the request. "Which brings us right down to your point, Stan, doesn't it? What do we tell them?"

"I think our only option is to continue with the nuclear-reactor story, which they're going by already. We can keep everything under classified control, so there would be no reason to answer detailed questions. If the press pursues its curiosity, we'll simply fall back on this being a matter of national security."

"That's been tried before with little success."

"True, but, again, we don't have many choices."

Lansing sighed deeply. "I guess we'll have to proceed with that." Then he turned to the two space-agency directors in angry resignation. "Gentlemen, this whole affair is incomprehensible. You're both charged with saving the world from what I've been told could be environmentally terminal. The whole matter must be taken care of immediately. Within a few months a sophisticated space operation must be designed, developed, and flown. And there cannot be the most remote possibility of its failure. There seems to be one and only one shot at this thing. You offer us no alternatives, no further guarantees. We are completely at your mercy, since there are no other options. This office can do nothing to prevent probable disaster other than handing you more money. I wonder, Chris, how your people can be expected to accomplish all of this, and do it perfectly, without any knowledge of how critical the mission really is."

Brookhaven cringed. He could say very little to assure the President. Their deadline was real. There was always the possibility of mechanical or human error.

Sanders made his decision. This was the time.

"Mr. President, Chris and USSA can only do what is humanly possible, given the lateness of the hour. Yet I sympathize fully with the concerns you've just expressed. For those reasons it's appropriate to present you an alternative we're developing within DISA. A backup. Since its classification is of even higher order than what we've previously discussed, I think you should hear the details first, in private."

"Well, I'm interested. But you can speak freely before my advisers. Please go ahead."

"Since this is strictly a military matter, what I have to say is not relevant to USSA, and I believe my colleague should be excused."

"Does it relate to the Orion operation?"

"Yes, of course."

"Then I think we can assume Chris may have a need to know. You are cleared for such things, Chris?"

"I am. And I'd like to know what DISA has been up to."

"Go ahead, Mr. Sanders. We're all waiting."

Now Sanders was in a box. It was more than risky having Brookhaven privy to his plan—it would certainly produce the unnecessary tensions between their agencies he had hoped to avoid.

"If you are willing to take the responsibility for insuring that security is preserved by all in this room, I will."

"I'll do that. Go on."

Sanders wasn't to have his way. And they all were waiting for his story. So he went directly to the point.

"From the beginning, when we first recognized there was a problem, I've been concerned about the USSA operation. It's basically a sound mission concept—send the Space Tug up onboard the Shuttle, maneuver it beside the Orion Platform, relocate the biology payload using crew support, then have the Tug boost the package into deep space. I helped develop the plan. But there are two serious flaws. Contamination could make the EVA activity extremely difficult. And there is no backup, as you already noted. Chris and I exhausted every conceivable solution to the second problem, and could not find an answer. DISA has therefore pursued a way to resolve the dilemma of a USSA mission failure. None of this has been cleared through regular channels. I hope you understand the constraints we were under."

"I can imagine."

Sanders hesitated only a second. "We are now in the process of preparing a special version of our SCEPTER surveillance spacecraft, which will be redesigned to monitor the USSA-Orion operation closely. It will also be able to evaluate the conditions on the Platform beforehand. The vehicle will have a full complement of biology sensors which can pick up the smallest trace of organic contamination. We can feed that data directly to the Shuttle crew before they prepare for their EVA."

He spoke without a trace of emotion. "The satellite will have another important capability. We've borrowed particle beam-laser technology from Land Technics, and are planning to incorporate into this version of SCEPTER a high-intensity neutron laser, weapons class. Its function, if approved, will be to vaporize the Orion Platform and its biological payload in the event of a failed boost attempt. All aspects of the design and mission operation are now under test at various facilities."

Lansing shook his head grimly. "You realize, of course, that this office has vetoed every single request the military has made to put strategic-laser-weapons systems in orbit. We have a firm agreement with Moscow on that."

"I understand and appreciate the situation. But this application is an exception—intended for a purely humanitarian purpose. There is no intent of aggressive use here. It will only be considered in a last-resort scenario. And if used at all, used only once. Then deactivated."

"Of course, if it were used the Soviets would be able to deduce what we were up to from their tracking data. What other conclusion could they come to if a huge U.S. military satellite were to quietly disappear?"

"That is probably true. Some explanation would no doubt have to be given them before, or shortly after, this option were taken. But to stress my position, the plan does offer us an effective backup, which simply doesn't exist in its absence. All other options are unworkable. Using the laser, we avoid the problems we would generate with any nuclear detonation. The neutron laser gives us surgical accuracy. Another important factor to consider is the fact that the SCEPTER effort is on schedule. Our launch vehicle is ready, and we simply don't face the same problems Chris has. There does remain more testing to be done with the laser directed against various target compositions . . . especially against forms of the bacilli itself, but so far those experiments have progressed well."

Adviser Abrams interrupted excitedly: "Unless this ties in with those reports out of White Sands this morning."

Lansing stared at the DISA director, waiting for an answer. Sanders was thrown off stride. They had him. His face flushed for the first time in many years, and the President picked it up. "Jesus, that *was* a laser-weapon accident. The very one you're talking about. Right, Sanders?"

He had to pull himself together and go on. Confidence was essential. "That was an unfortunate accident. The real problem at Sands was that our test was mishandled by a ground crew, a support team not entirely under our control. One target was put in the firing line that should never have been there under open conditions. A biology sample. Its release was the cause of the deaths. The laser itself performed perfectly."

"That's great. We certainly can't worry about the ten who died. I expect all the details on that incident promptly." Turning to National Security Adviser Berringer, Lansing continued: "Stan, I want you to determine exactly how all of this was carried on outside

White House authorization. A full report on all aspects of what we've just heard."

Then to Sanders: "As for you, Mr. Sanders, I have to do some serious thinking about your proposition. It seems to be as risky as the problem it's meant to solve. I want a complete briefing on this entire SCEPTER operation as soon as possible. But for now . . . I'll just have to think this over."

Sanders knew everything could slip away. "Mr. President, the SCEPTER operation, its development, hardware build, and test are all currently in progress. We have a project staff of five hundred scientists and technicians working it. We need a decision on whether to continue, delay, or cancel."

Lansing took a minute to consider that request. "In that case I suppose we have no other choice than to give your people a tentative go-ahead. At this point it doesn't seem wise to cancel our only backup. But . . . if my decision is eventually to cancel the project, at any time in the future, it will be done without question. And if I decide to give you a firm approval to continue, consider yourself personally under Presidential directive to consult with this office at every stage of development, and on a regular basis. Abrams will be assigned to monitor every activity on this. He'll be my personal liaison. You can report to him."

"Certainly. This should be handled in that manner."

"One final note. You'd better consider this, too. God help us, but if we ever come to the point of granting approval to execute your plan in its totality, this office will disclaim any knowledge of it. Do you understand?"

"I believe so."

"I mean precisely that for the record the SCEPTER solution will be treated as DISA's surreptitious attempt to resolve its own problem, with your agency as the sole responsible party. That implies, Mr. Sanders, all repercussions will fall directly on your shoulders. It won't go back to any past President. It won't go back to this President. It will be entirely your affair, and if any sacrifice is needed, you'll be it. Think that over."

"I'll consider that. Although, respectfully, the position is not justified to that extent. Our involvement originally was forced upon us."

"That may be, but now it's a matter of national integrity. The entire affair from beginning to end seems to have involved so much deception, and broken treaty obligations, that in the interest of world peace —if that somehow survives this operation—there can be no other approach. Given the path you people have followed to this point, I believe my stand is more than justified. So consider my terms seriously. I'll be doing some serious thinking before giving you final approval. Yours is, after all, only a backup. Hopefully your SCEPTER mission will never be needed."

He then spoke to Brookhaven: "Chris, you were unaware of this plan?"

"Totally. I've had other things to keep me busy. It's a damned surprise."

"Well, take care of your schedule problems. It appears the Shuttle is the only sane way to resolve the immediate danger. We'll give you our full support. But you'd better not let us down."

"We don't intend to."

"What I really wonder, you two, is when you would have come forward with this horror story had I not called you in—had McAndrews not lifted the rug covering your secret. What do you think?"

Neither offered an answer. They sat in silence.

"I thought so. From now on, keep this office informed of your every move. I plan to keep personally in touch with the details, of both operations. Greg, from you I want a complete briefing on the biological threat, as well as on SCEPTER and the laser testing. Tomorrow. Shortly after that I'll give you my own decision on your future. Good day to you both."

The space-agency directors were escorted out of the Oval Office. Brookhaven seemed pleased—a large part of his burden had been removed. Sanders was bothered only slightly by the President's final cryptic remark about his future. Basically he felt confident that now DISA could be free to proceed with the SCEPTER deployment, a prospect he was looking forward to.

He also knew, regardless of presidential interference, he himself retained the power to make the final decision. The only remaining question, one that he had to admit was far from being resolved, was whether or not, given the failure scenario, his neutron laser could really break the resistance of anthrax-r.

Chapter Eleven

Laine Jeremy's face reflected the pulsating field of digital displays that danced around the circular control panels of her executive monitor. The flashing circuit boards enclosed her in an electronic nest, which itself was at the center of a Stonehenge ring of software peripherals—mag-tape exchangers, liquid memories, micro and macro processors, and the new DEC metassembler. She was fully absorbed by the process of verifying the final links between biodata records and the adjacent recombination chamber, far too distracted to notice Daren Gray pass quietly through a corner entrance into the large room. He counted on her attention being held there—fixed just long enough to allow his unnoticed approach to a position behind her command chair.

Gray softly placed a hand on her shoulder beside a fall of auburn hair, and said a gentle "Hi." It had the desired effect.

"Damn." She turned, startled, then with recognition gave him her usual warm smile. Now only pretending irritation, she said, "You realize that trick probably dropped the entire link with biodata. Which took me a good half-hour to set up. Cute, Daren." She turned back to her displays.

"Sincerest apologies. But you looked as if someone should rescue you from this obsession."

"This obsession has been one of the few things holding your research together the last weeks. And you couldn't resist disrupting it. Well, if you'll give me a few minutes to make sure we haven't lost anything, and can behave yourself that long, I'll put the exec

on hold and we can talk. It's certainly been awhile—
and we do have something serious to discuss."

"I guess I'll try to restrain myself. How serious?"

For a moment she ignored him, moving her light
pen over the board on her right.

"Very." She scanned an illuminated array of circuitry. "Do you feel the trip accomplished its objective? We watched the debate, and your *Face the Nation*
spot. You and Severinson at least sounded convincing
against PAGENT. You were very impressive, in fact."

"Well, thank you. It went fairly well. We kept their
lab open, for the time being. And I think preempted
any similar action against ours. But I'd better let you
concentrate on your operation."

"Good idea."

Gray looked over the computer layout, critically
examining the arrangement, noting its order, its design.
The organization of all elements was visually and
technically perfect. He hoped Wilson had arranged the
recombination area as well in his absence.

"If this will take awhile, I think I'll check with Mark
in the chamber. I am anxious to see our own final
product."

"No. Wait here. That's part of the problem."

"It is? The lab's not ready yet, after two weeks?"

"The lab's been done just right."

"Then what?"

"Two more minutes, okay? Patience, please."

He waited in silence, watching her manipulate the
myriad controls with the skill and precision of a pianist,
fingers reading in the complex commands with only
slight touches of the pressure switches, guiding the
operation with a determined confidence that Gray was
forced to admire.

"Okay, done!" She was satisfied. "We're now 95%
through the checkout of central. By tomorrow it should
be totally verified. Then we can finish your demonstration sequences."

"So you're ahead of schedule by three days. Which
puts us well ahead of the game. Not bad."

"Thanks. But your excitement may be premature.
You haven't talked with Mark since you got back?"

"No, I just got in a few hours ago. Time only to unpack at my place and drive out to see what's become of my abandoned project."

"Sit down, Daren."

"Can't be that bad." But he sat down next to her.

Laine turned her controller's chair to face him. "During the last four days you've lost nearly your entire staff. Lewin and Cary resigned Thursday—they've accepted positions with the government. That's all they would say about it. Gave Stanford one day's notice. They're already gone."

"I can't believe that."

"You'd better. Mark is seriously considering the very same thing. I convinced him to hold off at least until your return so you two could talk it over. Daren, their offers were astronomical. Mark gave me some details the others wouldn't. The government is offering him a one-year-contract assignment for a salary of 15,000 in new currency. Lewin and Cary got 10,000. Mark wouldn't say what agency was behind the recruiting. Just that it involved some crash research project in biochemistry."

Gray was stunned. They had reached him too. There was no protection, no way to resist. His warning had been sheer futility.

He muttered to himself, "Jesus Christ. Exactly what they hit Severinson with. There's something damned ominous going on here. Maybe the McAndrews piece wasn't all that preposterous."

"You're losing me. What is going on, Daren?"

Gray was trying to arrange a pattern in his mind. The gathering in of researchers. Severinson's paranoia about military involvement. The *Post* story.

He thought aloud: "The Maryland lab is losing its scientists, too. Probably to the same place. While I was east, McAndrews came out with a story that sounded like sheer speculative journalism. But it sure as hell begins to fit together. Space Shuttle has had a last-minute redirection for its next flight, and all details are being kept secret. The military-space people, DISA, seem to be involved. And, by coincidence, they are also collecting a team of biochemists for a crash effort in classified research. The military hasn't been allowed to meddle in that area for over a decade. Now it's suddenly turned on again. McAndrews tied this all together to arrive at a potential problem with contamination in space. And then—then there's the GODS Effect. Spacecraft coming down from orbit every few months. That has got to be it."

He looked up. "Is Mark in the lab now?"

"He should be in the offices, documenting the test data we've gone through so far. He'd better be doing that, anyway, especially if he's leaving us soon. But perhaps you should talk him out of getting involved with this."

"That may take both of our best persuasive efforts. Damn, he can't go. We'd have to delay the mainstream studies for at least weeks."

"Well, if there really is military involvement here, that could make a difference."

Laine's thoughts were busy in another direction, free-associating with his story.

"Daren, there's something else you may be able to factor into this—something that came up while you were away. I heard of it from a friend doing postdoc at Las Cruces. Apparently there was a major incident at White Sands, a tragic explosion from some weapons test. Ten people were killed, and the Army tried to hush it up. The reason I mention this is because my friend heard the affair was in some way involved with biological contamination. Speculation at the university was running in that direction, although of course no one would officially confirm anything. Everyone was apparently very skeptical about the Army's version. The local newsmen were digging into it."

Gray stored the information away for future reference. "It wouldn't surprise me a bit if this were all connected somehow." He stirred in his chair. "I think I'd better see Mark now. Do you want to come along?"

"I need to continue with this right now. But I'll be glad to offer my own persuasion and moral support if you think it will help. Let me know."

"I will."

Gray left the computer complex in a state of increasing concern and headed for the walkway connecting Laine's building with the Recombination Lab. For them to continue into the next phase of research with any hope of making reasonable progress, Mark Wilson could not be lost. Gray could not spare the time to locate and train a new staff. Or to do all the experimentation himself.

As he approached the lab, he studied it from outside. The imposing facility would now be under his personal charge, and its potential nearly limitless. It would be criminal to interrupt the activity at this point. Their chamber structure was a full three stories high, a cylinder which contained the original setup for spacecraft-vacuum testing, and the support offices used for conducting the sophisticated operations. He neared the entrance and noticed the prominent warning sign to one side of the doorway advising, *"Caution— Recombinant DNA Research—Stanford University— Access Controlled."* Gray was glad to see that reinforcement. It was nearly a direct warning to PAGENT. The research team would require that degree of protection and isolation. He opened the door, entered a small lobby where a young woman, dressed in a Coast lab uniform, greeted him respectfully.

"Dr. Gray, welcome. We've been expecting you."

"I can imagine. I was supposed to be back a week ago. Is Mark in the control offices?"

"Yes, Mr. Wilson's been in since seven. Seems to be very busy."

His attention went directly to the corridor marked *"Vacuum Chamber."* A green light glowed above the opening, indicating there was no depressurization testing in progress.

"Assume it's okay for me to take a look at the chamber?"

"Well, green conditions are in effect, and I can't very well prevent the director of this facility from making his first full inspection. Go on in. Shall I call Mark, tell him you're back?"

"Thanks. Yes, please do. Tell him I'll be up in a few minutes, after I look over the laboratory."

Gray entered the corridor, noticed the light-scan

device pulsing as he passed through. The security system was apparently fully functional. A door at the other end buzzed as he approached. He pulled it open, stepped through into an observation room.

The arrangement was what he hoped to find. Black absorptive walls surrounded the chamber, with conical protrusions studding their upper surfaces. A muted light system encircling the ceiling illuminated the entire area for operational viewing. The effect was that of an unearthly medical operating room. In the chamber's center, along a raised platform, were the biology and recombination vaults. Surrounding this central table, suspended from above on mechanical arms and booms, were the sophisticated tools of his research. There was the enzyme-reaction module directly ahead. To the left the ionizing radiation chamber. Further back on the right the electromicroscopy systems. The most awesome item was located toward the front center. There he gazed down upon an elongated cylinder stretching eight meters in length. This intricate, tentacled apparatus would be used to effect his delicate microsurgery. It was the multipath laser borrowed from Stanford Physics. He continued his visual survey. An elaborate system of conveyors threaded its way around the sides of the center platform, the arteries for delivering and retrieving samples. Automated manipulator arms ringed the platform from above, along with TV cameras arranged at various spots about the area. The glint of spotlights produced a myriad of highlights from this collection of aluminum, titanium, and plastic-alloy research equipment. It gave Gray a reassuring feeling.

The entire system appeared to be completely in order, and fully capable of sustaining the demanding level of testing that Wilson had begun in Gray's absence. Both Mark and Laine had done just the degree of professional job he had expected of them. He was satisfied with his delegation of responsibility. They had carried out his design beautifully.

Gray took the exit that led from the observation room up a stairway to the main control offices, located midway up the building and sharing a common wall with the chamber for direct viewing during operations. He found the office door open and Mark at his desk, poring over countless pads of notes, which apparently contained the results of his recent test sequences. Wilson, looking as if he hadn't left the office for days, glanced up as Gray came inside.

"Hello, Daren. Welcome home. I knew you'd be anxious to hear the preliminary checkout results, so I've been trying to get summaries ready for you. You'll be happy to know that the entire operation is checking out perfectly. I've done twelve simple recombination steps with all the equipment modules, and everything functions smoothly. Actually, we're doing better than the design predicts. I think all our homework has paid off. My humble conclusion is that you've got just about the perfect setup."

"Sounds great, but of course I really hadn't expected less with such good people in charge. Now we're ready to get on with the real business of science—testing my hypotheses. Which, I understand, leads us to our only real problem." Gray's stare expressed his knowledge.

"Yeah. You've seen Laine already."

"She told me the story. Lewin and Cary have left. You're considering it. Mark, this is really unbelievable."

"Daren, you know how involved I've been with all of this—with you and this damned research. It kills me even to think about leaving now. But you have to understand the temptations—they're overwhelming. The government is offering me money that it would take five years to make at Stanford. For only a one-year stint. Christ, I could retire after that."

"But do you have any idea what they want you for?"

"Well, I confess that does bother me some. It's all classified. Their people were very stingy on details. Just that it's an intense effort to solve an immediate problem in the general area of biochemistry. And that we'd all be carrying this study out in virtual seclusion from the world, or from the public, at least."

"Doesn't that suggest something about the motivation behind it, the general nature of the study?"

"Well, that it's secret business. Beyond that, I honestly don't know."

"Look, I believe I've pieced together enough of the story to know what's going on. Some of it comes from my trip back east, and what I learned from Miles Severinson. Some of it comes from simple deduction. You need an idea of what you may be involved with before making a final decision."

"You're going to make this difficult for me, aren't you?"

"I'm damned sure going to try. I can't afford to lose you. You're just too valuable . . . and then I'd have to work that much harder."

"Hell, I wouldn't want to force that on you."

"The agency you'll be with is military—probably the Defense Intelligence Space Agency. I suspect they have a problem of biological contamination in space, one they no doubt created themselves. Anyway, it's something the next Shuttle flight is designed to solve. My educated guess is that there's something orbiting which is dangerous, perhaps toxic, that could be about ready to fall back to Earth. Whatever its exact nature, it has both space agencies running at a fever pace. And enormous amounts of money have been made available to bring in the right scientists to support the effort."

"Does this necessarily have to be a military problem? Couldn't we simply have contamination resulting from some old USSA-manned mission? An athlete's foot fungus out of control?"

"I suppose that's possible. Yet, if that were the case, what reason would there be for keeping everything under wraps? And for the DISA people to be so intensely interested?"

"But are you sure of that connection?"

"There's one hell of a good case for it."

"Well, if true, it would make my decision even more difficult. But Jesus, what an opportunity to miss. How can we really find out? I doubt I could extract any more info from the recruiter."

"That's a problem I need to resolve. For all of us."

Wilson thought about the situation for half a minute.

"You know, if the Shuttle's involved with this operation, you might put some direct questions to USSA at Houston. Aren't you and their director working together on a conference? You could try to pry out some details from him."

"Good man. That's a definite possibility. USSA has been conspicuously maintaining silence, refusing to talk with anyone about their planning. Which could be a break. Chris Brookhaven and I are slated to co-host the Science Symposium at Berkeley next month, and he's been trying to get out of that on the excuse of having too much to do at the center. I just may be able to use some leverage there, and pursue this a little further than the press has managed to."

"It would be nice if you could verify the facts of this story before I turn down a cool 15,000 new dollars. That is, assuming it will be conceivable for me to do that."

"I certainly understand the temptation, Mark. But consider what will be left after taxes."

"I'd income-average, or find a job in Swiss research."

"Can you put off the recruiter for a while?"

"They wanted a decision by the end of the week."

"That should give me enough time. I'll call Brookhaven today. Damn, this means I may be traveling east again. Just when I thought I could finally return to work. Do you have enough to keep busy with in the meantime?"

"Plenty. Still the last phases of demonstration. Then writing up all these damned results."

"Well, in case we can convince you to stay, go ahead with the first experimental series setup. I want everything ready to go once I get back and have a chance to go over your demonstration tests."

"Will do. Maybe in the course of all your maneuvering, you could manage to talk to the Dean of Science about a healthy salary adjustment for me. Might contribute to my making a more responsible decision."

"H'm, seeing that you've done such a great job with the Recombination Lab, we may be able to justify something like that. Just please don't expect a six-figure increase."

Wilson chuckled. "I'd be satisfied with what you make. I realize Stanford can't compete with the government."

"I'll see what we can do."

Gray stopped by Laine's offices, let her know of his plans, and told her of the conversation with Mark. She thought it was a worthwhile approach, wished him another successful trip—but requested that he not stay two weeks this time. He then drove to his old office at Stanford, where he still had to collect and pack dozens of documents and procedures that needed to go over to Coast Research. There he quickly located the phone list he sought, carefully tucked away inside a desk drawer. Gray turned a few pages until he spotted the extension of Chris Brookhaven at Johnson Space Center, Houston.

He placed the call through the Stanford operator, who asked if he wanted satellite relay or land. Gray said land lines would suffice—he resisted using the relay system as an unnecessary luxury, regardless of what Bell's advertising campaign tried to make you believe. All West Coast government and university and many private corporate institutions were now linked with their counterparts in the East via the sat-phone network, but half the time transmissions were rather weak, sometimes broken by local interference. There were still some bugs to be worked out.

A JSC secretary came on. Gray identified himself and asked to speak to Chris Brookhaven. Immediately she came back advising him that the USSA director was conducting simulation testing, and could not be contacted for the next three days. Gray then asked her to tell the director of his call, and to give him the message that he would arrive there tomorrow to meet with him. The subject concerned their hosting the Science Symposium. She said the message would be delivered, but the probability of a meeting was slim. He understood, and left it at that.

Gray called SF International, reserved an early-morning flight, then threw himself into the job of reorganizing his old office and collecting the part of it that would go over to Coast.

It was 1 P.M. Houston time before Gray could get to JSC, after making all the necessary connections between his place in Woodside and Nassau Bay, Texas. He went directly to the Administration Building and Brookhaven's office, where he was told his message had been given and the reply was that any meeting would have to await the finish of their current testing. Gray asked where the simulations were being held. Brookhaven's secretary gave him a building number, but cautioned him that he could not enter without special clearance. Gray thanked her anyway, found a waiting electric, told the driver his destination. They rode along the roadways of the campuslike facility, passing the lush green of its lawns and commons, by the pond, past countless white buildings, and finally out to a remote section of the center.

Gray jumped out, adjusted the coat and tie he wore especially for this occasion. With attaché case in hand, he headed straight to the lobby of the silver and white building. He wasn't sure how this would go, but he had a plan he'd put together in his Stanford office the afternoon before. It would be interesting to try. At worst, he would be put off for three days until Brookhaven was finished with his project. At best, it would get him inside immediately.

He approached a guard at the admittance counter. "I'm Dr. Daren Gray, of Stanford, to see Director Brookhaven."

The guard, to his amazement, seemed to know him. "Ah, yes, sir, I saw the TV interview last week. Very interesting."

"Thank you."

"Is the director expecting you today?"

"Well, yes and no. It is important, though."

"I'm sorry, Dr. Gray, but without his personal authorization, I can't let you in. The current sims are closed to everyone but those directly involved."

"I understand. Can you reach Chris with a message from me?"

"I guess that's certainly in order."

"Please tell him Daren Gray is here on a new assignment with DISA. That's D—I—S—A. And it's very important I see him immediately."

"I'll communicate the message." The guard stepped into a booth behind the counter, closed the glass door, and put through a call.

Gray reconsidered the chance he took, and the boldness of this approach. He really doubted it would cause him serious trouble. After all, McAndrews had supplied at least that much information.

The guard stepped away from his booth. "I guess it's all right. You're to be escorted in. I'll have to call someone over here for that." He put in a call this time from the counter phone. Asked for an official escort to come to the main lobby. In a minute, a second guard appeared from inside a hallway behind the receiving counter, asked Daren to follow him. Gray picked up his case and was led inside the sanctuary.

He smiled faintly. The deception was working. The first confirmation of the power which lay behind the suspected connection.

They took an elevator up a good two levels, to a waiting area outside a double door marked only *Shuttle Mission Sim.* He was shown a chair. The escort left him alone while he entered the closed module, was gone a full three minutes by Daren's watch, then returned through the door with a very irritated Chris Brookhaven. The director of USSA strained a half smile through his haggard countenance. Then lit a cigarette.

"Well, Dr. Gray, so they brought you in too. At least they're getting the best and the brightest to work our problem. But now, what was this earlier story about needing to talk details on the Symposium. Are you here for that, or as Sanders' personal envoy. Which is it?"

Gray vaguely remembered the name—and made a quick association with the directorship of DISA. He'd play this scam through to its completion.

"Both. I'm consulting for Sanders and was asked to be here in that capacity. To sit in. The Symposium story was something for the telephone communications only. But, we do have to talk about that also."

"Well, I'm far too busy to worry about science conferences. Now tell me why you are sitting in on our operation. I wasn't told anything about this." Brook-haven was puffing his smoke furiously.

"Last-minute request from Sanders. He wants me to become familiar with all aspects as soon as possible. I just came onboard this week. Probably he couldn't reach you to let you know."

"That's likely. I haven't been returning any calls."

"I don't have the proper access cards—he said you'd supply those."

"Okay, okay. I will. But for now it's too much of a damned hassle. We don't have the time to go through formalities. I'll let you in today. You'll have my personal permission to attend. I guess tomorrow we'll work all this officially. Now let's get back—I've got a sim in progress, and things are not going well. Not well at all."

Brookhaven pushed open the doors, and the two walked inside. Gray was led to a short row of observers' seats, out of the way to one side of the room, as Brookhaven resumed his place near a central command station. Daren took in the hectic activity. It seemed almost frantic. There was a high level of noise, considerable random chatter—most of it being created by the thirty engineers and technicians seated at various consoles scattered in a disorganized array around the room. There were display panels and screens everywhere, but the focus of nearly everyone's attention was a gigantic ten-meter-square monitor in blue and green on the wall opposite him. Gray studied that closely. It was a video-graphical representation of the manned Shuttle Orbiter, in fine detail. The aerodynamic craft was in the process of rolling itself about in a variety of attitudes and positions. Brookhaven could be overheard commanding vectoring optimization. Gray missed the exact detail. He tried to sort out the chatter—but what he could pick up was technical language and escaped him.

He continued to watch the giant display that was drawing most of the attention. Soon the Shuttle craft slowed and steadied itself, locking into attitude hold. Minutes later the rear of it began opening, swinging out great wide doors. Soon after that, an object emerged from within, something he couldn't identify—a crude, blockish module that seemed to be a conglomeration of tanks and rocket engines. He then heard someone refer to "Tug deploy," and made the association with the Space Tug. As the display zoomed in closer for a detailed view of that module, he studied it carefully as it was detached from the mother ship and began to roll through a series of its own maneuvers. The control engineers were apparently searching for some ideal starting condition.

That sequence lasted about five minutes. Then the display broadened again into a wide-angle panorama, capturing both the Tug and the Shuttle spacecraft in the view. It continued to broaden, increasing steadily to a point where the vehicles decreased in visual size to nearly unidentifiable objects. Then, very slowly, at the upper right corner of the screen, a third object drifted into the field. Gray couldn't begin to identify it. Someone mentioned over the background chatter "XO acquisition." The view remained wide-angle, and the Tug began a slow translation maneuver away from the steady Shuttle, gradually moving the distance toward the mysterious XO object. As those vehicles began to close, the zoom process was resumed and compressed the field for a better focus on the two.

Gray could then begin to study the features of this mysterious orbiting target. It was huge in comparison to the Tug. A large, flat rectangle, with various bulges and protrusions located along both faces. He was distracted by the background commotion. The noise level was becoming even more intense. He heard fragments such as "twenty-degree pitch," "yaw eighteen right," "velocity too high," "vectoring errors," "back-off position." The Tug seemed to be doing an orbital dance about its target, not able to get into the right position relative to what they desired. Gray glanced at Brookhaven. He was in a state of heightened agitation, waving his arms about, shouting commands directed at no one Gray could identify. The Tug on the large screen repeated its strange motion, closing in, then sweeping off in a curving movement. Finally he heard Brookhaven angrily command, "Go with automatic station-keeping—initiate next phase."

The screen blinked and returned to show the Tug in position just over the flat object, held firm and motionless directly above one of the prominent bulges on the platform. With both vehicles now steady, Gray could see more clearly. The flat station seemed to be a tubular trusswork of some sort, supporting a collection of separate modules. The one directly under the Tug's position appeared to be a stand that held a long, projecting cylindrical form. The display was held fixed moments longer, and Gray studied it closely as the technicians continued to talk about station-keep operations and commencement of EVA.

Entering from the left of the field were two very small objects, barely noticeable. Gray had to strain to see them from his position. Then it became clear. These were representations of suited crewmen, drifting toward positions on the structure. As they stopped at selected points onboard this still unidentified XO platform, Brookhaven's announcement boomed over the racket.

"Termination of automatic-phase simulation. Hold all positions and attitudes. Make notes of all nav errors, orientations, miss distances. Reports by everyone are due in an hour. Then we try again. We're still not anywhere close with this damned thing."

He removed his headset, stepped down to talk to one of his deputies, then ambled over to Gray. "Christ, this is exasperating. The control algorithms are just not converging."

Gray tried to console him: "Well, it appears you at least have enough professional help to make it work. The process itself is impressive. When does the rest of the operation go through sims?"

"Not until we get this part cleared up. Probably not for a few days." He pulled his attention away from the simulation to Gray himself. "Are you here to observe the whole thing?"

"No. In fact, this is probably all that's necessary. We do need to talk some business, though. Is there somewhere nearby where we can have some quiet?"

"Sure. I have an office one floor up. I could use a break from this as well."

Brookhaven led him up the stairs, avoiding the now-crowded elevator. Then into a rather modestly sized office cluttered with computer printouts, papers, and a scattering of red-covered reports. The USSA director sat down at his desk, while Gray took a chair in front, removing a pile of reports to the floor. Brookhaven pulled out a fresh package of cigarettes.

"So, what is it you've been ordered to do? Or need to know? Surely Sanders has briefed you about the whole operation. I hope that's not my job."

Gray looked at him directly. The man was nearing exhaustion. He could probably be pushed very easily.

"Chris, I'm not here on official business."

"What the hell does that mean?"

"I'm not with Sanders. Or DISA. This is on my own."

"Jesus. What's going on here?"

"I've seen enough today to answer most of my questions. I had to understand what you people are involved with. Your operation is playing havoc with civilian research, as you must know. I've just lost three of my own team to—I suppose it's now clear—to DISA and their biological studies. We've guessed the basics of your operation. It wasn't too difficult. Today's visit has confirmed a number of things. Your Shuttle is intended to retrieve, or remove, something of a biologically dangerous nature from this orbital platform known as XO. And whatever it is represents a cooperative effort with the military; otherwise there would be no reason for DISA to be so heavily involved. I want to know all the details."

"Goddamn, as if we don't have enough problems. This is all classified business, national security, secret. This little game could mean big trouble for you, my friend. I'd advise you to stay the hell out of it."

Gray wouldn't be intimidated. He knew the man was vulnerable. "It will mean even greater trouble for you, and for DISA, if you don't let me in on this. I want you to explain the whole operation—or I go to the press with what I already know. With my status I can make a lot of noise. You surely don't want that."

Brookhaven sank into his chair, and sighed deeply. He shook his head in disgust. "I really should call this into DISA, and let their side handle it."

"Go ahead—if you want to complicate things further. If you'll talk to me about this as a friend and convince me that security is really an issue, I'll keep quiet. But I need to understand the nature of the problem. And if it's real, not just a military exercise."

"There's a real problem, all right."

"Well, if you'll give me the details, it's just possible we may be able to contribute toward its solution from our own lab in California. We're set up to handle just about any kind of biochemistry." He waited a moment, then added, "If you'll be straight with me, I may find a way to replace you as conference host."

Brookhaven turned his chair to one side, then unlocked a drawer near the bottom of his desk. He reached inside, and withdrew a small vial. The powdery substance was shaken into the palm of one hand, then placed against his nose. The director of USSA took a swift inhalation.

"My own personal stimulant. Would you like some?"

"Too early for that."

"Never too early, in this business. The pressures are getting to be ridiculous. Have you ever tried to redesign a seven-hundred-million-dollar Shuttle mission at the last minute?"

"I suppose it's close to an impossible effort."

Brookhaven put the vial back inside his desk, and looked intently at Gray. "If you were less well known, and I wasn't trying to escape from co-hosting that goddamned symposium, you'd be talking to the FBI or DISA instead of to me."

"If it weren't for my association with you, Chris, I'd be back at Stanford still playing a guessing game, and wondering which news service I should contact."

"You're leaving me no alternative, then."

"I hoped you would be ready to tell someone on the outside."

"This can't go beyond you. The security is extremely

tight."

"Okay."

"All right, young man. You're about to hear a god-damned good scare story. One that's guaranteed to make you proud of what your country's been doing in space."

During the next forty minutes Gray sat in quiet astonishment. As Brookhaven told him everything, his worst fears were confirmed and exceeded. It was far more than he could have expected, or been prepared, to hear. The whole thing seemed to be an outrageous fantasy, too incredible to believe. But it was an un-avoidable reality. The rambling stream of information flowed nearly uninterrupted from Brookhaven, broken only by an occasional clarifying question from the young scientist. He was beginning to wish he could be somewhere else. But he had to know it all.

Finally the USSA director's narrative ground to an exhausted termination, concluding with a lengthy description of all the problems he was having with his sims, and the control algorithms for the mission. Then he stopped suddenly, and asked Gray what he intended to do with his newly discovered knowledge.

Gray's response was unsure, distracted: "I'll proba-bly use it to keep one of my assistant researchers around. Beyond that, I confess I honestly don't know." It was an accurate statement of his feelings.

Chapter Twelve

Anatole Karenov leaned forward onto his ski poles, face thrust against the warmth of a late February sun. It was a rare opportunity for him—to simply enjoy. He concentrated on the feeling. On the crisp air. On the dark blue above. He savored the visual effect of the surrounding peaks, sparkling in their bright white. The powder was good, deep from a fresh snowfall the day before. Karenov appreciated that. It slowed him, softened his occasional falls. He was not an expert at this sport—there weren't that many opportunities —but he was sufficiently skilled to derive considerable pleasure from Zermatt's intermediate slopes.

Karenov focused on the quiet. Especially the quiet. It contrasted so perfectly with the harsh, crackling voices of the synthetic translators he had been forced to hear for a week now. The tone of the dialogue, on both sides, had been irritating. And the Americans were proving to be more difficult than usual. But his side had refused to be put off. The issue was too important.

He watched a figure far down the hillside as it carved a graceful trail through the fresh snow. Yevchenko was younger than he, a much better skier. He would make two or three runs to Karenov's one. Except for that small incompatibility, he was an enjoyable companion, and the only other member of the negotiating party who fully appreciated taking time away from the continuous tension of the proceedings within the Diplomat's Room of the Bergdorff Hilton.

It was now only five days since he had been directed

to leave Novosibirsk and was delighted to learn that his destination would be Geneva. The political business he had earlier planned to engage in Moscow would be postponed indefinitely. His energies were now turned elsewhere.

Unable to deflect his ordered assignment at the Space Center, Karenov had dutifully spent two weeks carefully evaluating the KGB reports, which did, as promised, continue to flow in to him. He folded all the material together, cross-referenced their recent suspicions with archived information held in the Center's databank. Within a week, Karenov had absorbed everything available and was forced to concede a major reevaluation of his initial reaction. The picture of an American space intrigue was becoming more clearly developed. Indeed believable, even to him. The Kremlin was not overreacting this time. There was very likely a serious threat to be dealt with. From two very different sources.

He sent these conclusions to Moscow. Within a few days they responded, ordering him to Geneva, where he was to brief the Soviet negotiating team at SALT. A list of questions had been prepared for him to pass on to the team, questions to be posed to the American side. The issue was directly relevant to the current round of talks—SALT IV was addressing space-weapons deployment, with the intent of finding a compromise holding position on both sides regarding further advances in that direction. Up to this point the negotiations had gone reasonably well, from the Kremlin's point of view. But now there were serious concerns. And the Americans seemed to be unprepared, and reluctant, to offer meaningful responses.

Karenov and Yevchenko were in fact allowed this day of recreation because the U.S. delegation had called for a temporary recess, requesting time to consult with officials in Washington. That had been precipitated by the Soviets' rejection of the American reply to their set of questions. Soviet intelligence knew full well that the objective of the next U.S. Shuttle mission had nothing to do with the rescue of a nuclear reactor. They had refused to accept the official U.S. line, or to continue the mainstream SALT negotiation in earnest until details of this operation were presented.

The KGB reports and Karenov's own work had revealed the more sinister reality. Originally Soviet intelligence identified the military station Orion as an experimental weapons test bed, and surveillance of its telemetry had suggested either nuclear or biological processes onboard. Information from the U.S. Nuclear Regulatory Commission verified that no reactor had been built for that mission. Orion therefore became a strategic concern—its character had to be assumed offensive. But then the station had been deactivated—seven years ago. After that it was no longer considered an active threat, but more of a lingering mystery. Surveillance had been continued up to the present time.

Until the loss of Cosmos 1134, which triggered a renewed interest in what that satellite was observing. A directive went out to intelligence to determine whether a need existed to redeploy another inspection satellite. That produced a string of rather disturbing reports. First it was learned that the Orion Platform was itself in jeopardy, would be coming down in only a few months. Second, a closer watch over U.S. space operations yielded signs of intensified activity within both space agencies, civilian and defense. It was soon learned that the Shuttle program was being reconfigured in ways intelligence could interpret as having a potential application to the Orion Platform orbit. The modification to include the Space Tug was apparently associated with a boost or retrieval of something from that station. But intelligence could learn little more to supplement that story.

Then the Western press pointed the way for the continuing intelligence survey, for speculations centered around biological experimentation, and the military's renewed interest in that field. The KGB quickly confirmed the hypothesis. It was soon clear that the Orion problem was of a biological nature, and equally apparent that the Shuttle mission was being redesigned to deal covertly with that condition.

In Karenov's summary to the Kremlin, only that much was known. Less clear to Soviet intelligence, and to himself, was the closed activity connected with the defense space agency. There was more to that than a simple support of the Shuttle-Orion operation. They knew of a last-minute redesign of a surveillance satellite known as SCEPTER. But no details beyond that were available. And probably would never be. Intelligence had not been able to reestablish contact within that organization after the effective security tightening. Now they could only guess, and hope other sources could be developed to provide the remaining information.

So Karenov had briefed the SALT team on these matters, and they in turn queried the American side. The U.S. reaction was initially one of complete surprise. They had been caught off guard. There was dismay expressed over the allegations, which were dismissed as preposterous. Then followed a flurry of satellite communications with Washington, and the next day the Soviets were given acknowledgment of a nuclear-reactor retrieval. This story was immediately rejected, even after the Americans continued to insist on its validity. The stalemate held for half a day. Until the Soviets refused to continue, and the Americans responded with their call for recess.

Karenov flexed his knees, now stiffening in the cold breeze blowing forcefully against him. He pulled the visor down over his face, looked again at the surrounding scene of white peaks, then with a slow, deliberate motion, propelled himself down the slope in a quiet, graceful series of turns. It took only five minutes to reach the château. He locked his skis, then waited inside for an hour, sipping Courvoisier before a warm fireplace. Yevchenko would take his time returning from the slope. Karenov could relax.

After the limo ride back into Geneva with his companion, Karenov found a message awaiting him at the desk of the Bergdorff. From Moscow, encrypted. In his hotel suite he located the proper decoders, carefully moved the electronic scan-converter over the page, and read the resulting sentences. He would have to brief the negotiating team immediately. Nothing in the cable was to his liking.

The mood of their conference room was already strained as the negotiators took their places around the long oak meeting table. Aides in charge of communications busily readied the synthetic translators, which crackled abrasively while being forced through their test sequences. This meeting had been specifically called by the Soviet team—the Americans had hoped to stay in recess somewhat longer.

Karenov found his designated seat along the table at the end of their team—in the area reserved for consultants and technical support. The negotiations were structured according to a very formal protocol. A tone was sounded, indicating it was nine-thirty, time to begin. Since the Soviet side was the initiator, their delegation chief, Vasily Kuchevitch, would lead off as first speaker. Kuchevitch began, reading in an unemotional monotone from the prepared statement that had been drawn up the previous night.

We recognize these talks are in temporary recess at the request of your side. I must announce that this condition will become more than temporary if there is not an adequate reply to certain issues which are of a major concern to us. Part of this we have already gone over in specific. The Soviet Union is fully aware that your defensive space station referred to as the Orion Platform contains within its structure some form of toxic biological element, and that the mission of your next Shuttle is that of eliminating the expected problem of the spacecraft's reentry. We demand to be given all the details concerning this operation, and the exact nature of the organism involved.

Further, we have just recently learned that your Defense Intelligence Space Agency has been engaged in the testing of a restricted class of laser weaponry which has a direct applicability to orbital use.

Both of these issues represent violations of previous international agreements. They are of grave concern to us. It is not clear whether the incidents are linked in any way, although there is an obvious connection in time. In either case, our country has a vital interest in understanding your intentions in these activities. The future progress of our negotiations toward a SALT IV agreement will depend on your response. We expect completeness, and honesty.

The delegation chief looked up from his notes. "How do you respond?"

Karenov felt the hush on the opposite side of their table as the electronic translator flickered quiet, transforming the last sentence into English. There was no move toward consultation. Instead the American chief, Bryant, produced a typewritten paper from his brown folder. He adjusted a dial on his voice-mike.

The United States has no knowledge of the accusations made by your side. We have disclosed to you that the upcoming Shuttle mission has been redesigned to accomplish the retrieval of a small nuclear reactor deployed ten years ago during our Skylab program. Our intention is to remove the reactor from its near-Earth orbit, and using Space Tug propulsion, place it in a very high, safe orbital storage condition. The danger posed by this operation is no greater than that of your own Cosmos satellite entries.

We have no knowledge of any biological problem concerning the Orion spacecraft, nor of any attempted activity with Orion during the Shuttle exercise.

He paused to add, not from his notes: "Nor of these new accusations regarding the alleged testing of a space laser system. Your intelligence is quite obviously in error. We advise that your sources be investigated to determine the cause of such a mistake. And further request that our talks resume their formal schedule and primary purpose, with no further attempts to divert us from our very important task."

Karenov glanced at Kuchevitch as he waited for the

response to come through. Kuchevitch looked angry, and truly disappointed. He concluded only, "These negotiations will then remain suspended."

The Soviet delegation arose, and with Anatole Karenov, left the conference room.

His stay had been too brief. The final paragraph of his encrypted message from the Kremlin had been a directive for him to return immediately upon suspension of the negotiations. He was to return to Novosibirsk. His new assignment would involve a Soviet space response to this latest example of American aggression.

Chapter Thirteen

The phone inside the Recombination Lab offices rang ten times before Daren Gray gave up in frustration. He hadn't slept well for two nights following his talk with Brookhaven at Houston, and his usually well-ordered mental state was reaching a point of becoming unproductively disjointed.

There had been just too much to absorb at once. He went to USSA prepared to confirm a sketchy theory concerning an isolated contamination problem somewhere in Earth orbit. Instead he was presented a scenario for the world's end. And a complicated history of military and political blundering which had set the stage for that possibility. As if that weren't enough, now there was another military plan for compounding the existing terror by producing a new weapon, using wholly unproven technology which Gray suspected might, in untrained hands, prove to be even more dangerous than the problem it was meant to resolve.

Slowly the obsession began to take hold that he should do something—but defining what the something could be was proving to be incredibly elusive. How much time was there? April or May, Brookhaven had said. That was only about three months. What could possibly be done in three months to reverse the process, if indeed it should be reversed? There was probably very little he could do.

If USSA's Shuttle accomplished its mission, then the problem disappeared, and the military horror show would fold up and disappear. Unless, of course, another use was found for it. What probability could be attached to a Shuttle success? Ninety percent? Fifty percent? There was no way to tell. Given any major delays, any of a million problems that could cause USSA to fail, DISA would proceed with their solution—a solution he felt might lead to uncertainties that were monumental.

Brookhaven's hasty description of the DISA laser scheme was sufficient to reinforce Gray's skepticism about the wisdom of those guiding military thinking. They hoped to achieve sterilization of a toxic biological strain inside closed metallic containers within a space environment, using laser and particle beams which were never intended for that purpose. To Gray it sounded like using an artillery piece to control mosquitoes. These people were meddling with delicate interactions at a subatomic level which few totally understood. With apparently very little understanding of the conditions they expected to find. The biological responses would be unpredictable. They would be firing in the dark.

A feeling of powerlessness hung over him. Now that he possessed the knowledge, what was he going to do with it? He had not found a satisfactory answer to Brookhaven's parting question.

Gray needed to talk, and Laine wasn't available. She'd been called to San Francisco by Henry Jeremy —something about settling an uncle's estate. Again he put a call through to the lab. Still there was no response. Wilson was probably having troubles obtaining the anthrax samples from the Oakland Disease Lab.

The immediate problem was to figure out the most productive way to redirect their own study. Since his return, Gray had invested two days toward developing the key parts of that redirection, leading to a new series of experimental sequences. They would try to model, in a very crude way, the biology of Orion. And perhaps not so crudely, typical laser/bacilli interactions.

Adding to Gray's unsettled state of mind was the persistent scarcity of time to do everything that needed to be done. Wilson would have to be placed in charge of the new studies—with Gray able only to contribute

toward developing the procedures and interpreting results. His own attention would soon be divided between
Coast Research and the approaching Science Symposium.

He had not been able to find an adequate replacement for Brookhaven and so was left to undertake the
entire organization alone. It was only three weeks
away, and much had to be done, the room schedules,
the security arrangements, his own presentation—a lot
of busywork. All to be arranged under the cloud of
this one overriding distraction—what the hell should
he really be doing about the impending disaster?

Gray phoned Wilson's apartment this time. No
answer there, either. Tried again at the lab. Fifteen
rings and nothing.

He took another Heineken from his refrigerator,
twisted off its cap, then picked up a jacket and went
outside to his campervan. The night air was crisp and
cool, with a steady breeze coming down from the north,
filling the valley. He drove the nearly deserted parkways to Coast Research, left the car in a closed lot,
and went directly to the Recombination Lab offices.
There, in the quiet emptiness, he finished his beer and
scrawled two pages of additional details for one of
their first laser sequences.

Twenty minutes later he left the note pad of instructions on the top center of Mark's desk and walked
the corridor to the computer support building, up
three levels, then through a doorway into Laine's now-
darkened central executive room. Gray typed a short
message onto the main console screen, the letters standing out vividly in orange, pressed the hold switch at
one side of the function board, then left for home
hoping to find a much-needed rest.

The alcohol was beginning to achieve its intended
purpose of numbing his mind. Yet even completely
sober he probably would not have noticed the dark
brown van that kept a discreet one-block distance between itself and his Toyota.

Two day-packs were stuffed into the rear deck beside a bundle of hiking equipment and a large cooler.

Laine studied the arrangement, then adjusted things a bit until she was satisfied nothing could move out of place. She swung the rear hatch down in one fluid motion, until it responded with a reassuring click. Adjusting her blouse into the wheat-colored cutoffs selected for the trip, she then turned to Daren, crossed her arms and tried to look impatient.

"Well, are you about ready?"

"I think so. You've taken care of everything."

"Then put your body inside and let's be off."

Gray opened the door and crawled into the comfortably molded passenger seat of Laine's turbo-dieseled Porsche. She turned the key and it growled softly to life. From Woodside they quickly found the San Gregoria Highway, which twisted through miles of foothills on its way to the coast and California 1. It was Wednesday and there was little traffic away from town. Laine enjoyed the chance to put the vehicle through more challenging exercises—her drive to San Francisco and back over its crushing freeways had provided none of the excitement she was used to deriving from trips in the high-performance machine. That, coupled with Daren's uneasy mood, created the perfect excuse to delay resumption of work one more day.

She looked over at Daren, concerned, thought about his message, the one she could not have missed. There had been only four short lines, neatly centered in her control screen.

> IT'S WORSE THAN WE THOUGHT.
> I NEED TO TALK.
> I NEED A WOMAN.
> CALL ME, D.

Gray was still asleep when she called at eight-thirty and suggested they take the day off to do some hiking near Big Sur—that she'd be there in half an hour to pick him up. Now he sleepily gazed out the window as they passed from congested subdivisions to residential hillsides, then soon entered a series of ascending switchbacks by La Honda Creek that brought them above the busy flow of life in the valley.

Gray's thoughts drifted lazily, still slightly affected by the alcoholic overindulgence of the previous night. "What do you have planned for this trek, and does it take into account my current debilitation?"

"I think it does. There's a lovely stream-side hike that begins a little past Pfeiffer, up into the forest to the east about six kilometers, to a very nicely secluded hot springs. Which, if it warms up enough, we might try out. Can you handle an elevation gain of five hundred meters for that?" She smiled teasingly.

The thought of floating languidly in a warm forest pool, in the middle of February, seemed delightful. "Sounds absolutely rejuvenating. Just what I need to get the mind and body pieced back together. Yeah, I'm ready for it. Excellent choice, Laine."

Foothills and open meadows were now streaking by as the turbo-diesel was put through a tortuous series of downshifts and hard corners. Gray let himself share vicariously Laine's nearly passionate involvement with the car's performance. For him it was a pleasure simply to have someone else take charge, completely. He looked up at the sky—a few clouds, but mostly a clear, pale blue. Far behind them the city's atmosphere had already transformed into the familiar sullen shades of purple-brown. He wondered what it would be like to retreat permanently into this lofty purity.

They came to a straight, open stretch, and Laine pressed the vehicle into full acceleration. In seconds they were traveling at a speed double the national limit. It continually amazed her that this rich response and raw power was available from a machine that used no more than a gallon of fuel every hundred kilometers. The auto world had finally found a partial solution to OPEC. She felt only slightly guilty about being able to indulge herself with this four-thousand-new-dollar diversion. It had, after all, been a gift from Henry. And she knew how easily he could afford it.

As the straightaway began to curve into another round of hills, she slowed down to a more respectable pace, and glanced at Daren to see how well he had taken the outburst of velocity. "If this is too much for the stomach, let me know. I might consider slowing down a bit."

"No. Don't on my account. The sensation is close to erotic, and I'm enjoying it completely. No complaints. Just please keep the tires somewhere in the vicinity of the road. I've had enough air travel to last awhile."

They made their way quickly and smoothly over the coast range, and in fifteen minutes had merged with Highway 1 heading south along the beach parks above Santa Cruz. For most of the trip the two had spoken very little, Laine respecting his own private thoughts and the need to unwind, and Daren attempting to do just that. It wasn't until they had passed Pebble Beach that Laine decided she would interrupt his reverie.

"Mark said you were reworking the entire first phase of our research. Do you feel like talking about it yet, or should I just let you float awhile longer?"

Gray struggled himself back to reality. "Sorry, I was holding out on you, wasn't I?"

"That's okay. You're entitled to some quiet space."

"Yes, but I was the one who insisted on needing to talk. Yesterday that seemed a compulsion. Today, with you, it's just as important, but I'm beginning to feel the reasoning powers slowly mending themselves. I think my silence and neglect of you have been an attempt to let that process happen. Also, you're the one person that I can rely on to help me sort this business out—I may have been holding you in reserve."

"Well, whatever your excuse, when you feel comfortable about it, let me know. I'll turn up my empathy and understanding controls."

Gray knew they should get into it now. There wouldn't be a better opportunity, or a better setting. His mind would just have to pull itself together for the effort.

"Let's talk."

"All right."

"Mark did tell you that he is staying with us?"

"He said probably. If you could work the raise from Stanford. What was it . . . 40%? Can you do that, Daren?"

"It'll take special approval from the College of Science, but yes, I can do it. The discouraging part is that he'll be making more than I."

"Yes, but he doesn't have royalties from a best seller to supplement an expensive life style, or to support jetting around the country on missions of high intrigue."

"Okay, enough. You've made the point."

"I only talked with him a few minutes. He mentioned some virus you were trying to get from the Oakland Disease Lab. That, I assume, ties in with what you found out in Houston," Laine guessed.

"I'm being unfair, making you play Dr. Watson to my Sherlock Holmes."

She just smiled knowingly, and Daren continued: "Basically I conned my way into JSC to see Brookhaven—used the cover that I'd been hired by the defense agency, DISA, and was there to observe the Shuttle simulations. That opened the door, literally, and I eventually found out enough of their game to prod Brookhaven into spilling the entire unbelievable affair."

"It's that bad? Of course your message suggested it was."

"Bad enough that I've had a hell of a time digesting it. It took me five beers to get to sleep last night. It's unnerving. Accumulate in your mind all the evils we've suspected the military of doing over the last twenty years, and put that into space."

During the next ten minutes he told her Brookhaven's story. Laine listened intently, as all of Gray's earlier speculations now fell into place. When he was through, she could only ask the obvious questions.

"When did you say it will reenter?"

"End of May."

"Wonderful. And there is no antitoxin?"

"No—that's why the virus was originally sent into space. There's nothing to counter it. And they apparently looked for years."

"Jesus, Daren." Laine was now close to the same state of shocked numbness that Gray had given in to. "This is incredible! Is this all taking place with full government approval? I mean, does the President bless the activity? Does Congress know of it? Or is it all standard military intelligence, cloak and dagger, and come May we're all going to get a big surprise?"

"Brookhaven kind of hinted they had Lansing's authorization to go ahead with the missions, although there apparently was a lot of reluctance about the DISA laser deployment. Breaking of international treaty, that sort of problem. But apparently it's felt that the situation is so dire, they have no choice. Congress, it seems, does not know anything about the real situation."

Laine's mind was churning. "You realize that the consequences of this story coming out will be devastating."

"I know, I do know that. It's one of the things that's really getting to me. We have an ethical, moral duty to do something, but what, exactly, still escapes me. I could go directly to the press, but what does that accomplish? Worldwide hysteria, mass panic. Obviously that's why the secrecy has been held so tight."

"Well, what are you planning to do?"

"Christ, Laine, I don't know. That's where my reasoning breaks down. I've got Mark going after anthrax samples. I've completely restructured our first phase of recombination study to look at all sorts of laser-stimulated reactions in the space environment. I guess my first inclination was to help the DISA side with an independent check of their solution. But, damn, that's just not right. What they've done in the past with this is flagrant immorality. Their intention now is no better. Very simply, the defense people are deploying a new weapon to neutralize an old and dangerous weapon. And using a method which I believe is extremely unpredictable. They expect to obtain sterilization. What they might end up with could be something far different."

"In what way different?"

"I can't say for sure. Let's just say that there are

parts of my theories which give me serious doubts about their approach. I could be all wrong, but that's what our studies are hopefully going to resolve."

"Daren, it seems to me we do have a responsibility to take some sort of stand on this. Look, as you mentioned, both of these military deployments—the biological agent and the laser system—must be violations of SALT and other accords with the Soviets. If that's the case, they surely won't tolerate this nonsense if and when it becomes known what's happening. There could be some retaliation. I'm sure we can expect much more than a strongly worded protest."

"I can't argue with that. But if the Shuttle mission succeeds, it is possible that the problem may go away."

"What do you expect the chances are it will?"

"That's the guts of the issue. We can only pray they make it. This becomes a real moral dilemma for me. I simply can't go along with their space-laser solution. Once the military has it up there in orbit, I suspect they will find all sorts of ugly uses for the thing. I suppose we could marginally justify its use on the biology, if I could be convinced of its effectiveness, and if it were disabled immediately after that use. Realistically, that's not likely. But what do we do in the meanwhile? We look at some basic laser-anthrax interactions, and then come to conclusions. If we conclude that they would obtain sterilization, then we've opened the door for them to go barreling ahead with their deployment —if we make those findings known. On the other hand, if we discover some organic resistance to the laser, how do we make that input into the system? How could we get them to change their course? This is all supposed to be secret. Who would listen to an independent research laboratory? In either case, it's questionable that our findings would have much validity. There's no way for us to know either the exact DNA blueprint of the specific strain in orbit, or the complete spectra of their neutron laser capabilities. All we could do is generalize. I think you can begin to appreciate why I haven't gotten anywhere with this. And why I needed some help resolving it all."

Laine understood completely. She was quiet for a

long minute, deeply immersed in the essence of the problem.

"Clearly we have to make the right moves. In a way, the scientific community has contributed to this potential catastrophe. Simply by virtue of our developing the knowledge which has been used to bring us all to this point. And we therefore have a responsibility to undo it."

"I accept the premise completely. But what do you propose?"

"Well, I have to look at the problem logically. Which is hard to do, since it apparently involves the survival of life on the planet. But let me try."

"Good luck."

"First, if what you've suggested about the unpredictability of the biological response to laser stimulation is valid, and given the unquestionable fact that our deployment of still another weapon in space will surely contribute to increased great-power hostility, I think your research should demonstrate that it's a counterproductive alternative. One that should be done away with."

"I agree partly . . . but I can't force our conclusions."

"I know, but you'd better think along those lines. Second, since it's possible we *will* need an alternative in the case—God help us—the Shuttle plan fails, I think it would be better to work toward a natural, organic way of neutralizing the strain. Some sort of biological antitoxin. That's the direction toward which all this high-powered scientific research by the military should be headed. Perhaps ours, too. But realistically, we first have to discredit the laser solution before they would be ready to listen to that. So again, your current research is vitally important. And third, we probably should do everything within our power to make sure the USSA mission succeeds. And support that effort however we can."

"That's logical, Laine, but unfortunately not realistic. What do we know about manned space missions, or orbital mechanics? I think all we can do there is hope."

"Perhaps. But then we have to think about the basic realities, and consequences, of all this. If we are incapable of making any impact, or moving toward any positive change in policy, other things become clear. I think one real concern is the Soviet reaction. My own feeling is they should be made aware of this business in a way which would moderate that reaction. And now I'm stretching. But there is a new element in Russia which might deal more rationally with the situation. The Alternatives. If there were some way to let them understand that we have a basic problem of our own creation, not intended as a direct threat against them, that message should get through to the places in their political system which might treat things more calmly than the old Politburo."

"Again, your plan is perfectly logical, but how the hell do we accomplish that?"

"I think I might have part of the answer. But let me make my last point. One more thing we have to consider. If all else fails, what is our moral obligation to prepare the world for its potential annihilation? If that is really a possibility."

"I don't believe we can know that. There's just no historical precedent. What sense would it have made to warn Europe of the Black Death? Nothing could have been done. No lives saved. The technology simply didn't exist to do anything about it. We're probably facing the same condition now. Even if we were to announce the problem, there's only three months to prepare. That just isn't enough time for science to come up with the answers. But it would be time to throw civilization into chaos and confusion. We can't make that decision. It's out of our hands."

"I guess I accept that." Laine had paid almost no attention to the drive down the coast—but now they were approaching the outskirts of Seaside-Monterey, and she was forced to slow the Porsche down to the legal limit.

Daren Gray was staring out toward the ocean, his mind struggling with the points Laine had made. "Then are we right back to square one? We do our part at Coast Research by trying to understand the effects of laser stimulations, and attempt to prove its undesirability. And in the meantime search frantically for some organic solution that the defense people would probably pay no attention to. Somehow it all seems hopelessly futile."

"No, it's not. We do everything we can to avoid compounding a tragedy."

"I could, I suppose, try the direct approach and make some contact with DISA, to express scientific concerns. Let them know of my doubts about the laser solution, and make them aware of the independent research we plan to do. Somehow I'd have to do that in a way that wouldn't get me locked up, or worse, forced into government service, behind their closed doors. I can't imagine they will be the least receptive to our moral arguments."

"That might be productive. Worth a try, anyway."

"What was your idea about the approach to the Soviets?"

"Let's consider this. We do have an important contact within their scientific circles—Marya Scherensky. If somehow I could bring this to her in confidence, present the facts in a way that she could believe, it could be a way to carry a message of moderation to, at least, the leaders of the Alternatives. Depending upon the power held by that group, it might become a moderating influence. It would involve some risk. But it's probably all we have."

"How would you make that contact? You certainly couldn't travel there in the little time we have. There are passports, visas, government approvals. And anything but a face-to-face meeting would be unthinkable. Just too sensitive."

"No . . . but, maybe she could come here. Your Science Symposium is international in scope, isn't it? Possibly we could use that as a convenient excuse. I'd have to give her some indication of the importance of a meeting, and then hope she would respond. But she does have a Soviet travel visa—we got together just six months ago in Pasadena, at a computer specialists' conference. That just might work. When is the Symposium?"

"About three weeks. Starts March fourteenth, to be exact. And I like the idea. If anyone can carry this off, you're the one to do it. By then I may have even made some progress with the research, possibly even with DISA. But that is, I think, a long shot. We'll just have to hope our studies produce the right answers. Your story to Scherensky will have to be very convincing."

"I'm capable of that. In fact, tonight I'll try to send a satphone message. Guess it should be late tonight. They're eleven hours later than us."

"Laine, I admire your logic, and your courage. Don't be disappointed if mine falls short."

"Hey, in the final analysis we're only human. We're just trying to cope with the possible end of the world. We do our best."

"Thanks. Speaking of being human, how far are we from the Pfeiffer, and the hot springs?"

"Well, this is Monterey. Thirty kilometers. Fifteen minutes by Porsche. And then three hours by foot. Are you ready to throw yourself in?"

"Yes. Right now. Let's just find a secluded hot tub in Carmel."

"No. You need the nature experience. I promise the hike will be worthwhile."

"You're promising a communal swim when we get there?"

"Of course."

"And other diversions?"

"We'll see about that."

Chapter Fourteen

Greg Sanders had much more pleasant business to attend to at White Sands this visit. Clint Robinson, Simpson's replacement as military liaison, had yesterday given him the welcome report that Land's second version of HIMNL-9 had now completed all final verification testing against the inorganics. And had done so at performance levels exceeding 105% of design specs. All beam frequencies had been achieved. All fine-tuning and precision-beam-separation modes were verified. With Sanders' approval after a careful review of the results, the neutron-laser system could be made ready for its air transport to Dugway, to the sealed underground facility for the long series of organic tests.

Sanders was supervising the packaging preparation of HIMNL-9 that clear, cold March morning. Approval had been easy. Robinson and Land Technics had done a thorough and professional job with this phase. Since the early mishap, on Sanders' insistence everything had been forced into tightly controlled procedures, with triply redundant checks at every stage. Testing personnel had followed those without a slip, and the entire operation had progressed smoothly. Everything was again falling into an orderly, natural sequence.

After the White House meeting, Lansing had quickly given DISA the green light to proceed with the full SCEPTER program—both bio-sensing and neutron-laser functions. Sanders had really expected nothing less, since their options were so limited. Redesign of the SCEPTER spacecraft itself was progressing ahead of schedule, thanks to the effectiveness of Manning and

Du Priest. Now the only system whose design was still incomplete was the bio-sensor array. And that could be slipped to a point very late in the program—attached to the primary vehicle at the same time the laser system was mounted into its structure. The basic spacecraft assembly was in fact about ready to leave the Washington clean room for Vandenberg, to be placed in their deep-space chamber at the Western Test Range for environmental testing, vibration checkouts, and mission sims.

What remained as the only unresolved issue was the actual biological response to neutron-laser stimulation. With the rest of the program going so well, they would now have a full month and a half to clean that up. Dugway had been given a microscopic sample of anthrax-r, and the procedures to be used for guarding against any possible contamination problem. The setup there was ready for shipment of HIMNL-9, and many of those connected with the bioresearch team at Fort Gabriel had a week ago relocated to Dugway with their experimental systems.

Sanders did have some nagging concerns about that phase. So far the theoretical studies had not yielded the positive results he had hoped to see—results that would confirm the laser bombardment would guarantee sterilization. Some very peculiar ambiguities had been disclosed by the preliminary research. Those could only be resolved by the field testing. But Sanders was optimistic they would be. And in his favor. It probably was a simple matter of selecting the proper frequencies, the exact beam resonance with the organism's molecular structure. Sanders lacked the scientific background to understand the details fully, but he was certain the team he'd assembled would arrive at the right answer. That team was as professional and competent as his own at DISA. The gathering in had produced its desired goal. Thirty of the brightest minds in the field of biochemistry and recombination were applying themselves to a quick resolution of the disabling of anthrax-r.

And each day it was becoming more apparent that they would have to succeed. And more probable that

SCEPTER II would become more than an alternative. Brookhaven was faltering. His USSA-manned simulations weren't converging to the desired result. EVA operations were proving to be more difficult than predicted, with the crew bungling a number of the delicate activities in training. Sanders tried to keep in touch with that side, more as a motivation toward ensuring his own success. USSA had discovered that operating the Space Tug near the Orion Platform was more than a simple matter, since there seemed to be some unexpected stability problems to overcome. Complicating matters further, their actual boost performance had diminished to a point which canceled any possibility of achieving a deep space trajectory for the biology payload. At best they could get an altitude boost of perhaps a few thousand kilometers—enough to provide temporary safety if all else worked, but certainly not the permanent solution they had initially advertised.

Only to himself would Sanders admit a certain pleasure at that development. For he was now seeing clearly the enormous power, and potential, that deployment of DISA's space weapon would provide the country. He began to view Orion's condition as a lucky opportunity to move into important strategic areas that, without the basic problem, DISA might never have been allowed to penetrate. A successful demonstration of this new capability could turn the executive, and the Joint Chiefs, around in their thinking, and lift much of the resistance that had formerly held them back. Beam weaponry was without question an effective solution to a host of space-defense situations. And Sanders, on his own, could never have devised a better scenario for the visible display of those powers.

His thoughts returned to the USSA director. Brookhaven's anticipated weakness had shown itself in another matter. The unfortunate business with the young scientist from Stanford was a serious slip, one that would take some effort to neutralize. Sanders still could not conceive how Brookhaven had been conned into disclosing the details of both their operations. Clearly the pressures were having a profound effect on his common sense. No longer could he be relied upon for anything relating to security. At least DISA was far beyond the point where public disclosure would interrupt its plan.

Still, things would continue in a more orderly way if security could be held as long as possible. Sanders had requested federal surveillance on Daren Gray with that in mind. They might not prevent a public statement from this man, but at least they would be prepared for it. Probably he would be a continuing irritation for them. Sanders was aware the scientist had tried repeatedly to contact DISA. He had directed his staff to ignore him. Later, perhaps, he would have to be dealt with more forcibly.

He watched as the last velcro strap was wrapped around the protective foam insulation covering the massive system. He observed closely the handling of the collapsible ten-meter acceleration chamber as the assembly was carefully guided into its cylindrical vault which would serve as a cocoon during the flight to Dugway. In twenty-four hours HIMNL-9 would be secured to new mounts, and attached to the monitoring systems that were waiting in underground bunkers one hundred meters below the barren ground of Utah. A place where biological testing could be done with the threat of contamination limited to, at worst, a couple of sheep straying too close to a remote exhaust port. There would be no more mistakes.

Chapter Fifteen

There was already more commotion than there should have been—more random stirring, agitation, and background noise than any scientific conference he could remember. These gatherings were usually remarkable for their civility. Daren Gray stared out into the huge auditorium, darkening now as a signal that the Twenty-second Annual International Science Symposium was about to get underway. From the speaker's podium he could see that the hall was filled to capacity, which meant nearly six thousand people in attendance. Scientists, researchers, industry and academic reps, observers from nearly all fields and from forty-two countries had been invited. Nearly every invitation had been accepted. The conference was expected to generate at least a little controversy, and few had wanted to miss that, or miss the opportunity to make some statement supporting their own parochial positions.

Although two-thirds of the week's activity would be devoted to a diversity of specialized fields, the remainder of the agenda was to focus on recombinant research and genetic engineering, in all its aspects. Gray, besides hosting and organizing, was to represent the Stanford research in one of the mini-conferences. Severinson would present results from the Maryland studies of _E. coli_ and extensions to human DNA. Lederhaupt, of Columbia, perhaps the most outspoken on their side, had assembled the leading specialists and theoreticians involved with genetic design. It had been set up to avoid none of the basic issues.

Gray knew some confrontation was probably inevitable. PAGENT had been visibly and vocally active, lobbying the state legislature for a cancellation. When that was turned down, urging a boycott.

They had been busy the weekend before around the Berkeley campus, lecturing and passing out information arguing their standard theme—an immediate end to all genetic research. Their pickets were that morning ringing the walkways in front of the auditorium, making it impossible to ignore their presence. Gray guessed they had certainly not overlooked the opportunity to scatter representatives throughout the hall for the introductions. He expected it might be noisy, imagined he would have to deal with some heckling.

Gray looked around at security—hoping the campus police would be up to the job. There seemed to be at least an ample show of force, with twenty uniformed officers stationed very conspicuously around the inner periphery of the hall. This would be the most securely protected scientific conference in the history of the ISS. Everyone entering the hall had been screened, passed through metal detectors, with all briefcases and packages opened and inspected. Gray wished it could have been different, but the precautions were necessary. There had been threats, and with PAGENT's emotions so high, some had to be taken seriously.

The room was now dimmed, but the noise level hadn't yet reduced with it. He decided to give that another minute. Gray wondered if Laine had made contact. If all had gone well, somewhere in the hall she would have located Marya Scherensky. He strained to look out over the still-stirring multitude, but found it impossible to make out anything in the diminished light, and with the spots now focusing themselves onto the stage. He briefly looked over his notes—but they were already committed to memory. Dissipating nervousness, he adjusted the mike, checked his watch. It was time to start.

Gray spoke directly into an array of three microphones, looking out into the continuing roar.

"Our meeting will come to order. Please take your seats." He had to repeat the message four times before there was quiet.

Gray made the standard introductions. He then gave a brief summary of the importance of their gathering, contrasting this particular conference with its predecessors—how it came at a time when major breakthroughs now appeared to be imminent in a number of important areas. Special emphasis was placed on the demonstrated advantages of sharing these developments among the international scientific community, and the importance of continuing to do so in the clear light of an open forum.

His delivery was smooth, controlled, with the presentation done in a way to avoid arousing emotions. The audience responded with respectful silence.

Then it came time to announce and describe the agenda for the week's sequence of papers, lectures, and discussion sessions. These were carefully arranged into six broad categories—had been done so in a way that would allow each specialist to focus on his own field, but with strategically placed cross-field sessions that provided for an intermingling of the various disciplines. Gray had designed the structure himself so the conference would serve to provide both an intense information exchange and the most comprehensive exposure of every recent advance to review by an interdisciplinary body. The imagination taken in this organization reflected what was usually reserved for his own research. Given the little time available, he felt it had been done well.

He began with brief descriptions of the six conference themes, falling into an almost natural alphabetical order—Alternative Energies, Biochemistry Technique, Cosmology and Space Physics, Environmental Medicine, Fusion, and last, Genetics and Recombination. Gray was allowed to go through the first five. Everyone in the hall had been given printed program summaries of the agenda, and so knew the order beforehand.

The very moment he was about to announce the sixth and last topic, a chorus of chanting arose from nearly every section of the hall, apparently at a prearranged signal. PAGENT's representatives were effectively deployed. He listened as the chant formed itself clearly enough to distinguish the individual words, still increasing in intensity as other voices merged into it. *"No more tampering. No more tampering. No more tampering . . ."* The noise soon drowned away any possibility of continuing. The crescendo rolled on, building even more, gathering momentum. Gray could do nothing but wait, hoping for some eventual abatement. There was to be none. He turned to one side of the stage, gave a signal to an officer of the security force.

The lights were turned back up to normal so security could get an estimate of the problem. It was worse than Gray had anticipated. People were standing everywhere, shouting, many holding banners. Nearly every twentieth seat was taken by PAGENT, each with a now prominently displayed black armband featuring the symbolic broken helix. There were just too many protestors to deal with, and too well distributed. It would be futile to order security into action. That could only produce mayhem. Gray checked his watch. And waited. Still the momentum continued. Two minutes. Then three. This would go on indefinitely. There was no way to continue. If the Symposium was to succeed, it would have to be in the smaller conferences where controlled access could be enforced, and disruption would be easier to quiet.

Gray spoke with the security officer who was now on stage with him, behind the podium. A signal was given to the stage technicians for the speaker's mike to be turned up in volume. The chanting was close to deafening. Others in the hall had already tried to work their way out.

Daren Gray approached the mikes, announced in strong, deliberate words, "We will follow the agenda." He repeated that message seven more times, each time with increasing volume over the speaker system. By the sixth, his booming voice was finally carried above the background noise, and the majority of the audience comprehended. They hesitantly began to rise from their seats, and slowly, very slowly, began the process of leaving the hall, pushing their way around the still-stationary, still-chanting, PAGENT force.

Gray stepped away from the podium again, and

huddled with the security chief. For the next ten minutes, as the six thousand conferees were guided out of the auditorium by the campus police, procedures were prepared for tightly restricting access to the rest of the week's meetings. It wasn't a pleasant compromise. Much of the free communication he had hoped to develop would be sacrificed. The cross-discipline sessions would have to go. But there was no choice. Even with that alternative, security would have to be doubled in manpower, with Gray personally in charge of verifying credentials for all of the attendees within each of twenty-seven conference sessions. It was going to be an enormous hassle.

Marya Scherensky located the prearranged meeting spot, and Laine Jeremy, only a minute before the introductions began. The women had only a few moments to find their reserved seats near the front of the hall, and no time to talk. Very late the evening before, Laine had managed to get a call through to Marya at the hotel. Marya cautioned then that she would have to be careful about any foreign contact—everything was being watched and reported. Standard practice. She explained how the trip had been made possible under the pretext that there was to be important new information revealed by U.S. scientists regarding theory revisions to the General Orbit Decay Syndrome—all of which was of vital interest to their own space program. Other harmless topics were also discussed during that call, which ended with Laine giving the Russian a seat location in the conference hall.

Now they found themselves in the midst of a crushing, pushing crowd, being buffeted on all sides by the mass of people insistent on withdrawing from the chaotic, deafening scene. The PAGENT people were blocking the aisles, standing in place, adding to the confusion. Shoving matches were erupting spontaneously throughout, and it seemed close to becoming a brawl. Laine realized what an ugly setting had been created for the appeal she needed to present to Marya. It would be best to sit this out, let the commotion die down a bit, before attempting their exit. She made the suggestion to Scherensky, who agreed with her judgment.

Laine sensed the Russian was seriously bothered by the outburst. It was something very atypical in Soviet society. In fact, almost nonexistent. These people, even the disaffected ones, still had difficulty comprehending the raw freedoms enjoyed, or tolerated, in the Western democracies.

Laine studied Marya Scherensky, her prematurely silvered hair, the blue eyes, a strong, attractive face. If the hair were ignored, her age could be properly guessed to be thirty-six to thirty-eight. This woman, Laine realized, had survived the crush of the Soviet system with quiet grace, and beauty. Her intelligence was unquestioned—she knew this from their previous encounters. And Marya's sympathies with the Alternative faction, which made her a subversive in the Kremlin's eyes, made her a heroine to Laine. Scherensky was a true warrior—the feminine example of what Laine idealized. Her own success had been achieved without the element of struggle, the edge of repression and danger, that accompanied the rise of this woman. The nature of their respective successes was qualitatively different. Laine felt considerable admiration for her, and a degree of envy. Perhaps mixed with a touch of physical attraction. She let the last thought drift to a softer place.

It was becoming possible to think of finding their way out. Two-thirds of the audience had finally struggled outside. And PAGENT's collective voice and stamina were subsiding to a tolerable level. She put her hand on Marya's shoulder.

"It's time we leave. If we can get out of here, do we have some time to talk?"

The Russian turned to her, expressing relief. "Yes, we have probably an hour. I agree we should find a quiet place. It is difficult to think in this environment."

It took them ten minutes before they pushed their way into daylight. Their exit, even after the wait, was still rough. Marya Scherensky was visibly shaken. On the walkway outside she stopped Laine, opened her briefcase, and produced a package of American tobacco cigarettes. She lit one immediately, taking a number of deep puffs.

"There is still one thing I can always appreciate about my visits to your country," she said, trying to smile away her nervousness. "These are no longer available in Russia."

"Well, enjoy them while you can. They are practically extinct over here too. The synthetic blends are pushing them off the market. At last. The risks of tobacco don't bother you?"

"No. These contribute very little to the existing dangers of life. Besides, I only smoke them occasionally. At home I'm restricted to the imitations."

"Marya, let's find a bench somewhere on the commons, away from this racket."

"Yes, and away from my guardians. I believe we have lost them."

"You're being watched at all times?"

"It is customary."

Laine led her to a location she felt would be just right to help dissolve the earlier hostility—she found a circle of rocks under a large cedar tree, removed from the flow of campus life. There were a few scattered students about, studying quietly but paying no attention to the two women. No one who appeared to resemble her vision of a Soviet agent.

Marya put down her briefcase beside one rock bench, and extracted another cigarette. Her first was only half finished.

Laine sat next to her, deciding how best to begin. She looked directly at the Russian woman. "We've been friends, Marya, for some time, and you have no reason to mistrust me."

Somewhat surprised by this, she responded firmly, "None at all."

"We may need your help, with a very important matter. A matter of science, and politics. Something which may have very serious consequences. And I must put considerable trust in you too. For what I have to say will be a violation of our own national security. But it has to be done."

"I know of discretion."

Marya Scherensky listened quietly, intently, as Laine revealed the basic story of the Orion problem. She absorbed every detail, and filed away each aspect of the situation. There was no shock, only a knowing understanding. After both potential resolutions to the problem were described, Marya was impressed by the openness, the sincerity of the revelation, but was uncertain why she had been given this information, and where the dialogue might be leading. She interrupted Laine in mid-sentence: "Why are you involving me in this?"

"Because we trust you, and understand your position with the Alternatives is one of some importance. Our hope is that you will somehow use your influence to moderate Soviet reaction to this before it becomes public knowledge, and precipitates unnecessary international tensions. As I say, that can only be our hope. It was the reason for requesting that you come here. We can do only so much on this side—the wheels are in motion, and there may be no way to stop that. It seems that as usual we are covering old errors with new ones—compounding the problem. Marya, if you can reach at least the scientific community, and whatever political contacts you have, and persuade them that no harm, no threat, is directed toward you by our side, it could make some difference. That our means may be suspect, but not the intended end."

"Certainly that is a concept I know."

"We are serious, Marya."

"I do understand. And I will consider your appeal. But unfortunately I doubt my influence is as great as you imagine, or as it has been in the past. You must realize we in the Alternative Party have very limited impact on political policy. We are of course all still considered dissident."

"But your party holds positions of respect and stature throughout the scientific community. It also extends into the Soviet political system, doesn't it?"

"To some degree that is true. It is now a rather erratic success story. The Main Party still holds primary power. Over police and military functions. And over international politics. But we do have the sympathies of many in science, music, and the arts. We are indeed posing a strong balancing ideology. And are making considerable progress in the professional circles. But you must remember we are the outsiders, and are all under suspicion. Some have been isolated from the mainstream, as was done in past eras. We still have to be extremely careful if we are to maintain any hope of survival. If we continue to produce effectively for the State, usually that is sufficient. But any slip, any error, and we lose ground. I myself am in a very tenuous position at present since the loss of our last Cosmos. I must be especially cautious about stirring the Soviet political waters."

Laine voiced her disappointment for them both: "I'm sorry to hear of your situation. I know there are so many difficulties for you already that in a way it seems unfair to even approach you with this. Still, an attempt had to be made."

The honesty again had its effect.

"My friend, I believe these cautionary remarks are necessary to condition you against overexpectations. Your cause is not entirely futile. I believe your story, and also that whatever mischief is being conducted in space, your country's intention appears to be more humanitarian than aggressive. There indeed are contacts which I can make, certain individuals who have other contacts, within the political bureaucracy. I will have to think seriously how best to pursue a course which will lead to moderation. It may be possible. You have my word that I will do whatever I am able. But you must not expect miracles." Marya gave Laine Jeremy a reassuring smile.

"Thank you. I suppose we both know what can be accomplished by reasonable people, on both sides of this world. Let's hope for reasonableness. The other alternative is far too depressing."

"How much time is there before the events unfold?"

"I believe the mission occurs in April."

"Then the details will be surfacing well before then. Our intelligence agencies are very competent. We should carry this message along as soon as possible."

"I know it's not much time. For any of us."

"Perhaps . . . there may be some cables which could be sent, discreetly. Laine, I will try. Now it is probably best for me to continue my intended purpose for being here and attend the first space-physics session. That begins soon. I will try to get back in touch in a day or so. We should avoid unnecessary contact. Which I consider very unfortunate." She grasped Laine's hand in her own, pressing it firmly.

"Thank you, Marya." She watched as the Russian replaced her cigarettes inside her briefcase, then with a smile and slight wave walked away into the bustle of the Berkeley campus on that warm Monday morning.

The timing could hardly have been worse. It was Wednesday, and Daren Gray was chairing a session in which Miles Severinson had just taken twenty minutes to develop the link between his *E. coli* findings and human DNA manipulation. Even though access had been strictly controlled, there were three hundred people attending the lecture. This was a key breakthrough, and had attracted considerable interest. PAGENT was there also. But quiet. They had obtained court orders allowing them into the sessions, with the understanding that any further disruptions would terminate that privilege. PAGENT had acquiesced, and members were in evidence only as observers, identified by their ever-present armbands.

Daren Gray had something close to a premonition that there would be trouble. It had bothered him for the entire twenty minutes Severinson took to set the stage for his major premise. He tried to ward off that distraction, but it persisted.

Suddenly there was a shout, a disruption at the door. Everyone turned. A young man was scuffling with the guards, demanding to be let inside. Gray stood up to see better as the man shouted, "I have something that should be read. Something you should all hear now, before this goes any further."

The guards finally restrained him, grabbed what

appeared to be a newspaper from his hands, began to pull him out of the room.

"If you silence me, someone else will bring you the truth."

One woman with a black armband left her chair and hurried to the doorway. She scrambled with one of the guards, retrieved the paper. There was a futile attempt by three of the audience to restrain her too, and move her out the door. She cried out, "Wait. Please. This is important for everyone here."

Gray spoke out. "Okay, let her be. What do you have that's so important? If we let you read it, will you let us go ahead, with no more interruption?"

She was reading to herself furiously, ignored his request. Then she looked up and around the room, as if anticipating the effect she was about to have.

"Yes. It's a very short article. Then you can resume this madness. That is, if you can find enough left to support the session."

Gray snapped, "Please get on with it."

Without further encouragement, the girl began: "This is the Washington *Post*. Today's issue. In it we find an article by the well-known journalist, McAndrews. It's entitled . . . of all things . . . 'BIOLOGICAL DOOMSDAY IN SPACE.' " She paused briefly for the effect. "I'll read it verbatim."

My initial paranoia has unfortunately been confirmed, along with my darkest fears for our survival. Again the deception perpetrated on the people of this country, and of the world, by our own government, goes unchallenged and continues to be unbelievable. Perhaps this is being done for the last time. Our next Shuttle mission is indeed being redesigned to fly a crucial assignment. Its objective is to rescue us from a biological catastrophe. Now many things become obvious.

It is now known, and confirmed by sources inside government, that we have secretly used space as a dumping ground for our most lethal biological warfare wastes—for one particularly deadly batch that was created over a decade ago. This little problem is now about to return itself to those who sent it up there—and, of course, to the rest of us who had nothing to do with it. These wastes are lethal to all life forms. They are currently onboard an abandoned military space station. That station, which the defense guys call the Orion Platform, is today three hundred kilometers above our heads, only about one hundred eighty kilometers from the upper reaches of atmosphere, and decaying fast. Sometime near the end of May, if the forecasters are correct, and if nothing is done, the whole mess will be dropping out of the skies to spread its deadly payload about the upper stratosphere. All life on Earth will be in jeopardy.

But there is one hope. Our secretive USSA now tells me they plan to retrieve this lethal payload from the station, and boost it into a safer orbit, and spare us from worldwide contamination. Good. Great. Let's hope it works.

What I'd like to know, and demand to know, is what level of insanity has taken us to this point? Why was it done? How was it done? Who has blessed this perversity? We would like answers. What motivates the space agencies to endanger the entire planet? How is the military able to carry out such unbelievable mischief? And we would ask the President and Congress, what was your participation in these events, and now what the hell can we do to prepare ourselves?

If there is any hope beyond May, and we somehow survive this tragedy, more than another presidential commission is called for. We would expect indictments of everyone ever involved with this mockery of human life. We would expect resignations of the current heads of our space agencies for their collusion in all of this. I believe even Lansing's resignation would be in order, since, I am sure, he has known for some time. Finally, if we should survive, it seems appropriate to then consider a complete overthrow of the entire military complex which has led us to the brink of annihilation.

If there is anyone left to do that. Will we ever, ever, learn.

The woman from PAGENT looked up again, at the room of stunned conferees. There was complete silence. She spoke, softly: "What more evidence do we need before it's clear where your activities are leading us? Now, you magnificent scientists, what will you do with all of your sophisticated research?"

One man stood up from the audience. Gray recognized him immediately. It was Joshua Wilkens. His graying beard and fierce eyes seemed to sparkle as he spoke out: "This has gone far enough. I suggest that any of you interested in putting an end to this incredible path into destruction withdraw now from the so-called Science Symposium, and gather with us on the Berkeley common, where we can begin to sort out a reasonable and humane direction for us to follow. You have tampered with creation too long. Now it may be too late. I believe we all share a common interest in the cause of PAGENT."

Another man stood. A scientist from Cal Poly. Not before known for any radical positions. "This *has* gone too far. We'll listen. We will be with you."

More of the audience rose, seconding that thought.

Daren Gray sat back in his chair, watching as the entire angry, frightened assembly of people made its way out of the lecture room. There was new determination in the faces of the PAGENT group. Shock, fear, disgust on many of the others. Nothing could be done now to reverse the trend. The herd instinct had turned. It was too late to apply reason. If any could be given the situation.

Miles Severinson slowly collected his notes and slides into his case. He looked over at Daren Gray, who was slumped in his chair, defeated. Severinson just latched his case, slowly shook his head, and walked out of the room.

The Symposium was reduced to shambles. PAGENT people had gone to every meeting, every session, and pulled nearly everyone out to their own spontaneous gathering. They attracted nearly another three thousand sympathetic students. Gray listened with Laine Jeremy from the steps of his lecture hall by the commons—listened as Joshua Wilkens, with the help of a hastily rigged loudspeaker, conducted his largest, most successful anti-science rally to date. He seemed well prepared for this day. The list of condemnations was endless. As was the list of informal resolutions passed by the representatives of the Science Symposium, now transformed into the Human Life Symposium. Resolutions denounced both space and military institutions. The use of space for malicious purposes. The current directions of biological research. The atmosphere of secrecy. The matter of the impending catastrophe. Everything seemed a good target. One resolution met with even more resounding support among the multitude. There was a call for an immediate end to any continuation of research in the fields of biochemistry, genetics, and recombination. The outcry was unanimous. Shouts of "Close them all down" echoed off the buildings surrounding the common.

Gray wondered aloud where they would be going from that point. Laine Jeremy could offer him no comfort. Everything was collapsing about them.

Chapter Sixteen

One week later the shock waves had still not diminished but had spread rapidly from McAndrews' article and the events on the Berkeley campus to swell into an international cry of outrage directed toward the United States and its now-discredited military, political, and aerospace institutions. A mood close to hysteria could be found in even the most remote corners of the planet, carried there by the news-relay satellites of the world press network. The climate of fear and uncertainty was further aggravated by the action of the American President shortly after the disclosures. Lansing, although forced to acknowledge the fact of the Orion problem and USSA's mission to resolve it, firmly refused to elaborate beyond that point. There had been a brief statement read at a press conference, an admission of the truth, followed by his adamant and continuing refusal to provide details in the face of unrelenting questions.

That week there was nothing else discussed at the United Nations. Every nation demanded its own statement, its own denunciation of the Americans. Each appealed to the United States to provide some means of protecting its people in the event of the formerly unthinkable—the random airborne descent of a lethal biological strain over lands and waters. Scientists from all countries gathered in Washington, Munich, Geneva, and London to debate the possibilities, frantically searching for some solution which might counter the consequences of a failure of America's crucial Shuttle mission. But they were grasping, operating with only

181

partial information. Conflicts raged continually between those factions who demanded an immediate end
to all biological research and those who saw that as
their only hope for survival.

In this country Congress was caught up in the same
hysteria. Indictments were sought of every official
remotely connected with the affair. There was a movement toward Lansing's impeachment. But the basic
issues went unresolved—how to pry the complete picture of the impending disaster from a silent administration, and then what could be done about it.

In the midst of this outcry, only two examples of
rationality managed to hold firm. Lansing refused to
be carried under by the events. He insisted that no
recriminations would be taken against anyone until
USSA had its chance to accomplish the vital mission.
He would not tolerate an inquisition while that was in
progress. The consistent message from the White
House was for all to retain a hold on sanity until after
the events of April and May had run their course.
Then, he declared with a dubious optimism, if the
public still demanded it, he would resign, and Congress
could carry out whatever executions they felt necessary.
Lansing appealed to all that the only sensible approach
now was to allow USSA the means to continue forward
with its solution in dignity and professionalism—without harassment. His advice always included the superfluous warning that the future of humanity was on the
line, and for that, reason had to prevail.

The other pillar of calmness and strength was Greg
Sanders, and his agency's orderly and uninterrupted
progress toward the SCEPTER solution. The Washington
Post and countless others had long since guessed at
nearly every conceivable aspect of Orion's predicament,
with the single exception of DISA's secret plan to resolve it. For some unexplainable reason their position
was still unshaken, their security still intact. Sanders
himself found this unbelievable—almost miraculous
—given Lansing's original threat to make DISA a scape-
goat, given the relentless probing of the press, but
especially given the fragile state of mind he understood
the director of USSA to be in. He knew that was deli-

cate even before the uncovering. Now the pressures had to be unbearable at USSA. But Sanders was not privy to everything.

What he did not know yet—what he would learn only a week later—was that Chris Brookhaven was no longer able to react to those pressures. Before presidential directives could be carried out, erecting a shield around his agency, the media harassment had been too intense. The director of USSA had already broken, had to be institutionalized, was now far removed from any possibility of further compromising their remaining secrets. USSA's directorship and the critical Shuttle flight were now in the hands of a presidential commission.

Fortunately for Sanders the shield had been extended to DISA in time. He, along with USSA, was now firmly protected—at least for the immediate future. Lansing had been forced to make the expedient compromises.

But there were other casualties. SALT IV quickly followed Chris Brookhaven into that category. The Soviets, now confirmed in their suspicions and outraged, had demanded of the U.S. team at Geneva complete explanations of America's admitted contamination of space. Their reasonable request was countered with no more than a superficial, evasive rebuff. The Soviets would develop a more accurate picture by monitoring the evening news. In anger and disbelief, the Russians announced they would develop their own response, and withdrew for all time from Geneva and the negotiations.

The hot line between Moscow and Washington was in use daily. Only Lansing and the Kremlin knew where those contacts were leading.

The casualty list extended to Daren Gray's circle. They could now only hope that Marya Scherensky might still carry their message to the right places in the Soviet bureaucracy. She disappeared without a trace the same day the Twenty-second Annual International Science Symposium collapsed into anarchy. Laine had gone to her hotel room that evening to find nothing but emptiness and signs of a hasty departure. There hadn't been even the normal checkout at the reception desk—nothing but a phone call from the Russian embassy promising to cover all expenses. Laine phoned the embassy, could learn only that Marya had been recalled—and had left no messages.

Their next day was equally unsettling. Daren Gray went about the unpleasant, necessary details of closing down the Symposium, notifying everyone involved of its termination, gathering all remaining papers and lecture outlines into something that could perhaps be published so that at least the scientific value of the week could be preserved for posterity. He pretended that still mattered.

Gray heard nothing from Laine that day. After wrapping up matters at Berkeley, he took an evening drive to Coast Research to see Mark Wilson and take his mind off his depression. They talked late into the night. There was a lot to go over. Wilson's first results with the anthrax were in. They were inconclusive, but still disturbing. There appeared to be a basic uncertainty factor within the anthrax laser response. Some irreducible ambiguity he could not filter out. Wilson was stumped. He had double-checked against error and found nothing improper. After Gray had gone over the preliminary data for an hour, he too was unable to make sense of it. Everything was in order. The setups were right. Chamber pressures tested clear vacuum. The problem resisted scientific analysis.

Gray studied the reports, baffled.

"We may be reaching the Heisenberg threshold," Mark theorized.

"I can't believe that. We shouldn't even be close."

"We have 29% reacting one way, 32% a second, and 39% a third. All under identical conditions. What else could it be?"

"Environmental factors?" Gray wondered.

"No. The environment's perfect. With the lack of gamma radiation, it's cleaner than space. I simply don't understand this."

"I can't explain it either. It defies logic. One thing is clear—the results differ significantly for the different strains."

"Completely different."

"Which at least tells us something. We obviously need to somehow obtain the exact DNA blueprint of whatever's up there. Not just its relative. We need the real thing."

"And we should also have some better knowledge of their combined neutron-laser capability. So we can model that more precisely," Wilson added.

"I agree. We seem to be dealing with very sensitive responses. But I'll be damned if I know how we get our hands on that information. DISA of course refuses to talk to me. And no one else has what we need."

"Somehow you've got to get through to them. Until you do, it's doubtful we can get much further."

They both went over the data, concentrating on every detail. Gray found that becoming more and more difficult. The distractions were interfering with his ability to focus. He had Wilson repeat a portion of the test sequence, and put his mind in neutral. The results were repeated down to the last data bit. The ambiguities would not go away.

By the time Gray returned to his house in Woodside, his exhaustion and frustration covered the concern he would have ordinarily felt for the absence of any word from Laine Jeremy. He collapsed into his unmade bed.

At ten the next morning Gray was still preoccupied with the strange outcome of Wilson's testing. Laine reached him at the Recombination Lab, calling from Moss Beach. She wouldn't be coming in. She was planning to get high, and unwind. Her voice wavered as she explained how the FBI had taken her in for questioning about Marya Scherensky. The interrogation had lasted the entire day. There were parts of it Gray had to know, but she wouldn't trust the phones. She suggested they meet on the coast, at their usual place for weekend dinners. And then hung up, offering nothing more.

Gray spent the rest of the day trying to lose himself in the science of anthrax responses. Trying to find some clue. And trying without much success not to worry about Laine, the FBI, or the growing line of noisy pickets forming around the outer boundary of Coast Research.

They met at seven at Frenchy's in Half Moon Bay. Laine was feeling better—the day's therapy had worked well. She was waiting for him in her favorite spot—a booth tucked away from the main flow of the restaurant's life, beside a picture-window view of the city lights streaming toward the ocean. Daren was glad to find her there. Evenings they'd begun in this setting usually ended well.

"How's your psyche?" he asked, forcing a smile.

"Much better." She returned more warmth than she had been given. "Today's healing achieved the desired result. It's amazing what the cabin and beach can do for an injured spirit. But what about you?"

"I'm a wreck," Gray said honestly. A waiter approached. Daren ordered a double J&B on ice. Then he turned to Laine, who was already sipping something with rum and exotic juices: "Can we hold off on dinner awhile?"

"Yes, that can wait—I won't starve." The waiter nodded, and promised to be right back with the drink.

"This is unbelievable. How much of a hassle was the questioning?" he asked.

"At the time, no worse than Kafka's *Trial*. I just wasn't expecting anything like it. Now it doesn't seem that severe. But yesterday morning, when the FBI showed themselves in my computer room at Coast and told me I had to come into town with them, was not one of my fondest experiences. I was already edgy after Wednesday's mess. Their timing was certainly perfect."

"You didn't . . ."

"No, I didn't. I didn't give away anything."

Gray sighed, relieved. The waiter dropped off his Scotch. "You're a strong girl."

"Woman." She smiled, and continued: "They didn't learn anything from me they didn't already know. But I'm sure they sensed my anxiety. Hopefully they attributed that to what I'd just been through, and to the setting itself. Somehow these guys knew I was at Berkeley Wednesday. And with Marya on Monday. And that I'd checked about her after the disruption."

"And that's why they brought you in?"

"Well, their pretext was my contact with her. They were concerned about her sudden departure, so they said. They wanted to know why she was there, what we discussed, our relationship and contacts in the past, what I'd found out about her disappearance."

"I guess we could expect that."

"That's where it started. And continued for over an hour, with the same questions repeated, asked in slightly different ways. But I was consistent, wouldn't let them trip me up. I gave them the cover story, that I thought she was there to participate in the Space Physics sessions, those on the GODS Effect and satellite perturbations. I was honest about our past contacts —nothing to those. Beyond that, I said I was surprised and concerned about her abrupt leaving, suspected it had to do with the way the conference ended."

"Did they buy all of that?"

"I don't know. In any case, they finally gave up on that subject. Then they went on to their next topic. Which is why you need to be aware of the details." Laine glanced at the people at all the tables within hearing distance.

Gray whispered, "Is that paranoia necessary?"

Laine's voice lowered somewhat, to just the point where the background noise would cover it.

"Yes. I think it's justifiable caution. Now." She paused.

Gray took a long drink. "Please, don't keep me in suspense."

"Sorry. But there's a troubling undercurrent to this. And it relates directly to you. More than just the FBI are involved in this. Sitting in on the questioning were agents from CIA and the Defense Intelligence Agency. And their interest went beyond my personal involvement with Marya Scherensky. They probed into our work at Coast. Lots of questions about the nature of the research. What I knew of the Shuttle mission. What connection existed between your work at the Recombination Lab and the space problem. Questions about you personally," Laine said, pausing to see if he had any comment.

When he remained silent, she continued: "I did ask

why I was being questioned about that. Their response was only that there were routine national-security matters to clear up. It was obvious they were stretching the point, fishing, and really had nothing firm. The questions were vague. But the interest was there, and they seemed determined to find something."

"Did they ever mention, or ask, anything related with DISA?"

"No. Nothing on that. But they covered everything else. Daren, the feeling I have is that you're likely to be their next candidate for interrogation. And you should be ready for that."

"I guess so. What did you tell them about our study?"

"Only that my role was one of computer support to the research. I played dumb. I know very little of the details, you see. But they kept after me about that. I suggested they read your last book."

"Gutsy."

"By then I was getting back my old confidence. And becoming tired of the whole affair."

Gray finished his drink, flagged the waiter, ordered seconds for them both.

"They must know about my meeting with Chris Brookhaven. That I know the whole damned story."

"That's a logical assumption. These people are definitely worried about our knowledge of the biology problem, if we've said anything to the Russians, and how your research ties in. I suspect we're headed for even more difficult times."

"Yes, it seems like it." Gray thought to himself a minute. "The climate seems ripe for all sorts of over-reaction."

Laine wondered, "You're thinking on our side, and elsewhere."

"Correct. I hope to God your friend Marya gets through to someone over there. In time. I can imagine how they're reacting to the current news. And hate to think what happens when they learn our defense people plan to play games firing neutron lasers at orbiting biological toxins."

"Well," Laine said, "there's no way to predict that.

I just hope Marya's safe. And still able to make those contacts." Her voice indicated real concern.

"What bothers me most is our inability to do anything of substance over here, on this side, where the monster's been created. Here we are worrying about the Soviet reaction while we have the fact of the American response. And with that knowledge, we're still in a hopeless, powerless position. There seems to be too much hysteria and confusion for any of us to move rationally."

"Daren, what are you getting at? It isn't clear what more you think we should do."

"You're right. What I'm trying to say is that even if we can come up with a sound argument against DISA's proposed madness, who will listen to us? Look, everything is out of balance. My own perceptions included. I'm worrying about a possibility that may never happen. PAGENT's clamoring about closing down all science. The FBI and CIA are worried about our research at Coast, probably have us under surveillance. DISA continues to charge ahead with its own plan in near total isolation from everyone, as if they were the primary solution, which may well be the case, since the USSA mission is having serious problems in simulation testing. So what the hell can we do? Besides continue with our studies and try to learn what will be the real outcome of the DISA alternative, and maybe come up with something better, less threatening than risking a confrontation in space. Do you know what Wilson's results are turning up? Anthrax sometimes doesn't respond to laser stimulation by letting itself be sterilized. In some cases the energy is passed right through. In other cases, it's simply deflected. The results are confusing, and totally unpredictable. Yet without access to the exact conditions, our conclusions are tenuous at best. And if they prove to be valid, we still have the problem of who would take us seriously. Jesus, I'm probably still not making sense."

"One thing does make sense, Daren. I think you'd better find a way to reach DISA. And soon. They need the perspective of an outside, independent source. I also feel that since you're probably under suspicion, you should present them with your honest concerns, before you're ordered to."

"But how do I do that? I've already tried to reach their director, Sanders, but can't get past his secretary's *hold* switch."

"Force the issue. Let this Sanders know you're aware of what's going on. Like you say, he may already know that. Tell him you have some results that may be of interest to them. If all else fails, suggest you'll go public if DISA won't see you first."

"I suspect that would get a response. I might be sitting this all out on some federal prison farm."

"You asked what you could do," Laine insisted. "I'm only suggesting an approach."

"I know. There really is precious little time left to make any impact at all—to change directions. To move toward a more effective, less hostile solution than deploying particle beam weapons."

"If you're ever going to make those points, you have to do it now. Daren, they'll have to listen, given your name, your reputation. They surely won't brush all that aside, and I can't see them locking you up. But you *should* make the first move, before things are totally beyond control and the chance is gone forever."

"You're right, of course." Gray searched the field of alternatives. There weren't any.

Laine took his hand. "You really haven't been able to play the scientist much since your return to our world."

"That's for sure." He thought about it, amused. "Things certainly were much smoother on the lecture circuit. Much more orderly. And to think I once looked forward to this period as a refuge."

"And now you've become a politician instead of a scientist."

"When it's all over, maybe I'll run for Governor."

"Let's hope there will be something left to govern." She stopped there, tried to change the mood. "Can we order now? I'm hungry."

"How about skipping dinner? Let's just go to your place."

"Oh no, you don't. I'm looking forward to Frenchy's

famous Tournedos Oscar. And you owe me that much for guarding your secrets so well. For being such a good agent."

Gray pretended disappointment.

She added, "We can consider dessert later."

A quarter moon had slipped into view from their window, haloed by the night's mist. Lower down in the city the lights were glittering, moving with the rhythms of that Friday night. The motions were more restless than usual, reflecting the new uneasiness of a transforming world. A world now trying to find some way of coping with this latest, and possibly final, threat to its survival.

On Saturday morning Daren Gray placed a satellite call to the office of DISA's director from his own link at Coast Research. He was again told that Sanders was unavailable. Gray left a brief message:

"Please advise Director Sanders that Dr. Daren Gray of Stanford requests an immediate conference. There are important matters of a sensitive nature that must be discussed, specifically involving DISA's approach to the Orion situation. This will be my final attempt to contact your agency. Await your quick reply."

Gray did not have to wait long. The message was picked up locally. Within an hour, two well-dressed government men entered his office flashing FBI credentials. They would be his escorts to Washington that afternoon. The flight was already arranged, as was his meeting with Gregory Sanders.

Chapter Seventeen

The FBI agents were careful with Gray, and professional. There was no intimidation, just firm insistence. They left no question that he was in their custody. Gray had just enough time to leave word with Mark Wilson where he was going and to gather a few summaries of their preliminary results. Within hearing of his escorts, he told Mark not to worry unless he hadn't gotten some word, or himself, back by midweek. If nothing had been heard by then, Laine was to have Henry Jeremy send his best attorneys to DISA headquarters in Washington.

During the flight east, Gray had plenty of time to review the points he planned to make. He would finally have his day in Sanders' court, and his case had to be well presented. There would be no second chance. The FBI agents were silent during the trip. Apparently they were only to be his guardians, with Sanders handling whatever interrogation DISA required.

By the time they touched down at Dulles, Gray felt he was prepared for the confrontation. He relaxed a bit, taking in the details of this adventure. From the United departure lobby the three rode a tram to the heliport terminal. The FBI had its own means of getting quickly around the hopelessly congested East. They boarded a ten-passenger Sikorsky with jet assist and U.S. government insignia, and lifted into the crowded airways. Gray never tired of the sensation of full three-dimensional maneuverability.

It took him a few minutes to realize the copter was not heading due east toward D.C., as he had expected.

Instead its course was south, over the entanglement of interstates and commercial development that side of the airport, then southeast through the flickering remains of Virginia countryside toward the Potomac. He guessed they were somewhere north of the Marine Corps base, on a direct line with Indian Head on the Maryland side. He watched the landscape flash by. Soon their destination was in sight. The copter banked and dropped lower, streaking toward a sprawling complex of buildings he guessed to be one of the proliferating military-research parks. He studied its contours and character, tried to determine the exact location relative to the landmarks he knew. But Gray wasn't that familiar with the government's network of bases, and after a quick mental search, he gave up his attempt to identify this particular one.

The Sikorsky circled once around the base as the airspace was cleared, then settled gently on the roof of what, by its size, seemed to be one of the primary buildings on the complex. Without further delay, the three stepped out onto the landing apron, stoop-walked no more than ten meters, and in a rush of wind felt the copter fly off to its next assignment.

Gray straightened to see the large figure of a man, hair graying, wearing an English tweed jacket, well dressed in dark browns. The man extended his hand to Daren, gave him a controlled, pleasant smile. His voice matched the visual image—low, steady, disciplined.

"Dr. Gray. I'm Greg Sanders. Welcome to Fort Gabriel. You're right on time."

Gray shook the outstretched hand. Hoped the encounter would continue to be as pleasant.

"You certainly transport your people with style and precision."

"In this business we can't afford anything less than that. Time is usually at a premium. Please come along with me. We're going to take a brief tour. There are some things which may interest you." Sanders gave a slight wave to the FBI escorts, a signal they would not be needed for a while. They disappeared into a rooftop lounge.

Sanders led Gray into an elevator, in which they descended in one continuous, stomach-twisting motion for twenty levels, to a floor marked *U-2*. Gray guessed correctly that meant they were below ground. They stepped out into a hallway where Sanders nodded to a uniformed guard, who let them pass into a circular glassed walkway surrounding a central core of countless partitioned working modules. This was clearly their bioresearch area—Gray recognized the paraphernalia of his profession. But this place was much more well-equipped, better organized, than anything he had ever encountered. The setup was an elaborate honeycomb, with each cell representing a different specialty, and all arranged neatly into their logical and natural relationships.

The level of activity seemed unusually high, considering this was Saturday and government had long since adopted a four-day work-week. From his initial vantage point, Gray could see thirty or more people busily engaged in various tasks scattered about the honeycomb. They all wore color-coded lab coats in white, blue, and pale yellow.

Sanders stopped at a point about ninety degrees around the circling walkway—a place Gray recognized as the heart of their bioresearch complex.

The DISA director pointed into its midst. "This is, of course, our research center for the study of Orion's biology. This particular area before us is the recombination and microscopy specialty. Everything here is very new. We've assembled the entire operation in less than two months. State-of-the-art hardware in all sectors, as you can see. All together in the most efficient configuration."

"The organization and sophistication are impressive. My own lab seems crude by comparison."

"Color coding helps with functional identification and communication. Blue are the lead scientists, white the next-level assistants, yellow the technical support and computer specialists. The organization was necessary to maximize results in a minimum of time. The partitions allow each specialty to isolate its area when necessary—the large video screens in each module provide cross-communication and conferencing."

"You're very active here for a weekend."

"We don't have the luxury of recognizing weekends. Actually, those working here today represent only half of the entire staff. The others have been relocated to another facility. But let's continue our tour."

Sanders led them another sixty degrees around the walkway, then stopped above an area which was apparently a data-analysis sector and gestured toward it. Gray looked down at the tables covered with computer-enhanced representations of biological structures, and stacks of numerical information. Three people were seated around one large table, studying the material intensely, discussing the results of some current investigation. Two wore blue coats, one was in white. He wondered why Sanders had singled out this particular module. Then he looked more closely.

A lot of years had passed, but there was no question. One of the blue scientists was Mel Dankin. He could not have forgotten the face, the mannerisms. It was the first time since his abduction that Gray had seen him. None of the three looked up to return his stare —the glassed wall was obviously one-way viewing only.

"You recognize someone?" Sanders asked knowingly.

"Yes. Mel Dankin. We used to work together. He was once part of the Stanford team. Along with Don Walters, Cary Latham, and Lewin Greenwalt."

"Greenwalt's over in data-processing sector. Latham and Walters are now working at the other facility. Unfortunately I can't allow them to be distracted by your presence; otherwise you could chat with the two that are here."

"Surely this is all classified anyway."

"They understand what's to be kept out of unofficial conversation. But let's continue on. There's more to see."

Gray was led past the computer area, packed with the latest bubble memory systems, overlaying central processing units, suspended disks, data-retrieval devices. Then on to the biology storage vaults, where

Sanders explained in detail how the test units were kept in perfectly climate-controlled cells, each able to be retrieved instantly and transported via sealed canisters to the appropriate test assembly.

"All bio-test subjects are carried through a contamination-free tubular network. The network flows above the working area, totally isolated from the team. Samples are fed from above directly into the appropriate modules. We have the luxury of operating in a shirt-sleeve environment, while the biological specimens circulate through the sectors. The most compact, efficient approach we could design."

Gray was in awe, and envious. No expense had been spared. Clearly his own lab could never hope to compete with these extraordinary conditions, this highly sophisticated environment that the government could offer its researchers. As they continued the full extent of the circuit, there were more faces he recognized— formerly from other labs, other universities. He wondered what would become of it all, of them, when the problem that currently warranted this great cost, this investment of scientific talent, was over.

When they had completed the round, only one item struck Gray as conspicuous by its omission. Every other ingredient was evident, with the single exception of a vacuum chamber necessary to simulate orbital conditions. He made a mental note of that.

"Well, Dr. Gray, it is a respectable facility. We've not done too badly, given the time available. Even up to your high standards, I would imagine?"

"Well beyond them. You've applied your resources well, Mr. Sanders. And you certainly have been effective in bringing together the right people to operate all of this."

"As you know, they are all being well rewarded."

"Yes. I know."

"Now, about the purpose of your visit. You seem to think we need to talk. I have an office on the perimeter of the core laboratory where we can do just that." Sanders motioned to follow him. They walked further on, then came to a doorway. Sanders inserted a plastic card in a thin slot inside the door itself, a brief light flickered from that point, and a few seconds later the door opened itself with a slight click.

Sanders motioned Gray inside, then clicked the door closed again. A red light glowed ominously overhead.

"Don't mind that—it's necessary whenever we have uncleared visitors present."

It wasn't much of a bother—the other hidden light sources now coming on made it almost unnoticeable. Gray looked around the office. This was Sanders' personal command room, from which all the activities at the center could be monitored and directed. It was round, like the inner research circle. TV monitor screens covered the entire periphery of wall space. No doubt each set of screens and panels correlated exactly with a sector of the research lab. He noticed vertical panels labeled *"DISA-Washington," "Sunnyvale," "Vandenberg,"* and *"Dugway."* Most of the visual displays were switched off. But the constellation of lights and digital readouts made the walls alive with energy.

In the room's center was a circular couch, where Sanders sat down, turned a switch imbedded into an armrest, and triggered a large screen to descend on a wall directly in front of his viewing direction. Sanders asked Gray to take a seat on the couch opposite him. Another switch was turned, and an overhead fish-eye view of the entire lab appeared in color before them. The DISA director searched for something inside his jacket pocket, produced a tobacco pouch and pipe, which he began to fill.

"So, my friend, you've seen a glimpse of our operation. You know we are doing a very professional job here. That should put some of your fears to rest." He finished tamping, flamed a pipe lighter into the bowl, and puffed gently until he created the proper cloud of smoke.

"Now, what is it you have to say?"

Daren Gray tried to withdraw himself from the overwhelming display of technology that he suspected was meant to be intimidating. He had to focus on the basic reason for this meeting, on the appeal he had to make. He hesitated only a moment, considering again how best to proceed. There was no other way than the direct.

"I have serious concerns about your agency's proposed solution to the biological problem on Orion."

Sanders didn't show the slightest trace of surprise, confirming he was aware of the conversation with Brookhaven.

Gray continued: "You of course know I understand the details. My concerns are both those of a scientist familiar with the field you've entered and those, very simply, of a citizen. Of this country. Of the planet." He paused a moment to gauge the reaction. There was none.

"Let's first address the scientific side of the DISA alternative." He pulled folded papers from inside his jacket pocket. "As you probably also know, we have been doing studies parallel with your own in our Stanford-supported lab at Coast Research. We lack the technical sophistication you have here in Fort Gabriel, and of course don't have details of either the exact genetic blueprint of the strain involved or the range and character of energies available from a neutron laser. But we have enough information to pursue the fundamentals of this problem. In a very conscientious way. What we've discovered so far leads to some rather disturbing conclusions—for this particular application."

Gray handed the papers to Sanders. "These are the summaries, and our preliminary conclusions."

Sanders speed-scanned the pages. At first he seemed puzzled, then appeared to resolve some of his private discomfort. He looked up from the report. "Well, you should certainly expect ambiguities when you don't, as you admit, have the proper initial conditions for this equation."

Gray was not to be put off so easily. "But we do have adequate intelligence to make deductions from very similar conditions. Especially when such a surprising result is uncovered. Tell me, Mr. Sanders, what have your people resolved so far about this matter? Or have you obtained positive sterilization of your anthrax strain?"

"We have yet to determine that. We're only now going into actual field testing. So far everything has been theoretical, using computer simulations. But based on those we expect to find no problems."

"I honestly don't believe you can trust theory with this. The interactions take place near the submolecular level. We suspect there are Heisenberg threshold factors involved. And that you may never be able to obtain predictable results."

"Dr. Gray, I'm not a scientist, but I do keep well informed. So far we have no reason to believe this particular organism onboard the Orion Platform will be able to resist direct applications of neutron-laser energies. All we have left to develop are the correct resonant frequencies which are most effective. That seems to be a simple enough matter."

"But, again, have your people been able to discover those yet through a theoretical approach?"

Sanders shook his head slowly. "I suppose I have to say honestly that we haven't. But that's to be expected. There are clearly some issues that only the demonstration testing will resolve."

"So you're not the least bit concerned that no positive sterilization mechanisms have been confirmed?"

"Not at all. We will find those. Your perspective is too confined. There's no way for you to fully appreciate the power and versatility of this unique system we plan to use. There are no intensities, no resonant frequencies, no spectra that cannot be achieved. Its capabilities are nearly infinite."

Gray began to realize the man's obsession. It would be virtually impossible to get around that, but he had to try. "I noticed the absence of one particular item in your lab. There seems to be no provision for testing in a simulated space environment. How do you intend to do that?"

"Our conclusion was that that would be superfluous, an unnecessary expense. Again, the laser is so intense there are insignificant differences between in-atmosphere and vacuum reactions. If anything, we are underestimating its power."

"I disagree completely," Gray said, his voice rising.

"Our research, and nearly all my recombination work of the last two years, suggests that difference may be a critical factor. One which you especially should be considering."

"Dr. Gray, our people are capable of making the correct decisions on these points. You may indeed be a specialist in this field, and a gifted one at that, but we have assembled here at Fort Gabriel a degree of intelligence equal to your own by its quantity, quality, and diversity. I have no reason to doubt their collective judgment. The problem of space environment was addressed," Sanders stated with assurance, "and eliminated as a concern."

"Then let me try another way. You're dealing with an extremely sensitive biochemical reaction, so sensitive that the slightest imperfection can swing your results one way or the other, depending on the direction of the biases. If you ignore these fine points, the results can be completely misleading."

"I'm sure the problem is well understood here."

Gray sighed deeply, frustrated with his inability to get through. "Okay, then please do me the professional favor of having your group review our report on this. And let them decide for themselves whether it's a valid issue. It could make a great difference."

Sanders picked up the papers. "I'll consider it." He folded them neatly, slipped them into a coat pocket. "Now, what's this nonsense about your concern as a citizen?"

Gray recognized what he had to say on that subject would not make the slightest impact on the man sitting across from him. His ideas were too well entrenched, the plan too firmly set in motion. DISA would not be even slightly receptive to classical arguments for common sense. But he was there. He had to try.

"First of all, there is the obvious. Deployment of a neutron-laser weapon in space violates our country's stated position on orbiting aggressive weaponry. Then, of course, we both know the Orion problem itself represents a contempt for international agreements on the nonstrategic use of space, and on the preservation of the biosphere's environment. Your approach, even if it's never used but merely deployed, compounds the whole problem of transforming near-Earth space into a potential battleground—moving the concept of mutual, assured destruction into that region. Already we've driven the Soviets from any desire to continue SALT negotiations. When they learn of this new threat, this additional provocation, I think you people can expect a significant retaliation. Surely you've considered that, and don't expect the Soviets to ignore your activity."

"We expect them to recognize that the deployment of our system is in no way a threat to them, and that there is no implication of aggression or provocation. Its purpose is strictly the resolution of a very unique problem. All internal to our own space program."

"But the issue is one of demonstrating capabilities. Once your neutron laser has demonstrated effectiveness, it becomes a possessed capability. A new ingredient. And gives us an edge. Which the Soviets will have to respond to. That's been the nature of the business for thirty years or more. You can't deny it. This precipitates the next round of escalation."

"My friend, there are things in the world of space defense you have no way of appreciating. The Russians have, for ten years at least, been regularly deploying and testing, in this sanctity of space you speak of, a variety of aggressive terrors you couldn't even guess. You express your concerns with our deployment of one particular weapons system—worry about our potential capabilities and where that might lead. But you must be aware that their side perfected offensive disabling satellites, killer-sats, years ago. Do you know that they now have the capability, if they so choose, of neutralizing nearly every spacecraft of ours in a matter of twenty-four hours? They have the potential to shatter worldwide communications within six hours. There are Soviet satellites in orbit now that can direct their ground missiles, using evasive guidance, to every strategic target in the West with pinpoint accuracy. Their surveillance satellites are now able to penetrate even the ocean cover of our nuclear-equipped subs, and neutralize the advantage we've had with those."

Sanders paused for effect, noting Gray's surprise, then continued: "The entire building of this network has gone on continually during the last eight to ten years with only the slightest countering force on this side, while we have been held back from any significant response by pacifist critics, thinking just as you do. For you to suggest that a single deployment of one neutron laser could be a dangerous provocation is, to be mild, absurd."

Gray resisted the force of his arguments, determined to push on. "But wasn't the primary issue of concern to SALT IV the termination of all that activity?"

"I suppose that's what the politicians like to believe. But their intentions are more toward holding onto current positions, and so we end up at a disadvantage once again."

"It seems as if, given a spirit of trying to slow needless escalation, the neutron laser tips the balance far in the other direction. You yourself admitted its capabilities are limitless."

Sanders nodded in agreement. "I perceive that as being healthy. If the talks ever reconvene, we can negotiate from strength. Something maybe our side has grown unaccustomed to doing. Historically that has been very effective."

Gray groped for something, anything, to add. "Even granting that perspective, I believe you still should consider this a provocation. You know damn well their side will see it that way. And if the Soviets are as advanced as you say, surely this episode will push them toward an even more advanced state, even more lethal countermeasures. To something perhaps even more effective than you, or your agency, has yet had to contend with."

Sanders leaned back, put down his pipe. "Perhaps that's your only sound argument."

"What I would like to offer, Mr. Sanders, is that it seems possible to develop an alternative backup to USSA which could be as effective, but less of a threat, less likely to spark an overreaction on their side, than your current approach."

"Such as?"

"Since you're dealing with a biological agent, turn your research toward developing a detoxifying agent —chemical, biological, organic. Something that could be introduced to the strain and neutralize it. An agent you could disperse around the station, and inject directly into the existing biology, which would accomplish organic sterilization."

Sanders looked intently at the young scientist. "Military research has tried for years to find that solution. With absolutely no success. This strain is simply too virulent, too resistant . . . too perfect. It was evolved especially to be just that. It can survive antitoxins. It can survive nuclear radiation. There is, in fact, only one resistance that was not intentionally programmed into it. That, of course, would be resistance to the energies of a neutron laser. It's the only viable alternative. In the beginning of this mess, we considered others. And gave them all up. Our approach is really the only hope. Unless, of course, USSA succeeds, and they carry our little bundle off into deep space, or at least into a high enough orbit so we don't have to worry about the damned problem in our generation."

Gray realized the ultimate weakness of his arguments in the face of such determination. Greg Sanders would not now, or ever, allow the possibility of any direction but the one he had decided to follow. The attempt to change his thinking had been a complete waste of time.

"I recognize your disappointment, Dr. Gray. But surely you must realize we are facing a very time-critical, and very real, problem with this thing. We have to take the most readily available, and effective, approach—the most practical solution. If we had a year to study the matter, perhaps we could develop your proposed solution. But there simply is no time."

"And you won't reconsider, regardless of the consequences. Regardless of the uncertainties of its effectiveness, or the likely Soviet response."

"I don't agree that its effectiveness is in question, since your preliminary results are no more than that, and are based on incomplete knowledge. As for the Russians, I frankly can't be bothered even by your best arguments. They will pursue their own devices regardless of what our side does, or doesn't do, and regardless of how many SALT agreements are signed. None of your points wash against the reality of the situation. Sorry, but no, I won't reconsider."

Gray stared at the overhead screen, studied the thoroughly organized activity of DISA's research bees scattered about the honeycomb. This madness would proceed to its final conclusion. It was inevitable.

Then Sanders presented his offer: "Now, Dr. Gray, I have a counterproposal for you to consider. If you sincerely wish to act on your honest desires to contribute to the aversion of a real catastrophe—the biological one—those desires would be better served if you were to join our effort at DISA. There is certainly a place for your talents here. Although the recombination positions are all fully staffed, we could use your expertise in the area of bio-sensor development, which will be onboard our spacecraft. You could possibly have an easier time working that part of the problem, given your philosophic bias, since it's basically disassociated from the weapon itself. The sensor array is intended purely as a monitor, used primarily to detect contamination possibilities so we can accurately advise the Shuttle crew how best to proceed. Of course, in the event of a need for laser activation, the array will record the effect of sterilization, and monitor the process, allowing us to guide the radiation to accomplish total irradiation. It's an intriguing problem, certainly sophisticated enough to usefully engage your talent. Please think about it. Helping us could be a better use of your time than second-guessing what we're doing here from your lab at Coast Research."

Gray needed to think about it only a moment.

"Mr. Sanders, I don't want anything to do with your operation. It violates every principle I believe in. It's closed research, and in direct support of the military. There's no way I could convince myself that this particular application is not a convenient excuse to test a new weapons capability. In good conscience I can't justify giving that my support. Whatever your rationalizations, every new weapon system that goes into space brings us a step closer to annihilation of Earth life. You know that. And don't care. Well, some of us have to care. Someone has to resist. I won't be part of your plans."

"I'm sorry to hear that. Your type of philosophy is obsolete in today's world. A balance has to be preserved, and advancing our technologies to their limits is the only answer to maintaining that balance. I'd advise you to reconsider my offer. I'll leave it open for a while."

"I can't, and won't. The offer is unacceptable."

Sanders relit his extinguished pipe.

"This is not meant as a threat, Dr. Gray. But given that attitude, life will be difficult for you, and your research, during the coming months. Out of necessity you will not be allowed to interfere with our program in any way. You have knowledge of its nature, and that knowledge is now a national-security problem. You have already been, and will remain, under surveillance. That will be intensified. If you make the slightest attempt to disclose our activity, expect to find yourself in custody, and forcibly held silent. We have full authority to make sure you don't represent a risk to our position. Even if you remain silent, you will find that your research at Coast, if you are able to continue that, will be of no consequence, to us or to anyone else. There is no room for tolerating your continued meddling in this matter. I sincerely hope you understand that."

Gray was now close to despair. His failure was absolute. As was the government's power to carry out Sanders' threat.

Sanders continued: "Now, given your position, I regret that we'll have to give the FBI some time with you, to determine exactly the limits and extent of your potential harm to these operations. I advise you to cooperate with them completely. That will cause you the least grief. Resistance to their questions will likely put you out of circulation for some time."

Sanders pressed another switch on his armrest panel.

"I will still leave open my offer. For at least a week. If you should reconsider, get in touch with me directly. But do that soon." He studied the younger man in his silence. "I'm truly sorry our encounter could not produce a better understanding between us."

There was a light signal at the door. Sanders arose, opened it from inside. The FBI agents appeared outside, waiting.

"Dr. Gray is in your hands now. Proceed with the planned questioning. I would like a summary as soon as it's available." He turned to Daren. "Good day, my friend. Please cooperate with them, and you should be able to return to California by late Monday."

Gray took a final look around the command room, stared at Greg Sanders a long moment, and then was led away.

Chapter Eighteen

The most extraordinary aspect of the test was its silence. There had not been even a muffled shock felt by those inside the bunker. Karenov had not expected this complete absence of physical indication of detonation. Although it was underground, as with all the others, and admittedly a small device for its devastatingly lethal potential, he had never before personally witnessed the force, and had anticipated some profound sensation. They were, after all, only thirty kilometers from the zero point.

Alexis Duryanov approached him, his expression one of obvious pleasure.

"The first reports are in, and the test has performed perfectly. The warhead achieved its design specifications in both radiation spectra and particle output. We can expect certification for our use to proceed quickly from this point, given these preliminary indications of success. It has been a good morning."

Anatole Karenov did not completely share his colleague's enthusiasm. Somewhere inside, his emotions were still knotted. Although he now recognized the new development was probably necessary, he had to struggle with a lingering resistance. Karenov could not quite suppress that, and understood too clearly its recurrent nature. He was feeling a definite reluctance to throw himself into this new round of escalation, their new version of terror.

But as was always the case, he was given little time for the luxury of indulging in such doubts, pursuing such reservations. It was best to simply get on with the job at hand. He, with Duryanov, would return immediately to Novosibirsk, following this apparently successful test of their Petrograd series payload.

Duryanov's recent reinstatement as director of Spaceflight Control was a less than ideal solution. The man was not, to Karenov's displeasure, compatible with his own personality, or his working routines and attitudes. But there were no other choices. Kremlin was beginning to exhaust the supply of acceptable candidates to manage their various departments and programs. The repression of the Alternatives was beginning to become embarrassingly counterproductive.

Karenov would have preferred to work the new program with M. Scherensky. They had struggled in the past, but always with mutual respect, and shared complementary styles. More importantly, they had been productive together. Karenov realized her strength, intelligence, and competence would be a real loss to his department. He regretted that. But the matter was out of his hands. She had simply given the KGB more than sufficient justification to move against her.

The political winds were now blowing even more strongly, and he had to expect sudden changes. There would be no stability until one of the competing parties established clear dominance. It could be no other way. Coexistence was inconsistent with their structure. Karenov knew his own sympathies. And where his support should be going. But he simply could not afford the time for that involvement. It required a careful, calculated, and patient investment. And demanded a complete dedication in order to carry it off effectively. He had neither the time, energy, nor courage to go through with it. The last period at Novosibirsk had convinced him of that. The younger guard would have to carry on the political struggle for liberalization. He sincerely wished them success, but now was not the time, for him at least, to declare himself.

Karenov was a realist. Development of the Petrograd satellite constellation would absorb his energies for the foreseeable future. Thoughts of revision would have to be set aside temporarily.

He looked about for Duryanov. The man was now

across the room, thumbing through the first series of test reports. Karenov studied his actions, which seemed disorderly, too exuberant. If their working relationship were to succeed at all, he would have to conform to a more disciplined, reasoning style, closer to that of the director general's.

"Alexis, we should get on with our business. Please have our jet made ready for the return to the Siberian Center. I will take the reports. We can discuss them during the trip back."

"Yes, certainly, Comrade General." Duryanov hastily collected his group of summaries into a briefcase, handed that to Karenov, then disappeared into an adjoining room.

Karenov's thoughts wandered to Novosibirsk. This time he would be there indefinitely. He could not expect the reprieve of a week in Geneva, nor even an occasional weekend in Moscow. It had been far too long since he had been able to truly relax in the comfortable atmosphere of Moscow. Possibly he could do that after the current operation. But then again, they would have another assignment for him.

He thought of how the space centers had already adjusted in response to the new direction from the Kremlin. There had been a sweeping change of emphasis. All but the most critical Cosmos operations were placed on minimum-activity status. Each center had been directed to prepare for a separate launch—with a minimum of fifteen units planned in the first phase of the constellation, three onboard each of five launches. It was an ambitious proposal, but one he knew they were capable of handling. The option had been built in many years ago, but simply never tested. In the past that was not felt to be necessary.

But now the Americans, through miscalculations he could not believe, had precipitated this major escalation. There was the certain biological threat, and the suspected introduction of particle-beam weaponry. They were entering forbidden territory. Kremlin demanded that a firm response be prepared. As a counter to this new move on their side, the Petrograd system would be deployed in phases. There had not yet been a firm decision on its activation. But it was necessary to be ready for that, if that final step were deemed appropriate by Moscow.

Karenov understood full well the implication. As planned, there would be a global deployment at six hundred kilometers of intercrossing orbits, weaving a pattern which would envelop the planet between sixty-degree latitudes north and south. Each of the fifteen satellites held a cluster of seven independently targeted warheads, rated ten megatons each, with each warhead capable of reaching its carefully selected strategic target, either in space, on the ground, or underwater, within sixty seconds from command. With equal effectiveness, the warheads would disintegrate networks of electronic circuitry or human nerves, out to a twenty-kilometer radius. There would be no warning, and no defense for it. On their side.

Duryanov reappeared inside the observation room where Karenov waited.

"We are cleared for the return, Comrade. Everything is onboard, awaiting only us."

"You are ready yourself? And we have all necessary information?"

"Yes, I believe so."

"Then let us return. There is much work ahead of us. And the time, as usual, is short."

Chapter Nineteen

A lazy suspension of seagulls scattered in random directions as Laine swung the cream-colored Porsche up the winding driveway to her hillside cabin. On reaching it she slowed just enough to carefully maneuver under the shelter of her carport. Their local weather satellite had located an approaching cold front and was giving the coast a 90% chance of precipitation. It looked as if the forecast would be right this time.

She had driven more aggressively than usual to get them back from San Francisco International. The drive had taken only twenty minutes—through San Bruno, Pacifica, then down along the Cabrillo highway at 130 k.p.h., watching the radar monitor all the way. The entire trip had been traveled in silence. She left Gray brooding to himself.

It hadn't been easy to give him the bad news, but that couldn't be avoided. She found him in the arrival lobby looking exhausted and defeated, and trying unsuccessfully to hide it, talking instead about what they needed to do in the Recombination Lab. He had immediately begun rambling on about experimental details which would be necessary in their next research phase. Laine understood his desire to lose himself there. But it was not to be. For his own sake she would keep him in touch with reality, and accept the responsibility for that decision. They would find a more healthy distraction. As they had gotten into her car at the airport, she told him how Coast Research, under pressure from PAGENT and the Governor, had closed down his lab.

Now, under the shelter, with the first drops of rain beginning to come down, she turned off the engine, and spoke to him with a gentle firmness. "Let's go inside, you can start up a fire. I'll program something mellow on the System, and we'll concentrate on pure relaxation."

Daren nodded a vague yes, and forced a smile. He picked up his travel bag from the Porsche rear deck as he got out. Laine circled an arm around his waist and they walked together up the steps to the porch, and unlocking the oak front door, entered the cabin's living room.

"You can put your things in the bedroom. Then dig into the wood stack and get the heat going. Looks like it's going to cool off quickly along the beach. While you're busy with that, I'll find us some of Henry's wine downstairs. Or would you prefer a smoke?"

"Wine sounds better."

Laine went first to the kitchen console, keyed in a selection of commands, which activated a soothing medley of blues, and adjusted the lighting to a warm, muted glow. She then descended the redwood spiral of stairs winding down into the cool chamber where Henry Jeremy's insistent generosity, and precisely controlled temperatures, maintained an ample stock of California's finest fermentations. She found what she wanted—two bottles of a special estate Zinfandel—and carried them back up with her. Laine opened both, set one aside to rest, and poured two glasses nearly full from the other. Then with glasses and part bottle in hand, she glanced momentarily at a wall mirror on her way into the living room. She was pleased. The round trip to the airport had not taken much out of her.

Daren had carefully arranged wood strips over crumpled newspaper, was finishing off the assembly with three split cedar logs. He looked up at her.

"I need a match."

"Check the brass box on the mantel."

He found one; then set fire to the under-layer of paper. It quickly erupted into a comforting blaze.

Laine motioned him over to the cushioned sofa, where she had already collapsed. As he sat down, she offered him one of the full glasses. The rain was now becoming steady, audible as a soft murmur on the rooftop. Outside the sky had turned darker, and their view of the ocean was disappearing in the mist.

Laine shifted closer, moved so Daren could rest his back against her side. He fell easily into the offer, kicked off his shoes, and stretched both legs over a nearby leather ottoman. She was already comfortable, enjoyed serving as a refuge for his drained spirit. The first long sips of wine were having their warming effect on her. Daren took a tentative sip of his glass, approved, and finished half in one continuous swallow.

Laine let her arm fall purposefully over his shoulder, her hand sliding gently on his chest. She gave him a reassuring caress.

"You know," he said quietly, "I just don't know where the hell we go from here."

"I know." She looked into the fireplace, absently. "It must have been incredibly frustrating with Sanders."

"What I haven't told you is that your FBI friends had their turn too."

"Not surprising."

"Exactly what you warned me of. Complete interrogation about everything we were doing at the Lab, about everything I knew of the DISA plans. Now it's all down on tape, recorded for posterity. They should have a nice thick file on me."

"At least you're in good company." She tried to be light.

"The whole encounter was just so damned degrading."

"Yes. They certainly make you feel you've been violated."

Both let themselves be drawn into the fire for a long minute—the rain reinforcing the numbing effect of warmth and alcohol.

Daren broke the silence. "There's no way we're going to stop this. The DISA people are obsessed with their program."

"We can still hope they're not given the chance. That the USSA mission succeeds."

"I doubt the military will be held back even by that. I left with the impression they believe their solution is the primary one. It wouldn't surprise me to discover they have a plan to circumvent the USSA operation, just for the opportunity to use their own little weapon."

Laine searched for some positive counter. "Given time, we might still find a biological solution."

"Not much chance of that with our lab shut down. And the curtain of secrecy around everything. Hell, DISA probably had something to do with our lockout. PAGENT may have been used as a convenient front."

She thought about the call she made to Henry Jeremy that morning. He told her it was out of Stanford's control. The trustees had been directed by the Governor's office not to interfere. Apparently the PAGENT lobby had gotten some support from other, unnamed groups, and closure could not be resisted. He could offer her nothing in the way of encouragement.

"You know, that bastard Sanders even had the nerve to offer me a job working with them. So, in his words, I could help make sure their solution didn't fail, and contribute in a positive way to prevent the disaster. *Jesus!*"

"Doing what?"

"Oh, something connected with their satellites' biology sensors. Kind of on the periphery of the operation. Apparently the mainstream research is fully staffed. It is—with everyone who's been stolen from the independent labs. There were sure a lot of familiar faces around Fort Gabriel. Latham, Greenwalt, even my old assistants who were commandeered years ago. All part of their team. Now at least I know what they've been keeping busy with all this time."

Laine had been busy too, her mind probing at something, paying only partial attention to his explanation.

"Where is their activity taking place?"

"You mean all of DISA's operation?"

"Yes."

"The scientific research—all the biochemistry—is at Fort Gabriel, outside D.C., where I met with Sanders. Very sophisticated facility. Some field testing is being done in the West. Dugway, Utah, I think he said. Probably that's where they've got the neutron laser set up. Where that was developed I really don't know."

"What about the actual launch, and flight operation? Where would the software brains guiding the mission be located?"

"Well, the development of the software is probably being done back east, around D.C., close to the spacecraft and weapon assembly. I'd guess the mission will fly out of Vandenberg—that's usual for classified military launches. The software would probably move there."

"But will they actually control it from Vandenberg, or use the Satellite Defense Complex at Sunnyvale? That's been recently cleared for DISA operations, and I believe all the flights are now going to be commanded from that facility. They're tied in to all the software houses in Silicon Valley—from Palo Alto on down. I heard final linkups were put into effect two months ago, and DISA's been gradually transferring staff up here."

"Well, you'd know more about that than I would. Seems like I did read about the move in one of the journals."

"Vandenberg is supposed to become exclusively a launch pad, with minimal support personnel."

"So why the keen interest in all of this?"

"For now, just curiosity." She drifted more deeply into thought. Seemingly weighing alternatives. Then arrived at some internal, private answer.

"Daren, do you believe their offer? Were they serious about bringing you into the group?"

"I think Sanders was dead serious. He'd surely rather see me working with them than against them. Said he'd keep the offer open for a while, assuming I'd reconsider. But I, of course, gave him a flat no. Told him it was an insult."

"Did he react strongly to that?"

"Well, not emotionally. He's pretty cool. Of course,

that's when he turned me over to the boys from FBI. And got more heavy-handed with his threats."

"But you left feeling that the option was not closed."

"Probably correct. Your mind is really working overtime on something."

"Just its standard mode."

Gray took a long drink of wine and finished it off. He reached for the bottle she had placed near them on a table, refilled his glass. Laine offered hers so he could do the same. He rested the bottle back in place, then resumed his earlier position. And sighed heavily.

A muffled burst in the fireplace sent a shower of sparks swirling. Out the west picture window water was dropping in streams off the roof overhang. The warming influences inside, and the contrast, were filtering through them both, attempting to lift them from their feeling of despair and hopelessness. Laine's eyes reached out through the mist and streaming water, looking for some glimpse of the beach below, or of the white surf she knew would be breaking further out. She searched, as if needing to see a sign, some quiet confirmation. But everything was obscured—the rain now even more steady, more insistent. It would be up to them, alone, from this point on.

She knew the man beside her was lost. His unique genius would not find the right solutions on its own, because the game was now beyond the realm of strict science. A different force was required, another energy. One she could command, understood how to direct, but had never before had the opportunity to develop fully. They both would have to move together in a new direction, with new rules.

She gave him a strong hug, from behind.

"You and I are going to find a way to change this."

"We will?"

"Yes."

"And you have a plan?"

"Working on one. But first I need some perspective."

Laine found the buttons of his shirt, undid them one by one until she touched the soft hair of his chest.

"Mm . . . a nice attempt at distraction."

"Not *just* distraction. Put down your glass, Dr. Gray."

He obliged, turned his head toward her. "You're getting pretty serious."

"I'm always serious."

Laine curled herself onto the couch, put her lips against the back of his neck, brushing softly. Both her hands moved down his chest, pulling away the last part of his shirt until it lay open and she could follow his hair down to the belt. She studied the flickering light from the fireplace creating moving patterns over her fingers and his stomach. The warmth was building, doing just the right things for her. She reached his cool belt buckle, loosened it, and moved lower until she felt him, responding completely, then enclosed him in a slow, soft, gliding motion. Daren exhaled a deep, satisfied breath. Her fingers explored, touching everywhere. She shifted slightly, to one side, and let him lie back. With soft lips she circled his chest in moist kisses, then drifted down for long, sensual minutes, until he had to pull away.

He whispered to her, "Equality, girl. I want to see you too."

Laine smiled, then withdrew slowly, standing up directly in front of him. She let slacks, sweater, cotton pants drop smoothly to the floor. Now completely nude, she assumed a provocative pose, letting her hands play suggestively over her own body, fully enjoying the exhibition she offered. Daren studied her moving silhouette, illuminated for his view by the gray rainy light from outside. He watched, eyes transfixed, fascinated by her self-arousal.

Finally he spoke, weakly: "Damn, you're lovely. Come back down here so I can join you."

Laine stretched herself in one fluid motion alongside him, resting her head by his thighs. She felt his breath, then lips on her smooth stomach, moved her legs slightly as he began his own exploration, as the warmth began to reach inside her body. The background music of the System gave way to the sound of the continuing rain.

They had made love only twice before, and never with such abandon, or completeness. Both escaped this time into a passion they had not let themselves enjoy during those first encounters. Now it seemed a continuum of loving. Both wanted to be nowhere else, and had nowhere else to be. They concentrated on each other, exclusively. Feeling. Learning. Laughing at their own rediscovery. Morning drifted into afternoon, then evening, and sleep. The next day was clear and sunny, and they spent time on the beach, curled together in a secluded sandy cove, letting themselves play along the shore, exploring the tidal pools. Feeling only sun, sand, and ocean spray. And each other. Making love under the bright sun and pale-blue sky. They let their minds return to an earlier age. An accidental observer could not have guessed these were respected scientists—they were surely college sophomores on a mid-week adventure, escaping the pressures of undergraduate classes. Both had needed this, desperately, and openly delighted in their ability to make it happen.

Only on the third evening of their interlude did Laine feel it time to turn back to the other reality they both faced. Dinner had been exceptional—a crab salad and steamed shrimp—and they were relaxing on the cabin deck, Gray in a rope hammock and Laine in a lounge chair beside. The evening was clear, and the surf gentle against the rock and sand. Laine went inside for a moment, and increased the System's volume to a point where the music was carried more clearly onto the deck. Then she returned to her place beside him.

"Daren, I want you to listen to this. Carefully. What I'm about to propose is going to require a lot of ingenuity, and risk, from both of us."

"After the last three days I should be ready for that."

"I want you to accept that position with DISA."

He looked over at her. Surprised.

"Everything I'm thinking of depends on that. It's our only access. We'll get nowhere struggling against them from outside."

"All right. That makes sense. But where does it go from there?"

"They want you to work the biology sensors. And our lab, and computer support, is closed down. Tell them a condition of your acceptance is the reopening of the lab. You'll insist on working that part of their operation from Coast Research. The lab will have to be modified, of course, to handle all the equipment—and you'll see that it is. And, most importantly, you will need my computer tied in—and linked with the other software operations. For compatibility checks and cross-referencing mission sequences. You'll have to get that last done gradually."

"You want access to the entire nervous system of their operation."

"Precisely."

"And what will you do with it?"

"All I need are the appropriate computer links, and I can do virtually anything."

"But they'll have barriers, lockouts, codes."

"I'll have to work around those. Which is where the ingenuity comes in. Some of their codes I know already. Others, particularly those connected with the satellite sequences, will have to be deciphered. But we have systems at Coast that will help."

"All right. Assume you can eventually reconstruct the entire flight control software. What have you got planned?"

"We're going to alter a few logical command sequences. Specifically the arming sequences for their weapon. If I can make the appropriate modifications, it shouldn't be too difficult to reroute a few electronic impulses into whatever turns out to be a delicate link. If somehow we trigger a critical short circuit and a very high voltage transient runs through the onboard memory, we could take out the satellite's nervous system, for good."

"Goddamn. Your imagination has been active."

"Be careful with this, Daren. Because it's not just imagination. I've worked the same basic procedures before, on other spacecraft, but for purely constructive purposes."

"Yes, but there you had approval, and cooperation.

I just don't see it being easy to slip in unwelcome alterations. That's where you find the lockout problem."

"Consider this. You'll be working with the biology sensors. There will have to be a certain number of computer interfaces between that function and the rest of the satellite's main executive. In the course of all that, you, and your software team, which I'll be a part of, will be designing computer routines supporting the sensors, to be included in the main product. There should be ways to make hidden, subtle changes which stay invisible to the overall system, and are even undetectable by checkout and verification procedures. I don't claim doing so will be easy. It will be an enormous amount of work. But I know it can be done."

"And done in such a way that the instant prior to laser activation, their entire vehicle goes down. Absolutely remarkable."

"So are the risks. Keep that in mind. If we're discovered, we'll be out of this permanently. The plan has got to be precise, and perfectly engineered. I'll take the responsibility for unscrambling all the computerese, but your part is perhaps more delicate. You'll have to make sure I get access to whatever I need. We'll have to come up with logical justifications. And that goes even more for sneaking the alterations into their system. Your reasons have to be valid, and flawless. Do you think you're up to it?"

Gray lay back into the hammock, sorting everything out logically in his mind. Trying to imagine the problems they would encounter.

"My acceptance of Sanders' offer will have to appear reluctant. And I need to show honest resignation to their approach. I think I can sell the condition of doing it all at the lab. And DISA probably has the power to get it reopened over PAGENT's opposition. But . . . and this is the only part that bothers me . . . I don't know if we can count on having you tied into their network."

"We'll have to find a way. I suppose I could get around that problem. There would have to be some satellite data relay between the lab and the rest of the operation. We could, if necessary, tap onto that through an Earth-station set up at my place. But direct access would of course be preferable. Make a strong case for using the computer support that's already at Coast Research. Literally next door, in fact."

"Have you ever worked for the CIA?"

"No, not directly. But I have all necessary special clearances. I know how this business is done."

"Then realize you'll be working with a novice."

"I understand. Leave the devil's work to me. Most of the time you'll be concentrating on your mundane activity of building and testing biology sensors. Sounds like pretty mild stuff. You should do a fine job with that."

"But when I'm called upon, Agent Gray will have to respond."

"That's right. And it will all need to be done very diplomatically. And subtly. You'll have to control your behavior, and ego, very carefully."

Laine reached for his hand. "Are you willing?"

Gray gave her a squeeze. Then thought a long minute.

"We just might be able to carry this off. And it has other benefits. I should be able to obtain the DNA blueprints, and specifics of the laser energies, that Wilson needs for his studies, which we could probably continue with the lab opened up." He paused longer. "Have you thought of the consequences?"

"For us?"

"No, for civilization."

"If USSA fails and we've canceled the last solution?"

"Yes."

"Then civilization takes its chance with nature. It's possible someone may still find an organic solution. I'd rather go with the natural approaches, and risks, than see space filled with particle-beam satellites. I honestly don't see much future for us in that event. I thought you understood."

He sat up, looked at her, her soft hair draped carelessly over one shoulder. She was right. It was time to move forcefully against them.

Gray walked to her, gently pulled her close.

"For a computer specialist, you are truly marvelous. And courageous."

"For a mere scientist, you have a few redeeming features."

Arms around one another, the two walked down to the beach. And there they talked for hours.

Chapter Twenty

Gray shook his head in disbelief at the classified report Sanders had sent him. It had been prepared by Dankin at Fort Gabriel—their final summary of field testing at Dugway. He should have been more than amused, but it nevertheless bothered him how blind the military could be when they wanted to see only one side—the one that supported their position. The conclusions he read were entirely self-serving. Everything Wilson had found lately pointed exactly the opposite way.

He reread the one paragraph which summarized all five sections of bio-analysis and test-data interpretation.

After exhaustive field testing with the sixteen most probable biological states of anthrax-r bacilli, each subjected to varying intensities and proportions of neutron particle and laser irradiation, successful negation of each grouping was achieved in all cases but one, allowing a nominal energy envelope to be defined for the n-laser, comprising 94% of all expected encounter conditions. The single resistant example, although felt to be an extremely unlikely form, could still be reduced to a benign state by a specific, and easily achievable, shift in the laser/particle mix, toward the laser side of the stream. It is our conclusion, therefore, that virtually no possibility remains for varieties or mutations of anthrax-r to survive irradiation by the current configuration designed for the SCEPTER II spacecraft.

Momentarily he wondered if DISA could be right. After all, they had the benefit of actual test data. Wilson was forced to work with hybrids—a synthetic neutron laser and synthetic anthrax—with computer models used to project those into the correct conditions. In reality he and Wilson now found themselves relying heavily on those projections, and therefore, to a large extent, on theory. But one essential difference remained in their favor. They had held firm to the concept that all simulations be done in an accurately reproduced space environment, while the other side still refused to accept that doing so could have the slightest influence on the ultimate results.

Gray thought about it, grasping for objectivity. Given the game they were all playing, it shouldn't matter who the hell was right. But still, as an issue of science, it somehow did. He couldn't ignore that. And it nagged at him. Even with everything else progressing so smoothly. Sanders had given him his position, accepting all of his conditions. With virtually no DISA resistance, the lab had been reopened and the bio-sensor work shifted there with Gray completely in charge. A lower section, including the vacuum chamber, had been reserved for their original work to continue under the direction of Wilson, separate and sealed off from the mainstream DISA activity. Even PAGENT had been neutralized. After two days of noisy protest, several hundred had been arrested and jailed on DISA's insistence and their prodding of the FBI and local authorities. Now there were armed guards stationed around the lab.

After convincing Sanders that he was ready to contribute in any way he could, all of that had been rather straightforward. The one difficult issue, as he expected it might be, was the acceptance of their on-site computer support under Laine. Gray still did not fully understand how she had arranged that part. But after DISA's initial refusal, there had been pressures exerted from various sources—he of course suspected Henry Jeremy as one—to allow Laine's group the chance to support the lab activity, as they had done so well over the past two months. It then required a personal inter-view between her and Sanders before the DISA director, apparently impressed with her brightness and security credentials, granted his approval.

He stared down at the report again. Vaguely interested. Then looked out of his small office to the SCEPTER mockup, where a dozen DISA technicians in white coats were studying an array of scopes, busily reading and recording the sensor responses to various biology test samples. It had been three days now since he'd seen Laine. A week since they had spent a night together. She had warned him to expect that—that she would become totally absorbed with her own technical problem. Still, he thought it was a hell of a way to go through what was potentially the planet's last month and a half.

That was the point the media never let anyone forget —as if that would have been possible. Or who was to blame for the debacle. Lansing's resignation was now promised immediately after the mission. But that wasn't enough. The press had already brought down, besides Brookhaven, nine other ranking USSA officials, even two of the military's top brass who could be directly traced to the initial Orion program. Somehow, miraculously, Sanders had remained beyond censure, and the public still remained in the dark about the DISA alternative. Their security had been exceptionally tight.

Gray found himself in a drift, random thoughts entering and leaving. How close was Laine to finally deciphering the SCEPTER software? She offered so little —claimed he wouldn't understand the technical explanations she could give. How much time did they still have? The Orion Platform was only nominally given seven more weeks in orbit, nine at best. USSA would get there with the Shuttle at the very last minute, with no time to spare. SCEPTER, on the other hand, was right on schedule. The spacecraft and launch vehicle were to be mated at Vandenberg in four weeks, then would go through a final assembly checkout, ready for launch one week prior to USSA's flight. Gray was to be a part of that—and had been given his own control monitor station at the Sunnyvale Defense Satellite Complex.

So as he mentally assessed things, all appeared to

be going about as well as could be expected, with the exception of his infrequent contact with Laine, and the huge discrepancy between Wilson's and DISA's conclusions on the effectiveness of the laser system. He had no small difficulty identifying what was really troubling him. Perhaps, he speculated, it was the peripheral position he held. Nearly an outsider to the real developments—those that mattered most. It was becoming obvious that he was no longer a principal figure in this drama. Everything of importance had been relegated to others.

Gray reached for his phone, dialed Wilson's extension.

The voice answered quickly: "Hello, Wilson here."

"This is Daren. You busy right now?"

"Of course."

"I've just read the final report from Fort Gabriel's research on the effects of the n-laser against anthrax. They sound convinced they have the final solution. Would you like to read it?"

"No. But I'd like to talk to you about what I'm finding. Confirms many of our early theories. Naturally my conclusions are different from theirs. You'll be interested in them. Come on down."

"See you in a minute."

Gray left the office, walked down a corridor through two checkpoints, then down a short stairway to the sealed biology lab. There he waited for an electronic badge verification before a door opened, letting him inside Wilson's offices beside the vacuum chamber.

He found Wilson writing furiously, checking mathematical equations on his desk computer.

"Be with you in a moment. Got to get this last point down on paper while it's fresh. Results of this morning's hybrid runs."

"I'll wait. When you're done, just scan page twenty-seven of their report. I've marked it for you." He looked over the paper clutter of the offices. Then gazed into the vacuum chamber and experimental areas. Wilson had obviously been working at a fevered pace, witnessed by the apparent disarray of the lab's hardware, and the condition of the office. Gray envied him. It brought back the old days—the days of pure research, productivity—when he was thoroughly motivated. Wilson was now doing exactly what Gray had wanted—but to do himself. Testing hypotheses, confirming intelligent guesses, studying the subtlest of reactions and recombinations. Now, finally, the lab was being pushed to its limit, and Gray could only take pleasure in that he had perfected its design to achieve that very end. Now everything was working just as predicted, but without him.

Wilson wrapped things up in his notebook. Apparently satisfied, he slammed a pen down hard on his desk.

"That's it. Now it all makes sense. The ambiguities are finally resolved."

"Before I ask what, or how, do me the favor of scanning this report, because these fellows seem just as certain and confident as you. And we both know that's dangerous. Which is why I have to understand your results, completely."

Wilson reluctantly picked up the document, quickly leafed through the analysis section, stopping here and there to study certain portions. Finally reaching the marked summary of conclusions, he put it down, and chuckled softly.

"They're doing a fine job out east. Really thorough. Only trouble I see with it is that they're testing all the right factors in all the wrong places."

"Such as."

"Everything they say is valid if we were going to perform this operation on the surface of Earth. They've almost correctly identified all the anthrax possibilities, including the primary mutations. But they're totally wrong as to which have become dominant by this time. Turns out it's similar to the one which doesn't respond well to their weapon's nominal energy envelope. Worse, they have no understanding of the process that makes this the dominant one, and how it survives in space. Then they start with the same model of the neutron-laser energies as I have—which we would expect, since they've supplied it to us—except, and this is the persistent difference, they fail to account for the power degradation we find in the space environment, where we have to contend with interfering radiation."

"Can you be a bit more specific?"

"Sure, the last is easiest. My synthetic testing in the space chamber shows that the background gamma radiation of space will cause interference patterns with a neutron-particle beam, diminishing its intensity, and effectiveness, by about 30%. Which means simply that DISA is overestimating the effect of half their fire power by that amount. They get great results on Earth, which just won't happen in space."

"Sounds like one hell of a blunder."

"It is. Look, DISA in fact expects to get improved performance in space."

"What about the mutations?"

"That is the fascinating part. Let me show you a computer diagram of the DNA blueprint for anthrax-r_{14}. That's the variety, or mutation, which according to my studies should theoretically have become dominant in at least one of the four compartments. Statistically one of the four should in fact now contain only the r_{14} variety."

Gray drew his chair close to study the molecular blueprint.

"Let your mind search for a moment, and see what comparisons you make."

Gray looked more intently, but drew a blank. Wilson gave him a minute longer.

"Nothing, eh? Perhaps I'm expecting too much. You've been away from this for a while. Mind's getting soft." He reached for another figure. "Compare it with this blueprint. Same variety. But after the irradiation."

Daren shifted his eyes rapidly from one to the other. Slowly the pattern was coming together. A familiar pattern. "It's absorbing some of the energy—like a photosynthesis effect. A productive, rather than destructive, absorption."

"By God, you've got it. The scientific mind of Dr. Gray still functions. Allow me to go through the whole theory for you. First, we still have some Heisenberg uncertainties to deal with. The result you see here is still unpredictable, not deterministic other than statistically. If you'll recall my earlier studies, where I discovered certain reactions part of the time, different reactions at other times—well, for each positive reaction there are maybe ten neutral reactions. But I'm getting ahead of myself."

"I felt you might be off on a tangent."

"Only momentarily. The original anthrax-r sent up in orbit was already highly resistant to conventional radiation. Once in space it was subjected to even more intense varieties of particle bombardment. The 'shell' it already possessed, the key to its resistance, adapted and evolved over countless generations to a point where, unless it broke down at some early stage to form one of the other anthrax varieties, it became super-resistant to virtually every source of high-energy particle. And that is the mutation r_{14}. The neutron portion of your n-laser should be totally useless against that variety. Even at its full Earth-rated potential. Leaving—"

"Leaving only the photon stream of the laser portion to have any effect."

"Exactly. And that's where the oddity comes in. What you observed in the blueprints. For some intriguing reason that I cannot guess, the very same adaptive process which strengthened its resistant shell, in space, caused a biochemical transformation, creating a neat approximation of the photosynthesis arrangement. Just as plant chemistry on Earth accepts photons as part of the reproductive process, anthrax-r_{14} has the ability to do the same."

"Meaning instead of succumbing to laser-directed energy, it feeds off it."

"There's the catch. It's very choosy. It only does that about 10 percent of the time. Heisenberg again."

"The rest of the time destructive?"

"No. The rest are neutral interactions. The photons are passed straight through, which helps make the case for its dominance."

Gray was impressed. "This is truly incredible. A remarkable discovery. But . . . why doesn't this show up in DISA's Earth-based testing?"

"Because they miss the boat by ignoring the effect of space. Because this is the one variety of anthrax that must evolve only in space. They have simply not created the right blueprint. The photosynthesis feature only arises if it evolves in that environment. What the military tested against was almost, but not quite, anthrax-r_{14}. Their version lacks the photosynthesis response. Here, you can read in their report how after that strain resisted the standard energy envelope, they push to the laser side and convert it into a harmless form. It's a useless test."

"So how do you create the real item?"

"I don't, dammit. It's a projection via computer. But just as valid as if I had the living, breathing organism lying in front of me. Look, if I turn off the space evolution in my projection, I get the same thing as the military researchers, and would come to their conclusion. That is the essential difference."

Gray considered everything he had been told. He could find no logical inconsistencies. "If you're right about this, and anthrax-r_{14} is dominant, the weapon will be useless against it."

"That's the inescapable conclusion."

"What might be used instead?"

"Nothing. That is, nothing in the form of artificially directed radiation. It would take some organic form yet to be found which would merge into r_{14} molecularly, and neutralize its toxicity, much as a base into an acid."

"But such a substance doesn't exist."

"Doesn't exist, or hasn't been found, or would have to be synthesized from scratch. Take years of research."

"Can I have copies of your r_{14} blueprints? It may be time to go to Sanders with this."

"Sure, you can have copies. But I'll have a more complete preliminary report on it all by tomorrow afternoon. With all the supporting physics and simulation results. That would make a more impressive story. One even DISA could hardly ignore."

"I'm afraid at this point they would ignore whatever worked against them. But it is damned sure worth another try. Thanks, Mark. This was brilliant work. Wish I could have been part of it."

"You were. At least in the beginning. And in spirit after that. All of this brilliance has its origin in the theories you developed years ago."

"Ah, again, thanks. Keep at it, and I'll be back tomorrow."

"Okay. Say, how's Laine doing on the support of your new secret mission? She keeps very quiet about it."

"Afraid she does with me too. Very busy lady."

Gray left, taking the copies back to his office to study. He put in a call to DISA headquarters, left word for Sanders to get in touch, ASAP, concerning comments on the Dankin final report. Then he adjusted his chair into a recline, his mind still grappling with the DNA structure of r_{14}, and drifted into a sleep.

Somewhere within the network there had to be an opening. She had stared into the maze for nearly an hour, and the red-line trace she had begun twenty minutes before now trailed off into a hopelessly congested box of symbols and figures. The puzzle deliberately obscured itself.

Laine Jeremy's beach cabin had undergone a complete transformation. Where wood panels, artworks, hanging plants, and library shelves before had given off the ambiance of a rustic manor, these were now hidden behind enormous unrolled sheets of blue-on-white paper, taped to every wall—paper filled with the intricate diagrams and flowcharts understandable only to those specialists of the computer world. Her living room was now wallpapered with the charts, and the floor cluttered by others which had no other place to go. Her study had been converted to a computer center, with rows of display terminals, each linked to a different source, and a variety of printers, tape drives, and storage devices, all ringing the walls, set on top of desks and tables, stuffed into whatever space could be made available. Books which had previously filled the shelves were now boxed up and stored in the wine cellar. And with it all there was still barely room to move about.

She had no trouble quickly assembling the imposing

collection, all of which was quietly borrowed from Coast Research and Stanford. The move was made when it became apparent she had to relocate to the cabin and safety of Moss Beach. DISA security procedures had become too thorough for her to make any real progress at Coast. Now she could spend half of her workday and all of her evenings away from the commotion of Gray's lab. Assistants had been trained to handle the routine support needed by both Gray's and Wilson's operations. And they covered well for her.

By now most of the satellite's primary control system had been decoded and unraveled, thanks to the direct link Gray managed to set up with the defense complex at Sunnyvale. She now possessed a nearly complete working model of the SCEPTER central processor—its mind—which commanded every one of the vehicle's complex functions. The problem now presenting itself as her most difficult obstacle was the new military programming language known as DEFAUL. It had been created years earlier for the specific purpose of countering software theft and other varieties of espionage—exactly what she needed to accomplish. This clever language condensed all sorts of coded operations into tight packages, or bundles, which were then totally secured by automatic lockouts. And the lockouts were proving impenetrable. She had been able to maneuver around the system just enough to copy, using Coast's powerful computer deciphers, the internal logic patterns, and to reproduce them in her own model. Beyond that, Laine had been stopped. Any thought of introducing alterations directly into the central processor appeared impossible. There was simply no access. The problem had been apparent for a week, and she had gotten no closer to resolving it.

Their only hope, it seemed, would be to pursue the original plan of disguising the proposed modifications within logic modules Daren would make up for his sensors. And that too promised to be less easy a task than expected. DEFAUL had a nasty habit of scrutinizing and isolating any new software input so thoroughly that anything out of the ordinary, anything it deemed superfluous, would quickly be expelled from the central system.

As her reluctant admiration for the new language grew, her frustration mounted. DEFAUL was proving itself good, effective, efficient. Its development had been guided by the masters in the field, who were in touch with all the latest schemes, whose cleverness had evolved through years of practical experience. And she was right up against their accumulated wisdom.

Laine stared again at the chart before her—at the red line which ended in a hopeless tangle. She studied a possibility—one path which seemed to lead around the dead end. Her hand put the pen up to the original line drawn an hour ago, then traced a second tortuous path in red which appeared to bypass that area, leading toward places she knew would have to be entered. It looked right. A potential opening.

She moved quickly into the study, to a terminal marked IBM 3034. It was linked to the sophisticated main computer at Coast. The operation she was about to request would take up half of its core memory.

Carefully she keyed in a three-line instruction set. A test to determine whether her hunch might be correct. The blue screen blinked once—into its waiting mode— gathering supporting disk files for the operation. One minute went by. Then a second blink. Now it was into execution. The time lapse here seemed endless, but she had asked for an involved sequence of operations. The entire DEFAUL network was being automatically engaged. Five minutes passed as she nervously awaited some response. Another two minutes elapsed. She was about to go for a refill of coffee when the blue screen came to life, signaling its answer.

Laine sighed, and knew instantly. Her fist came down hard on the desk beside the terminal, breaking the electronic background hum of the room. Its message had been too simple, and familiar. NON-FUNCTIONAL OPERATION DETECTED BY DEFAUL—ACCESS DENIED."

She stood up in disgust, switched the screen to *off*, walked through the living room, passing rolls of charts, stacks of documents and computer printouts on her way, and went out onto the deck. She reached the lounge chair and collapsed into it. The possibilities were quickly running out. And there couldn't be much time left. The wall was there, firmly in place, formidable.

Gray was startled awake by the ringing. He groped, not finding the phone where it should have been. Finally realizing his chair was ninety degrees from where he had imagined it, he located the phone, switched on both voice line and video. He was still disoriented when the face formed slowly on the screen.

"You look somewhat shaken, Dr. Gray."

It was Sanders.

"Oh, it's nothing. Just dozed off a few minutes."

"We're not paying you to sleep." Sanders smiled wryly. "My office tracked me down with your message. Found me here at Vandenberg, inspecting the launch-support operations. Looks like they'll be ready for us. Now, what's on your mind?"

By now Gray had recovered, was fully awake.

"It's about the final report of Dankin's, which you had relayed yesterday. I'd like to discuss it with you, in person."

"Anything in particular that you can say over the line?"

"Well, there are some important issues we need to resolve. Some we've talked about before. You know Mark Wilson's been pursuing some independent checks with the synthetic models DISA supplied. Turns out we're coming up with some contradictory results. Discrepancies with your own testing. Before we go any further here, it might be useful to iron out some of our differences. It also may have some bearing on your conclusions regarding the nominal energy envelope selected for your—your configuration."

"You're not going to put me through another round of objections, I hope."

"No. Not at all. That's behind us. We simply need to work out a few problems that are surfacing here. It's up to you what you want to do about them."

Sanders looked down, appeared to Gray to be leafing through something before him.

"If I've got my schedule right, I should be up in your area in two days, anyway. Checking out the defense complex at Sunnyvale. Now, I'll be very busy there for a while. But by the first of next week we could get together. Might be a good chance to review the sensor status. You should be close to finishing that off. We could set up a briefing on it. How does that sound?"

"All right, we can put something together. We're still a ways behind with the software packages. But let's not drop the other issue."

"I won't let it drop."

"So I'll expect you Monday?"

"Afternoon. I'll confirm the time with you Monday morning. Guess I can copter up from Silicon Valley in about ten minutes."

"Okay. Let me know. Bye."

Gray switched off the line, and watched Sanders' image fade away. He would have to make certain everything was ready, and that he had a good story for delaying the software. Laine would need to be warned, and all loose ends gathered in. Wilson could give the report on his results. Gray would sit in on that—the sensor briefing would be routine.

Chapter Twenty-one

The Sikorsky landed gracefully onto the green circle, and without delay Greg Sanders stepped through the copter's open doorway, took two steps down, then walked briskly out from under its swirling blades. The craft lifted seconds later and disappeared into the sky above Coast Research. Gray was there to meet him, and together they walked the one block to the Recombination Lab.

Outside the fenced boundary, encircled by military guards, PAGENT's pickets had reappeared. But now their presence was far subdued from earlier episodes. They were holding a silent vigil. After the courts had once again sided with their plea for freedom of expression, Coast was forced to acquiesce with a PAGENT request to make a peaceful statement. They had been back for three days now. Today there were no more than eight in the group, each standing soberly, quietly, and each wearing a saffron robe and supporting an upright white cross. Their allegiance could be quickly identified by the familiar symbolic armbands.

Sanders and Gray passed by them in silence, then showed badges to the guards stationed by the entrance, and crossed into the lobby, where they were recognized and passed through without further delay. The DISA director insisted their first stop be the bio-sensor area, where he spent twenty minutes inspecting the device that was to become the sensitive biological antenna for SCEPTER. He chatted amiably with the technicians, and seemed genuinely pleased with what he saw and with the obvious progress made to date. After this, Gray gave him a half-hour briefing on the details of the sensor's functioning, and emphasized their success in tuning the instrument to search out every organic reaction which they expected to encounter, plus countless other capabilities that could be used in other operations. He concluded with a somewhat forced explanation of the reasons why they were still behind with the interfacing software modules.

Sanders was openly encouraged by what had been accomplished in the relatively short time given and reassured that his decision to let Gray carry the activity had been a good one. His comments to Gray afterward reflected that feeling.

"You've done an excellent job with this. SCEPTER II should be a very important contribution to this country's arsenal of space-defense vehicles, far beyond the Orion application. You and the team are to be commended for your part in it. Now just be sure the controlling software matches the ingenuity you've built into the rest of your work."

"That's our intention. We have the best people designing it."

"The group headed by Laine Jeremy, you mean."

"Yes. They're all very capable. But now we should get on with our other business."

Sanders' exuberance diminished somewhat. "I suppose I'm ready for that. Now that I'm here, it probably can't be avoided."

"No. It can't. And shouldn't be. Let's go over to the Recom section."

He led the way down the connecting corridor, and with Sanders present they were waved past the checkpoint. Gray triggered the Recom area access door with his Coast badge, then both stepped inside.

Wilson was introduced to Sanders, who had not yet met Gray's former assistant, as the new lead researcher in charge of the recombination studies that were focusing on the anthrax problem. Sanders greeted him respectfully, knowing this man was of the same competence as Gray and would also be just as convinced of his own ideas as his sponsor had been. But he had been able to handle that before.

Wilson went directly into the problem, presenting his whole story in a thoroughly prepared, logical sequence. He led Sanders step-by-step through all the complex projections of the n-laser spectra into the space environment, and when it was clear the director had the intelligence to follow him, he explained in even more detail the statistics on the evolutionary history of anthrax-r during its ten years in orbit. It was a clear, concise, and—Gray thought—convincing argument for their premise. The conclusion seemed obvious that any failure to account for all aspects of the space background would lead away from the proper estimates of n-laser effectivity.

Throughout Sanders listened attentively, had not raised a single objection. He asked the right questions at the right times. There was no doubt that he followed the thread of Wilson's logic. He closely studied the complications of the r_{14} blueprints, and inspected those carefully, along with the others. There had even been the impression of understanding, and heightened interest, when the photosynthesis factor was brought up. Wilson concluded with a rather thorough comparison between the Fort Gabriel results and his own, pointing out the areas of agreement, and of disagreement. When he finished, Gray felt it was now conceivable that Sanders could no longer ignore reality.

The director of DISA leaned back into his chair and reached for his pipe, which he then placed in his mouth, unfilled and unlit. He had been holding the r_{14} blueprints, and now set them aside on the table before him. Apparently some decision was being reached. Finally he turned to Gray, returning the pipe to his hand and gesturing with it.

"You realize, of course, that this r_{14} variety, which you believe to be dominant, is the most virulent, the most toxic, of all our possibilities. If we are to accept your conclusions, the strain will resist all attempts to control it. Our efforts will have been a total waste."

Gray said nothing, but looked directly at Sanders. The director dropped his gaze to the table before him, absently thumbing the pages of Wilson's report. He then studied the recombination area through the glass wall, with the office behind reflecting its pattern in a vague overlay. Then he spoke to them both. His voice was firm, deliberate, unmoving, as he looked at neither of them, but stared straight ahead.

"Your entire analysis and set of conclusions rest, in the end, only on theory and computer projection. Once, Dr. Gray, you warned me against making that very same error. The conclusions of our Fort Gabriel staff now derive from solid reality, based on real hardware and the actual organisms we face. Your hypothesis offers no hope. No solution. Ours provides the solution, and its effectiveness is no longer a matter of question. The Dugway test series has confirmed that. I would remind you again that I've assembled a team of specialists whose combined ability and competence is possibly greater than your own, which is in no way meant to downgrade yours. But they are the very best, and their experimental techniques are second to none. Everything Fort Gabriel has concluded supports my original concept that the neutron laser is our only way out of this dilemma, and I have no reason to doubt them."

He seemed to fix his eyes on something very distant, as if he were no longer speaking just to them.

"But there are larger issues involved beyond that. Issues which you cannot fully appreciate, or comprehend. The system we are sending up transcends the Orion problem. It is the answer to a multitude of issues of a highly strategic nature. Without the current justification for its deployment, there are forces in this country which would make sure it never became a strategic factor of benefit to our side. Now the system will be an accomplished fact. And demonstrated. A functioning element. It will be an unimaginably powerful bargaining point in any current and future round of negotiation. It is, you see, our most effective deterrent to nearly every conceivable threat, from the ground or from space. It is something that must be done."

Sanders stopped himself at that, satisfied with the justification, but internally cautious that he may have gone too far, given away too much. Wilson and Gray could find nothing to say. They had understood him too well.

"Gentlemen, I appreciate the thoroughness of your research, and respect your professional ability, but I'm afraid you're on the wrong course. The conclusions you've presented to me today are interesting, but of no consequence to the activity we're now engaged in. I can only suggest that you study more carefully the steps taken at Fort Gabriel, and especially the test results from Dugway, and try to convince yourselves of the correctness of our position."

Wilson now was shaking his head, and Gray was finally about to protest, but Sanders silenced him and rose from his chair.

"Now, I've got to be returning to Sunnyvale. I left before resolving a few items there which require my attention. Keep at it. This is, after all, a very intriguing piece of research."

Before turning to leave, he offered a handshake to Wilson. "I do appreciate the work you've done. It's allowed our Dr. Gray to do some real engineering. If you'd like, I can get you in touch with Mel Dankin to discuss his methods. I'm sure he'll be glad to share ideas."

Wilson gave him no reply.

Gray walked out with Sanders. He was in a state of disbelief, felt one last attempt had to be made. Talking as they went, he said, "I'm not sure you realize the importance of this. We're not saying the device is entirely ineffective. It's a matter of how best to use it."

They passed the checkpoints, then went into the main lobby. Gray went on hurriedly: "The point is that we can use this information to better focus the energy levels so it will have an even greater chance to accomplish its mission. Look at it as a matter of fine-tuning. What we both want is the highest likelihood of success against *all* the mutations which could be encountered."

Sanders said nothing, acting only politely attentive. He opened the doorway and continued outside with Gray close beside him: "The fact that r_{14} may be dominant shouldn't preclude its effectiveness against the other forms."

They walked past the fence and circling ring of guards. Gray was about to go on, then paused, sensing something was not right. He stopped Sanders.

"Wait. Please."

Sanders frowned, now impatient. "Well, what the hell else?"

The PAGENT people were gone. Their white crosses had been painted red. On the building across the way a large white banner was hanging from third-floor windows.

An instant later they were hurled to the ground by the shock. The blast sent bricks and debris flying everywhere. A deafening roar echoed from every building of the Coast complex. Gray found himself tangled in a group of bushes, with dust and glass and unidentifiable pieces of matter filling the air overhead. He covered his head with his arms, waiting for it all to settle. Then he heard the shouting.

"An ambulance, get an ambulance. We need help here. Get the lab paramedics." The voices were chaotic, coming in from all around, as the debris came to rest, and the cloud of dust began to disperse.

Slowly Gray pulled himself free of the brush, checking for signs of injury, or blood. He hurt all over. He felt battered, but that was all he could identify. Across the way he spotted Sanders walking quickly toward the building opposite. There were now people everywhere. Two sirens in the distance began to register over his numbed ears and the background commotion. His mind was still dazed by the shock.

Staggering to his feet, he walked unsteadily in the direction where he had spotted Sanders. It was only then that he saw the letters of the large white banner, and read the words: *"PAGENT WILL STOP THE GENETIC GODS."*

He continued on, was halfway to the other side of the walkway before turning to look back at his own building. On one side there was a gaping hole, with a huge mound of brick and rubble lying beneath it. It appeared that a quarter of the building, or the lower side, had been blown apart. Then Gray shook, a tremor of cold fear coursing through his body. It was the side where Wilson's section had been.

He turned back, and one knee buckled slightly. Still he tried to walk toward the blast area, but as he approached was held back firmly by a military guard. There was one momentary perception of a stream of people scrambling out of the lobby, but that was his last vision. His eyes blurred, and he crumpled to the pavement.

The next morning his only sensation was motion. It was not unpleasant. He would have drifted asleep again if the others had not returned. But slowly he began to smell, a foreign scent of leather. And then feel. The pain. Soreness nearly everywhere. His whole body ached. That brought him gradually into full consciousness. Sounds were back now, a soft rumbling. Then the voice. Laine's.

"Are you in there?"

He tried to turn toward her. No. Too much pain. But he was now awake. In her car. Heading in some direction which seemed vaguely familiar.

"Where are we going?"

"To Woodside. Your house. We'll pick up whatever you'll need to stay with me for a while. I'm going to play nurse, your keeper for a few days."

Gray focused his eyes with some effort.

"Mark? What happened . . ."

"He's going to make it. Actually he looks worse than he really is. A concussion, and a hell of a lot of lacerations. Mostly he's in a lot of pain right now. But okay. You were both damned lucky."

"I wasn't even in the lab."

"Still close enough to be done in by flying shrapnel." She looked at him, trying to assess his shape. "You spent the night at Palo Alto–Stanford Hospital. Had to treat you for a mild concussion, and shock. How do you feel now?"

"Sore as hell."

"Again, you were lucky. One of the military guards

was killed. Two others fairly seriously injured. They think the one died before the blast—they've found stab wounds. Looks like PAGENT may have killed him to get close enough to leave their plastic explosive."

Gray's mind flashed back to the scene. Something returned in a hurry.

"Was it definitely set off outside?"

"Yes. That's the indication."

For wild moments the day before he had suspected Sanders. Anything was conceivable. But he knew his thought processes had been less than coherent. A vision reappeared of the right side of his building.

"The recombination section . . . how bad?"

"It's all a ruin. Somehow they knew exactly how to take out your part of the place. It's a small miracle Mark survived. They've quarantined everything." She paused a moment, worried. "Was he working on active forms of the anthrax?"

"No, thank God. Only benign synthetics. And computer models of the r_{14}."

Laine whispered, "Good."

"The sensor section. Any damage there?"

"None. A few things shaken loose, but it got through in nearly perfect shape. The sealed walls of the vacuum chamber worked as a good buffer—your section absorbed it all."

"Jesus Christ."

He stared out at the houses passing by along the parkway. Focusing again at various objects.

"What am I supposed to be doing?"

"Rehabilitating at my place in Moss Beach."

"And helping you decode the software?"

"No, I wouldn't think of that. You'd be useless in your current condition."

"The sensor staff will be needing me."

"Not right away. Even DISA has to understand. Now calm down and let me do your thinking. You're in no shape to worry, or to make decisions."

He tried to smile at her comment, but couldn't make it form. Then he asked, "Are you making progress with the alterations?"

She sighed. "No. Zero. I've got a working model, but no way into it."

"The lockouts?"

"Yes. Dammit, I know exactly what sequences need to go in, but haven't been able to sneak them by their DEFAUL system. It's just too well designed."

His mind drifted again into the passing traffic. Everything now seemed to be running into barriers, going nowhere, falling apart. They were losing. The opposition was too much for them, too well disciplined. And his side so vulnerable. She was trying her best, but only encountering frustration. His own effort, with Wilson, was ended. There was so little he had been able to contribute, while he could. Gray tried again to turn toward Laine.

He groaned. "Oh, this neck is useless."

"Just relax. You'll recover in a few days."

"What I was trying to say was that I want to help you. To get right into the software problems. I have to be useful for something. Maybe the sum of our geniuses will find a breakthrough."

"Or breakdown, if you don't let me concentrate on the problem." She smiled. A minute passed.

Then she suddenly slowed the car, moved into the right lane, startling him.

"What?" he asked.

"Sorry, but maybe you've already done it." She was excited, deep in thought.

"What have I done?"

"You don't see it, because this puzzle hasn't been part of your blood. But I've lived with this thing for weeks now. Which is probably why I didn't see it before. All it took was the right catalyst."

"I'm lost."

"It's simple. The sum of the parts being greater than the whole."

"Still too obscure."

"I can't sneak in a single logic change to the arming sequence because DEFAUL recognizes and kicks it back. Even if it's part of one of your inputs. But—we do it in very small steps. Each package you submit for the biology sensors carries only a tiny part of the modified sequence. A part that we make sure is actually used in your interface. We make the change by increments. After all the biology modules are safely inside, accepted and bundled into their central processor, the separate pieces will link together naturally to trigger our voltage transient during the arming command. All you have to do is string out the sensor inputs long enough, let's say in six to eight stages, and we'll have it."

He knew she had discovered the key. Her optimism was rarely unfounded. "You really think you're good, don't you?"

"I won't argue." She was busy planning. "All I need are the basics of what you've already got designed. If they're in the Coast computer, we can pull them out over the link at my place. Do you remember the file names?"

"Let's hope that part of my memory is intact."

They had nearly reached his house, were approaching Mountain Drive, when Laine recalled she had not yet told him of the unexpected letter.

"There's some other good news. I heard from Marya Scherensky a few days ago. She'd gotten a letter out with some Alternative Party friends. Apparently they've had her released from the clutches of the KGB, and she's doing some political work. Better still, she mentioned that some progress was being made on our request, but the result depended on the success of a contact she was about to make with someone in the Soviet Space Program. Told us to hope along with her."

"Good. I hope her struggles against the bureaucracy go better than ours have."

"Well, she's trying. Which is all we're doing."

"I still wonder if we're doing everything possible."

"What else is there? Beyond disarming the weapon."

"Seems like I could do something with Wilson's results. He's got the actual molecular blueprints on what's up there. There's always the chance of finding—"

"It's all gone, Daren. You can't do anything without the lab. Besides, even if you could replace everything, there are only four or five weeks left. Remember, the military spent a decade and got nowhere."

"Well, it was an amusing thought. If Wilson could work on it . . ." His voice trailed off.

"He can't work on anything. And you're still in shock. Anyway, we're there. I'll come in with you to look for things—you can't be trusted alone."

Chapter Twenty-two

He allowed his mind to roam freely this day. Anatole Karenov, imagined, could feel almost personally, the intense pressures which his American counterparts must be experiencing. It was understood throughout the world that the fate of civilization was soon to be decided—that the U.S. station called Orion was only twenty days from its descent. And also known within the Soviet Space Command were the terrible, frustrating delays which had been encountered by their civilian space agency in its attempt to reach the lethal spacecraft in time.

He could only speculate, and not objectively at that, on the probability of success associated with their other solution. They had stubbornly, and needlessly, held a curtain of secrecy about it, although the principal details were now familiar to Soviet intelligence, and to nearly everyone within the political structure on his level and above. The entire controversy had brought the collective Soviet thrust of political and scientific energy into focus on two issues—what could be done to prepare for Orion's fall, and how quickly could a response be made ready to this American escalation of space warfare. Karenov's involvement had been directed only toward the latter and had now taken him —despite his insubordination of the last few weeks, despite every attempt of measured resistance—inevitably and finally to the Baikonur Cosmodrome at Tyuratam.

He looked about the control center. It was larger, of substantially greater sophistication than that of Novosibirsk. The current operation was being handled by a team from the PKO Division, one not under his direct authority. These were specialists, an elite portion of the Air-Space Defense Directorate.

Yet normally he would have held an important position within the governing committee for this flight series. Today that was not to be. Karenov had been stripped of any active, participating role. Instead he was assigned the harmless function of consulting deputy director—the title "consulting" being a Soviet euphemism for "inactive." He was to be no more than an observer. It was the Party's least embarrassing censure. Effective. Obvious. Yet not necessarily terminal.

The small monitor station which had been provided him resounded just as noisily as the others, but there was no place upon its panels of lights and screens for him to register a single input. The station was itself no more than a listening post. He had been relegated to passivity and impotence. Yet his presence had been demanded. So he listened.

Voices over the primary network gave details of the SS-24 launch activity preparations. The final countdown was only minutes away. He heard a clear confirmation of "Petrograd Series A–Vehicle One completing final flight readiness sequences." Then the phrase "Warhead status affirmative" echoed clearly over all headsets, including his own. Next the voice of Alexis Duryanov could be identified, advising of tracking station readiness. Duryanov had taken Karenov's place on the mission directorate. It was a move Karenov had again felt compelled to express objection to, given the man's inexperience with mission operations and dubious judgment. Yet his views on that, as well as others, were now totally discredited. This final complaint had done nothing to lessen the disfavor which surrounded him. But it meant little.

He thought over the last weeks, which had become so instrumental in causing his own internal pendulum to swing back; away from those who supported the Soviet hard line. After the contact with M. Scherensky in Semipalatinsk it had no longer been possible to continue the lie. Where he had successfully set aside political ideology for pragmatism after the Geneva confrontation, the private discussions with the Alternatives finally reached him and reawakened all his old doubts.

It was unavoidably true that the Americans had provoked the issue, and pushed the Kremlin at exactly the wrong moment, in the midst of their own power struggle, yet it was clearly done in a belated attempt to correct mistakes made years earlier, in still another climate of paranoia and distrust. There was apparent justification for what was being done by their side. But the outward appearance of aggression was too much for the conservative element still controlling Kremlin policy to ignore.

He had sent his communiqué directly to the Politburo against the advice of Scherensky. She had urged him to move discreetly. But he knew there was not enough time to handle matters in that way. And without question the report so intelligently drafted by the Alternative's committee on space had made a profound difference in his thinking, giving him an additional degree of urgency. His sense of being so wrong, of having violated humanistic principles for the past twenty years, was heightened to a point where it could no longer remain suppressed.

Duryanov's voice broke into his thoughts: "Tracking stations for Vehicle One are now on active status. Vehicle Two tracking to be initiated in two hours, forty-five minutes. All networks are screening external interference." Then the mission director for PKO interrupted the net.

"Launch area—check. Support facilities—check. Block One and Two initiate standby. Final guidance procedures—check. Internal vehicle pressurants—nominal. Final warhead conditioning—accomplished." There was then a brief pause as other voices filtered onto the open line. A flurry of incoherent comments seemed to permeate the air, but Karenov recognized these as commonplace while all aspects of the launch system received their last confirmations. Then the PKO director could be heard once more.

"All supporting systems report affirmative. Terminate

final hold. Commence terminal-phase countdown. At two minutes . . . mark."

Karenov's display began its slow step-down in seconds from one hundred twenty. He returned his thoughts to his appearance before the Central Committee, which the unambiguous nature of his communiqué had provoked. They had summoned him directly to Moscow. He still could not shake the overwhelming feeling of despair which he carried away from there. The images played games with him. The unforgettably stifled cloister of the aged Politburo, who desperately clung to their last vestiges of power as they realized a new order threatened from within. Their indifference to, or inability to absorb, the argument of reason which he tried so intently to bring them. A rigidity which someday would certainly collapse, but possibly far too late. For now their reaction could only remain as it had always been. Exaggerated. Motivated by fear. Overdone.

He had at least been allowed to present his argument, yet throughout his long cross-examination he knew quiet checks were being made with Soviet intelligence. Checks to verify the validity of his information. Reappraisals of his own service record with the Party, and of his performance as chief of Soviet Space Operations. Careful examinations of KGB dossiers. While nothing in his past could be found to devalue his testimony, the aging leaders of the Soviet high command remained unmoved. Intelligence could only confirm and reinforce the Kremlin's worst fears. The Americans were about to introduce laser, even particle-beam weaponry into their space-defense arsenal. It was immaterial what the alleged purpose might be. The mere deployment of such capability was an unmistakable signal that the Soviets must once again demonstrate their own strategic superiority.

The voice registered firmly in his ears: "One minute to launch . . . mark." Now the red lights on his display panel were turning green, and a silent, expectant hush replaced the chatter of the last four hours. The overhead countdown display was at T minus 00:00:58, and marching steadily down.

Deep within his stomach he could feel a sickness stirring. He thought again of the document he was given by Scherensky weeks ago—*An Alternative View of Space Ideology*—the report which had compelled him to take what now was clearly a hopeless stand. It had considered the theoretical potential of having diverted the countless billions of dollars and rubles, the entire decades-long investment of scientific innovation of both powers, away from the strategic abuse of space and into, instead, its exploration and constructive exploitation. Mathematical estimates had been developed of what could have been, based upon what had been accomplished by both sides on relatively so little. Their assessment, relying only on the most conservative projections, still to him seemed incomprehensible. Given a modest amount of cooperation, there would now exist colonies ringing the polar caps of Mars, sophisticated astronomical observatories on the Moon's far side, a doubling of man's lifespan to support interplanetary flight. In five years, working colonies on the Saturn satellite known as Titan, with smaller research stations on Venus and the Jovian moon Io.

The overhead launch counter reached the five second point, and progressed relentlessly down from there to zero. There was a low rumble through the control area, a simultaneous display of fire and cloud on the visual monitor at its center. A mood of controlled excitement filled the control room at Baikonur Cosmodrome. The chief of PKO Division announced, satisfied, the successful liftoff of Petrograd Series A–Vehicle One.

Chapter Twenty-three

A status bulletin flashed in yellow on the information screen to the left of his command console. Yellow meant "of immediate interest," but whatever it was would have to wait. Gray was into third-phase checkout of the sensor array—its last complete verification before SCEPTER's final orbit adjustment. He put a fingertip to the pressure square beside the screen, and its message was instantly copied onto a yellow-bordered paper, which then dropped silently into his quickly filling data tray.

Gray focused his attention on the graphical figures in green oscillating rapidly upon the large monitor directly before him. The bio-sensor was checking out well against preprogrammed test patterns stored within the satellite's main memory. He knew the responses had to match perfectly those recorded six weeks earlier. So far, in the initial phases, they had. Since the flawless launch of SCEPTER the day before, this was his first opportunity to determine how invisible Laine's alterations would remain, in actual flight conditions, to the DEFAUL system. And how closely the modified sensor logic would approximate the original.

While he watched the patterns change on his screen as he commanded various operations from the colored pressure squares, Gray knew the emerging figures were being not only studied by himself, but watched just as intently by the mission director, whose interest would be as high as his own.

The final two test sequences were crucial—they were the most closely and delicately interwoven with sections of their modification. He sent in his commands, and stared expectantly. Green waves produced curving patterns over a fixed blue boundary, and continued doing so for ten seconds—then finally settled down into their proper places. He was afraid it had taken too long. Moments later a message displayed itself across the screen, and the curves faded from view. It read: "BIO-SENSOR FUNCTIONAL RESPONSE NOMINAL—SENSOR ACCURACY 99.98% OF EXPECTED VALUE."

He sighed with relief. That was close enough. Gray relayed the results directly to the mission director's status screen. Sanders at once returned a signal indicating their reception. Then his voice directed itself over the net.

"Looks very good, Dr. Gray. Appears we have an accurate system to play with. Great work."

Gray relaxed for the first time in hours. He pressed two switches, transferring control of the sensors back to central operations. Then requested a coffee, with sugar, from the automatic vend on his console. He tried to convince himself there had been no reason for the tension—their exhaustive planning weeks ago was now proving itself.

He settled back in his chair, and retrieved the last message from his data tray. It was an Orion status update. Gray read the one-page briefing that had been given to the press. The Orion Platform was closing in on the outer fringes of Earth's atmosphere, orbiting currently at an average altitude of 244 kilometers. NORAD in Colorado Springs, which was doing the tracking, now gave the spacecraft no more than twelve days—only ten before instabilities would make it impossible to attempt the manned rendezvous. USSA reported its Shuttle would be there in eight.

Gray thought about that. It was the same unfounded optimism USSA had been pushing to the public for months. He handed the bulletin to his deputy at the adjoining console—a DISA engineer named Sheffler.

"What do you think of this?"

The man read the press report.

"Well, it just reminds us how little time is left. We both know how close it is for USSA. If they can actually get the damned launch off in eight days, everything from there on has to go without a slip. They've left themselves nothing in the way of margin. I sure as hell wouldn't want to be one of Shuttle's astronauts."

Gray glanced away, studying the central monitors for a moment, then turned back to him.

"Sheffler, how is your family preparing?"

"Hell, there really isn't anything to prepare for, is there? They follow the news pretty closely, like everyone else, I suppose. Do you mean if we both blow it, and Orion comes down?"

"Yes. If that happens?"

"They'll all be together, watching it on the home screen. Right there with all the network commentators. Waiting to see exactly where the thing will enter, and who will be first. But as I understand it, that won't matter much. The stuff gets spread through the upper atmosphere. I guess it would all end fairly quickly. Unless, of course, the scientists come up with something by then."

"Will you be with them?"

The man was silent for a moment. Uneasy. "Don't know. They're in Virginia. I doubt it would be possible to get back there. In time." He paused, then asked, "Why so negative?"

Gray let it be. He reflected on the apparent mood of calm anticipation that was settling over the world during the final weeks. Last night's news carried a two-hour special on the public reaction. Beside the continuing hysteria on the Soviet side, and the bizarre business in India with millions migrating into the Himalayas, the planet's peoples seemed to have accepted the threatening event with a surprisingly stoic resignation. There was, of course, the outcry after the first disclosures, when PAGENT had tried, and failed, to move this country and the Europeans into a revolution against what they called the "technological complex." But they were never taken very seriously. And the political purges were now far behind.

He wondered how much of that resignation was natural, and how much the result of propagandizing done by USSA and supported by the administration.

The rationalization followed a simple theme—during the history of the U.S. space program, never yet had they failed to produce near-miracles when the public well-being or their own prestige was at stake. Certainly that was supportable by fact. Hadn't Apollo 11 made its scheduled appointment with the Moon within the decade of the sixties, as promised nine years earlier by the young President Kennedy? A crippled and half dead Apollo 13 successfully returned its crew of three astronauts from a week-long lunar circumnavigation. The potentially devastating Skylab was somehow nudged into a harmless descent over the remote Australian outback. Only the Russians had been guilty of producing a catastrophe. It could therefore be assumed that good fortune would again prevail, that USSA's Shuttle would reach its target in time, and the biological time bomb onboard Orion would be carried safely into the depths of outer space. So the story went.

Yet everyone connected with the program was aware the chances were not that promising. Greg Sanders, and the entire SCEPTER flight team, recognized that all too well. The frantic last-minute chaos taking place in USSA mission centers could not easily be hidden from those on the inside, who understood the reality of the technical problem. USSA was still running behind. Had it not been for the massive infusions of money from a desperately frightened Congress, the Shuttle would not even be in the race. It was perilously close, and close to being scandalous.

Their mission had now slipped a full month, which was very nearly too late. Only one week ago Shuttle had blown out one of its three orbital insertion engines during a routine test at Canaveral. Now they were scrambling to refit a replacement. Gray again considered their official schedule—that they were only eight days from reaching Orion. It was no more than a hope.

Privately, he had to admit moments when the decision to disable SCEPTER seemed unwise, possibly proving to be the ultimate blunder. At those times he could only find internal reassurance by returning to those underlying principles which, for him, retained their absolute soundness. In the end the solution could not be still another agent of destruction.

Gray studied the overhead mission monitors clustered at the center of the large control room, located within Sunnyvale's elaborate Defense Satellite Complex. They were now only seconds away from final orbit adjust. Sanders was guiding the operation professionally, as tightly as an orchestra leader. Everything was thorough, precise, and efficient. There had not even been the slightest hint of an anomaly for the contingency teams to resolve. It was just that very perfection which nagged at Gray. So far he had slipped by three complete sensor verifications without error. Each had been more demanding than the last, and each probed more deeply into the modified logical interfaces now hard-wired into the satellite's memory. But as a result of the Shuttle's excruciating launch delay, there would be at least another eight days of that to get through somehow.

He followed the countdown to orbit adjust to zero, then watched the monitor screens flash details of the burn progress. SCEPTER was quietly maneuvered into its final position, only a few hundred meters away from the Orion Platform. Soon the central monitor began relaying the first close-encounter color video of the target. There were murmurs of satisfaction from the room as Orion slowly swung its great bulk into the live view of man for the first time in ten years. To Gray the structure seemed oddly archaic—an awkward assembly of tanks, spheres, antennae, and curious cylindrical protrusions. He recalled the simulation witnessed months earlier in Brookhaven's JSC control room. The prominent features were the same as he remembered, but the three-dimensional impression before him now was much more vivid, a more ominous reality.

Sanders announced over the open net termination of the propulsive maneuver, and gave confirmation of final orientation. The cameras onboard SCEPTER held Orion fixed against the background black of space, then began a zoom process, which continued until the Platform entirely filled the screens of three separate perspectives. Gray was enchanted by the scene. He looked closely at his own monitor.

Orion was there, right before him. Fixing one image within the circular cross-hairs of his sensor-directional controls, he enlarged the object to four-power magnification. Gray studied the payload capsule, still fitted above its long-ago-failed propulsion system. The curved aluminum covering was a dazzling white, glistening with solar reflections. He stared more closely. Everything appeared to be intact, from all survey angles. All of its surfaces seemed clean—free of any visible sign of leakage, or corrosion, or perforation. Gray rolled the scan over the entire outside area. He found two micrometeoroid dents, but no indication of penetration. He switched to ten-power for a closer look at the indentations. After a full minute examining each, he could find nothing to suggest the slightest tear or breach of the outside shell. It was an encouraging start.

Gray's visual inspection was interrupted by the voice of Greg Sanders over his local net.

"Bio-sensor area, I know you are enthralled with the scenery, but it's time to place your array into its first scan survey, and SCEPTER is in attitude hold—ready for you. We need to begin phase one contamination search, Dr. Gray."

Gray recovered from the start he'd been given. "Affirmative. First sequences will be powered on right away. Sorry about the delay."

Forty-eight hours later, and ten days prior to the predicted Orion descent, the sensitive biology scanner onboard SCEPTER had not found the slightest evidence of external contamination to Orion's structure. The sensors had been put through every level of their organic spectra. Not a single microorganism was to be found, and to Gray's relief, not a single accidental signal had been sent prematurely into the satellite's flight computer. The search had now moved through every specific pattern of expected anthrax mutation, and through a huge variety of other possible, yet more benign, contaminations, with nothing showing itself. Not a trace of living bacterial existence. Whatever had in the past found its way to the outside of Platform Orion was by now either thoroughly sterilized or dormant. These were the welcome conclusions of their external survey.

On the fourth day of SCEPTER's mission the sensors were then directed into the x-ray mode, allowing the biology scanner to probe beneath the outer covering of the payload, and to "see" within the four sealed containers. Inside Orion's intended launch package the results were disturbingly different. The containers were teeming with life.

So intense were Gray's readings that the makeup of each individual cylinder could not be differentiated from the others, nor could the composition of any be broken down in order to isolate particular anthrax forms. The results were delivered to an offsite computer for additional analysis. Measurements from other sources put the pressure within the compartments very close to, and in some cases over, the bursting point.

Mission Director Sanders relayed the day's results directly to an anxious President Lansing, and also to the USSA operations at JSC, where hasty final preparations were being made for the long-awaited flight of the Shuttle.

It began with a threat from the Soviet ambassador. He delivered his government's message in person to the American President, warning that there would be a limited retaliation, an example made, if any command were initiated to trigger the SCEPTER weapon. They were following our mission closely with the aid of a nearby Cosmos satellite, and would know the instant anything like that occurred.

Immediately thereafter, a presidential directive was received by SCEPTER Mission Control. It was clear in its intent. After summarizing the Soviet position, an earlier order was repeated—that under no circumstances was the neutron laser to be armed, or fired, without specifically coded instructions from the White House. And that direction would be treated in the same regard as the code triggering an American nuclear retaliation.

Sanders took the directive into a private office. There

he spent a half-hour alone with his thoughts. For him the events were moving too fast to redirect. They were all being drawn toward one unavoidable end. He saw the President bound by political compromise, and unable to see the clear reality that the weapon onboard SCEPTER II would reduce the Soviet threat to empty bluster. Lansing was far too timid to make the proper decisions in these matters. The director of DISA considered his options.

Sanders made his decision early in the fifth day of SCEPTER's flight, with Platform Orion orbiting Earth at an altitude of 230 kilometers, and descending at an exponentially quickening rate. The reports from JSC that the engine replacement had gone smoothly and they now expected the Shuttle to meet its launch deadline no longer seemed relevant to him.

While Daren Gray studied the results of his latest internal scans, trying to understand nuances which might enable him to identify individual anthrax responses, the SCEPTER control room was quietly cleared of all non-essential personnel. That done, Mission Director Sanders issued his first unauthorized instructions to the flight team.

"We find ourselves with a time margin of seven days. And so far every aspect of our mission, and the vehicle itself, has been tested with professional thoroughness and found to be flawless. Today we will go through a simulated execution of the neutron-laser sequence. You will proceed immediately under my direction, with all built-in holds in effect. Please use the next half-hour to prepare your systems. The simulation will begin in thirty minutes."

His directive caught Gray completely off guard. He lost hold of a collection of papers, which spilled in disarray onto the floor beside Sheffler. This exercise would push the software to its limits, testing every carefully hidden electronic path they had designed into their interface. Laine had prepared for this specific simulation, but only to a certain level of laser system activation. Levels one through four of the exercise would avoid calling the dovetailing logic into play. But a level-five sim—a step which so closely paralleled the actual laser-arming sequence that it was indistinguishable to all but the central executive—would trigger it. Gray knew that level five was forbidden by flight procedures—it was to be performed only in the event of an anticipated weapon activation. Yet something inside warned him that he really had no idea how far Sanders intended to carry this.

He sent a message over the net to the mission director.

"Biology-sensor area requests to know on what levels the simulation is to be conducted."

The answer from the director was immediate, and simple: "That will be determined real-time. For now, consider it open."

Fear crawled over him. He gazed over the heads of the others seated around the circular rows of consoles. Beyond them DISA security guards were being stationed beside all doors, and the control room was sealed up.

Gray called the simulation procedures up on his instruction screen, and read through them thoroughly. There would be little for his area to do but watch, listen, and stay ready if actively called upon for support. He could only sit this one out. The operation required the direct involvement of nearly all other elements of the flight team, and they would be very busy.

He thought about Laine. She would know immediately what he was going through. Her secret phone tap with Sunnyvale would surely indicate to her remote monitor what action the mission director had taken—how close the simulation was about to come to them. If level five could be avoided, which Gray tried to convince himself by all premission ground rules it should be, they might squeak through.

In the dim quiet of Sunnyvale's Defense Satellite Complex control room, Greg Sanders began his simulation at 10:00:00 PST, without the consent of the President and hidden from view of the rest of the world. Only minutes prior to that time he had received the response from NORAD tracking providing him the precise location, over the next twelve-hour period, of the Soviet Cosmos satellite monitoring their operation.

The flight team, working in its most intensive mode, carried SCEPTER II and its weapon system painstakingly through sim levels one, two, and three, and by 13:30 hours level four had been directed, and begun. This part of the exercise would be even more time-consuming, and exhausting. At every stage leading up to the simulated arming sequence, the built-in holds were longer, while more details of the logical processes were inspected and evaluated. The flight version of DEFAUL was operating at maximum screening sensitivity. Gray sat nervously as each segment took seemingly forever to work through. The amount of coffee he consumed was doing little to ease his emotional state. Only once was he given the distraction of activity as his team was called upon to give a mock verification of a specific sensor scan. But that had been routine, taking up only fifteen minutes.

By mid-afternoon, Gray was beginning to feel they had survived—there was no evidence that a level-five sim would be commanded, at least not this day. The flight team had now been through six strenuous and uninterrupted hours of training. It seemed unlikely that Sanders could ask much more. And level four was nearing its last twenty minutes—the set of commands prior to arming—the procedure which was to condition the particle-beam column to the extreme temperature conditions necessary to generate the deadly stream.

And there it surfaced. A red alarm appeared in an indistinguishable garble of letters on one of the central overheads. Gray was thrown into panic—he could only hope the anomaly report was for another system, anything besides the arming logic.

Seconds elapsed while the screen seemed to fight to unscramble itself. The red background was running too rapidly to read, overlapping messages with other messages. Finally it settled on two lines which could be read and understood by everyone: "FLIGHT DEFAUL PROJECTING CONDITION FATAL TO SUBSEQUENT ARMING SEQUENCE—AUTOMATIC HOLD NOW IN EFFECT."

It was over. Gray surveyed the agitation erupting about the control area. Sanders and his deputies were huddled around their command consoles, frantically calling in reports from all systems. When he decided there was enough random activity for him to move unnoticed, Gray handed control of the sensor array over to Sheffler, excused himself, and feigning a case of nausea to the security guards, quietly left the room. Within five minutes he was in his campervan headed north on the Junipero Sierra Freeway toward San Mateo, and then the coast towns.

It took the special team Sanders called in thirty minutes to identify the exact nature of the condition uncovered by DEFAUL after it choked on the spurious signal deep within SCEPTER's central memory. After another forty minutes, a thorough analysis by DISA's contingency software experts had traced the damaging logic threads directly to the bio-sensor interfaces. One hour later the alteration was purged by ground commands to the satellite, ordering its flight computer to bypass the fatal logic. Nearly the same moment agents of the FBI and Defense Intelligence Agency were moving with instructions to arrest Daren Gray and Laine Jeremy.

Gray had no way of knowing that despite everything they had attempted, SCEPTER's particle beam was about to perform its first real assignment flawlessly. By evening, the Soviet monitor Cosmos 1244—orbiting in formation high above the two U.S. spacecraft—would suddenly and inexplicably have been surgically rendered inoperable.

The town of Moss Beach, colored by a hazy late-afternoon sun, appeared tranquil enough as he passed through. Just beyond it Gray pulled over to the beach side of the highway. He looked up, but could not quite see through the cedars obscuring his view of the bluff. He opened the door and cautiously emerged from the van, gradually changing positions near it until he had a clear vantage point. The panic he felt in the control room returned. They already had her.

Around the Jeremys' driveway he could pick out three or four unfamiliar, innocuously colored sedans. Then, straining for a closer look, he noticed the highway-patrol vehicle further down the hill. Its lights were off. Gray thought it would have taken them more time. Maybe it had been the phone link.

Now there was nothing left to do but run, and disappear somewhere. Laine was lost. He had no way to change that.

He got back into the campervan. They would surely be looking for it, but it seemed unwise to be on foot around Moss Beach. He'd drive north, taking all the back roads he knew, then lose himself in the valley, or in the city.

Slowly Gray pulled onto the highway, hoping he could get by the Sandia Road turnoff to Laine's. It was now just ahead, and there seemed to be no sign of the police, or of anything else unusual. He drove past at a steady speed, fixing his gaze straight ahead. Then he was safely beyond the intersection.

From nowhere a dark brown car swerved directly in front of him. There had been no warning. He clutched the steering wheel, fighting for control, trying to avoid it, but the other car was now rubbing against his, forcing him over to the side. They slid together for forty meters. Both vehicles came to a dusty halt, far over into the dirt shoulder, and he looked about frantically for some way to escape, to pull away or turn around. For a brief moment he wondered if they would shoot him. He grabbed the shift lever, slamming it into reverse.

Then he glanced back for an instant toward the blocking automobile. Inside a figure was waving violently with its arms. The figure was female. He stopped. It was Laine. Within seconds of that recognition he left the van sitting where it was, engine off, and scrambled into the other vehicle, in the front seat beside her.

Still startled by the encounter, he could only exclaim, "Thank the gods you're all right, but, Christ, you gave me a scare."

She didn't bother with a reply, instead pulled at once into the northbound traffic, matching her speed with its flow. Then she looked over at him, her own relief showing on her face.

"Look, it's just a damned good thing you got here

when you did. I was going to give you a few more
minutes, and then vanish. That is, if I had been able
to."

"Whose car do we have?"

"A neighbor's. That part, at least, went well. He
works in the city. Stays there all week. He shouldn't
be missing it until the weekend. Also conveniently
leaves his keys in the ignition, with the car locked inside his garage. The only tricky part was finding a way
into the house. I started on that soon after the alarm
was triggered at Sunnyvale."

"So you knew right away. I was hoping you would."

"Yes, goddammit. Gave me just enough time to
gather enough money to last us a few days. And then
get the car."

"I'm glad I was included."

"I still can't believe it. We should have been safe
through a level four. Something makes me think they
were actually carrying out level-five sequences."

"I wouldn't be surprised. Sanders was up to something beyond normal mission training." Gray thought
about the last hours inside mission control. "The man
was obsessed." He paused a moment.

"It's all over now, Laine. They've won."

She stared ahead into the oncoming traffic, carefully
searching for signs of police or highway patrol.

"Where are we going?" Gray asked her.

"North, hopefully. Far north. To my uncle's estate.
No one should be there—it's all tied up in escrow. And
too remote for anyone to find us for a while. I'm sure
Henry won't mention it. There's a small guest house
way back in the woods. Rough, but livable. Now all
we have to do is get there."

"What if they check your neighbor's place and contact him?"

"Unlikely. He's not that close to me. Over the ridge
and down a couple of houses. I can't think of any
reason why they would check there. Unless . . . unless
I was noticed driving away."

Gray tried to think rationally. "Okay, what's the
most likely thing for them to do? They have your car
sitting unused at the cabin. And mine should be dis-

covered pretty quickly. They'll decide either we're hiding somewhere in that area or traveling damned fast away from them in another vehicle."

"At least they have no idea what kind. To our advantage."

"Maybe, for a while. But there will be descriptions of us over the police net. It might be better to take the back roads over the foothills, then through suburbia, than to stay on the highways."

"Fine. You guide. Just get us into Marin County, and from there we should be all right."

They turned off California 1 at Vallemar, and Gray picked out a way along dusty farm roads until they reached the outskirts of San Bruno. From there, with the help of a city map, they gradually wove a path through the suburbs, avoiding all the primary boulevards. The drive circled through Serramonte, Broadmoor, Daly City, then right up through San Francisco. At Marina they had to move back onto the highway leading toward Golden Gate.

Finally they were on the bridge. Far behind Laine spotted the flashing lights of a highway patrol car.

"Christ, turn on the CB scanner. There's something coming up way behind us."

Gray looked back. "Still quite a distance away. This traffic won't bother to let him through until we're past the bridge. But you'd better get lost immediately once we're over there, just in case he's looking for us."

She kept driving, and the flashing lights moved insistently closer, now perhaps a tenth of a kilometer back. Gray switched on the scanner, but found the police bands conspicuously silent. When they reached the last portion of the elevated, the siren became audible. But the heavy flow of traffic continued, and they stayed sheltered in its midst.

At the state-park exit she turned off, swiftly dropping down along the exit ramp, hugging the inside rail. Gray watched toward the rear—about thirty cars behind them the highway patrol vehicle, with its lights still flashing, had taken the same exit.

"It's looking worse. First turn you come to, take it. We have to lose him."

"All I can do is head into the park."

"Do it. But open it up."

She swung the car past the park entrance, and took a long winding road to the right. They came to a string of parked cars, and Gray had her stop there, and pull in beside them.

They both jumped out, and headed into the woods. They ran for a minute, then out of breath, stopped to look back. Seconds later the patrol car moved rapidly past the parking area, then beyond. It slowed, hesitant at first, then backed directly in reverse to the end of the row of cars, stopping beside theirs.

Gray, his heart pounding, pulled her with him further into the trees.

"What now?" she said, still trying to catch her breath.

"We get the hell out of here. That's what. We'll have to find our way back through the park, and get to the freeway. Then hitch a ride north. But we'd better get moving—it's going to be dark in a hurry. You good at running?"

"I'll make it. Just find the right direction."

They ran, walked, and stumbled for half an hour through Headlands State Park, until they had reached its north border, by the highway. It then took fifteen minutes before they caught a ride with a computer salesman going to Petaluma. There they risked a Trailways for the trip north along 101. Twelve hours later, with only occasional sleep, they had reached a restaurant on the outskirts of Eureka, still hours away by car from Burnt Ranch, out 299. After a quick sandwich, Laine made a phone call to Mark Wilson, trying his apartment first, then his Stanford office. He answered at neither place.

A young vacationing couple from Illinois carried them to Burnt Ranch, and from the main road they hiked the last six kilometers to the estate, and then another kilometer to the guest house beyond the main building. She opened it up, and they collapsed, exhausted, into a large, quilt-covered bed.

During the long bus trip Laine had explained Wilson's final research to Daren. Later that evening he reached Wilson by phone. They talked for over an hour. The following day Daren Gray put a call through to Washington, D.C., over the land line, which was all that was available from the estate. He asked to speak with someone on the President's staff.

Chapter Twenty-four

As far as Greg Sanders knew, it would remain for eternity his secret. He was never required to account for his neutralization of the Soviet spy satellite. Now SCEPTER had been returned, under his command, to its scheduled mission. While the onboard biology scanners maintained real-time observation of Platform Orion from half a kilometer away, he watched his monitors flash details of the long-delayed Shuttle launch from Cape Canaveral. Within the sealed confines of DISA-SCEPTER Control, Sanders felt confident his group was prepared for whatever might arise in the hours ahead.

Inside USSA Mission Control at Houston faces on their flight personnel were intense, strained, much less assured. The final delay was costly—they were now operating on the ragged edge of orbital instability. The Platform had already begun a slow, regular tumble. With all supporting systems active, Mission Director Kline made one last contact with DISA, confirming their target was still free of contamination, before giving his final *go* to the Shuttle crew of four. After all the frantic months they were at last in space, and approaching sight of Orion. Kline issued the commands which had to be accomplished within the next eight hours, before the entire assembly would dip into the Earth's atmosphere and be lost. He first directed initiation of Space Tug deployment, communicating with the Shuttle commander over local relay satellite.

The Shuttle stationed itself within EVA distance of the slowly turning target, at about one hundred meters standoff. Minutes later its cargo bay doors parted, then opened wide, exposing to the black vacuum of space the vehicle nestled within its cylindrical storage hold. The Space Tug rested motionless there, like a caterpillar suddenly stripped of its cocoon. Three EVA-suited astronauts entered the cargo bay, then began guiding the release mechanism which moved the Tug gently from its nest, into the openness. The bulky assembly of propulsion tanks and thrusters separated from its last link, unfolded, and now under its own awakened power left the mother ship, maneuvering purposefully into the close vicinity of Orion. It would wait there, holding tight formation with the structure, while the astronauts performed the intricate removal and transfer of Orion's lethal payload.

The operation required the involvement of all four men. Commander Erhardt, the only Apollo veteran, remained inside the Shuttle, controlling its orientation, providing the relay for all ground-space communication. Co-pilot Jensen located himself at his monitor station in the cargo bay, which was to serve as the primary television observation point. After all readiness checks were complete, the two astronauts trained to perform the mechanical surgery, Halverson and Garcia, activated the maneuvering units of their packs, and propelled themselves gracefully through the starlit void toward the imposing structure of Orion.

They carefully matched body rates with the turning Platform, and settled gently, equipment modules strapped in place, onto its cluttered deck. Immediately their work began—the equipment packs were securely velcro-fastened to the Platform, and tool units retrieved from them. Both studied the ten-year-old propulsion system that had once been intended to solve the problem they now faced. Its length was perhaps only four meters, with the biology capsule located that distance from the deck. A variety of instruments would have to be relayed for the final detachment activity. But they had spent months rehearsing the technique.

First the propellent-arming circuits of the old system were deactivated by Garcia, the electronics specialist. That operation proceeded quickly, smoothly, taking no more than fifteen minutes. Then began the more delicate procedure.

Halverson maneuvered directly to the payload, and thoroughly inspected the outside capsule. Its appearance was as had been reported—the aging process of space having done nothing visibly more than discolor a few patches of protective coating. He quickly identified the rows of aluminum connectors which circled in three lines just above the propulsion stage. With the special tools handed him by Garcia, he methodically released each one individually, until the upper package could be loosened from the main fuselage. Both men now used their pressure wrenches to pry the capsule to a point where they could access the internal harness of umbilicals.

It then became a matter of severing, carefully and in specific sequence, each line connection that existed between the biology compartment and its electronic package below. The process was slow. With both men working constantly, it still took over two hours to perform that part of the surgery. Then the last link was cut, and the capsule finally wrestled free.

Garcia returned to the deck, sorting and replacing his collection of space tools. Halverson alone carried the payload to one end of Orion, clamping it tightly in place for temporary storage. Mission Director Kline studied the operation over his monitors, pleased everything had gone so smoothly to that point. As the huge disk of Earth rotated beneath the astronauts, all eyes in the control rooms far below were fixed on the fascinating view of their orbiting workshop. Erhardt at the Shuttle's controls relayed a flurry of satisfied messages that passed among the participants of this drama in slow motion.

Garcia and Halverson felt it at once—the sense was an abrupt disorientation. Orion suddenly changed its turn rate. Erhardt immediately relayed the message to them from ground—his voice crackling over the headsets.

"We've hit a local density pocket. Your rate is up to three-point-four cycles per minute. Can you adjust?"

As Halverson steadied himself against a nearby antenna mount, he heard Garcia shout over the net, in alarm.

"Where the hell is the Tug? It's out of view. Behind us!"

The collision was violent. Halverson wrapped his arms around the mount as he watched the far end of Orion crumple sickeningly against the mass of the Space Tug. The jolt sent pieces of spacecraft hardware glancing away in all directions. He could do nothing but watch, and clutch the structure tightly, struggling to keep himself in place. Then he heard the horrible scream.

Where he had last seen Garcia there was only part of a spacesuit, covered in red, snagged between sections of both vehicles, which were now entangled in an ugly metallic crush. The ear-splitting scream died away into a low rumble, then was drowned out by the panicked voices relayed from Mission Control. Moments later he saw Garcia's tumbling, twisted form drift away into the eternal black.

Halverson considered going after him. But that would be difficult. He was still fighting to keep his own orientation. Soon the voices began to register in his mind. They should be told what was happening.

"Garcia's been hurt—broken loose. Somehow I should bring him back. It's a mess up here."

The reply from Director Kline was firm: "Negative. Stay where you are. The Shuttle position scan shows him moving out of range of your maneuvering unit. Just hold in place—we'll bring him in later. Are you okay, Halverson?"

He tried to determine that.

"Yes. Only shaken up. My suit and pack appear normal. Headset readings are all right."

"Good. Then just hold tight for the moment."

There was nothing but eerie silence for half a minute. Then another response from Kline.

"Can you give us a report on the Orion capsule?"

He looked for it. Part of Orion's structure now lay beside the unit, partially obscuring his view. But he could tell it was still there.

"We have it."

"Any apparent damage? To the capsule?"

Halverson strained to look through the tangle of hardware.

"None that I can see."

There seemed to be a reluctant pause from Mission Control before Kline made his next request.

"Halverson, as soon as you regain your full orientation, would you give us a first-hand assessment of what we have there? We need a damage survey of both spacecraft. How badly are they tangled? It doesn't look good from our perspective. Are you up to that?"

He steadied himself. The shock was diminishing. His balance mechanisms had nearly readjusted to the new motion of the spinning assembly.

"Yes. I can do that. I'm all together now."

After resetting his pack stabilizer, Halverson steadily made his way, hand-over-hand, to the crumpled end of Orion. There he closely inspected the area where the Space Tug appeared to be firmly enmeshed with the Platform. He relayed each observation back through the Shuttle cockpit to Mission Control. Then concluded, "It's too tight for us to work loose manually with the tools available. But the Tug engines seem intact, and the propulsion structure is in reasonably good shape. Looks usable."

There was another stony silence as he realized what was being considered. So he added, "A good blast from the main thrusters should force it free."

He understood that they would not ask him for much more—especially not what was obviously the next step. And he knew that all cameras and sensors were trained on him, waiting expectantly. He moved slightly, locating the attachment point designed to hold the payload capsule on the Tug's forward end. It was clear. Undamaged.

"I'm going to carry over the payload," he radioed back.

"We can send Jensen to help," the voice of Director Kline offered.

"Negative. Let's not risk anyone else. I can get it done."

Halverson moved carefully, deliberately back to the payload, pushing loose pieces of structure out of his way. It was still clamped firmly where he had left it. Then he noticed the tear.

"Christ! The damned thing's open." He hesitated for only a moment. Then his gloved hands reached down to undo the fasteners. "I'm going to finish this," he said, this time more softly.

The warning from SCEPTER appeared simultaneously inside the Sunnyvale complex—adding to the set of red alarms which had already been triggered—and on the control consoles of USSA-Houston, still reeling from the shock, then was relayed instantly up to the stunned Shuttle Commander Erhardt.

Director Kline at once shouted the message over all their headsets.

"We have positive bio-readings. Repeat, positive bio-readings. Terminate your activity now. Re-synch your pack stabilizer and return to the Shuttle."

The lone astronaut onboard Orion looked again at the gaping wound on one side of the package now in his hands. It seemed harmless enough. And it had to be done.

"I'm going to get this damned thing connected to the Tug. If you can blast free, we can still do our mission." He wrapped an arm about the capsule, and moved on.

Erhardt exclaimed from inside the Shuttle, "Let it be. For god's sake man, get the hell off there. We have biology escaping. Get off the damned thing now."

He ignored the plea, continuing toward the crumpled end of the structure.

Kline came on again: "Halverson. You are ordered to—"

Halverson switched off his headset receiver. Then replied, "We'll get this baby launched yet."

A minute later he was at the attachment point. With his body framed against the silver assembly, the dizzying images of Earth and Shuttle sweeping by at a terrific rate, he began making the three necessary connections in slow, cautious succession. He was too involved with the details to notice the blue film gradually forming about the payload capsule. Nor did he have time to be concerned when the light blue aura began to surround his space suit.

But Jensen could pick it out from his vantage point on Shuttle.

"Christ, Halverson, there's some sort of vapor condensing around you. Get your ass out of there," he shouted futilely over the net. The plea could not be heard.

Finally, after another long minute had slipped by, Halverson rechecked all his connections, and transmitted the message of his success with undisguised relief: "There. It's done. You should be able to send this thing off now. I'm leaving."

The entire Orion Platform was now enveloped in a glowing film of blue. Halverson reset his pack stabilizer, activated the maneuvering unit, and gently drifted off the tumbling structure. His form stabilized as he propelled himself toward the waiting Shuttle. Only then did he notice the waving arms of Jensen in the cargo bay, and his obvious agitation. He switched on his headset to hear the alarmed cries. They registered as he came to rest on the cargo bay deck.

Jensen was hysterical. "You're covered with the stuff, goddammit. Get off so they can analyze what the hell it is. Jesus, it's probably the biology."

Halverson steadied himself, looking down at his lower suit, then at his arms, haloed by the aura. The recognition was slow. He turned to look back at Platform Orion, now pulsing with the same ghostly blue light. An intense concentration of the mist began to build at a single point of his support pack—beside the external vent which provided him release of excess water vapor. The concentration grew more intense, enlarging itself into a bright sphere. Then in an instant, it diminished.

The infiltration was successful. And quick. Halverson had only one brief moment of comprehension. Then a sudden cold wave of nausea swept through his body. There were two convulsions, and he was dead.

Jensen dived toward the Shuttle airlock. But he was too slow. The blue film already filled the cargo hold, clinging to and seeking out everything within. It surrounded him in seconds. He had time only to shout a final warning to the last man inside: "For god's sake, stay in there. Lock it all up. It's all over."

The aura enveloping his suit formed itself again into a bright local concentration, then broke through his last point of resistance. He felt a cold tremor, like an icy wind, and was gone.

A stunned Mission Control had picked up only fragments of the conversation. Desperately they tried to communicate with Erhardt.

The Shuttle commander responded, in shock: "Some sort of mist out there. Covering everything. I think we're lost Halverson, and Jensen too. Can you see this thing over the monitors?"

Mission Control had seen it all too clearly. So had the sensors and video scanners onboard SCEPTER II. The biological intensities it recorded were giving readings ten times greater than what had been expected of the anthrax. That report was relayed by Greg Sanders directly to USSA-Houston, and then to the White House. Kline sent the communication to Erhardt.

"Shuttle, this is Mission Control. We have confirmed data from the SCEPTER flight team. What you have around the spacecraft, and your ship, is an active form of the anthrax biology." There was a nervous pause. "We can't let you bring it back to Earth."

Erhardt remained silent for grim seconds. Not fully believing. Finally he responded: "Okay. I have the commands ready to fire the Tug main propulsion. We can still tear it loose, and get the capsule off."

A helpless Mission Control did nothing to interfere. They all stood by passively as he initiated his brief countdown. At the signal every engine on the

Space Tug fired to its maximum thrust. But the vehicles stubbornly remained locked together. When the burn was terminated, the assembly was spinning even more wildly out of control. And the blue aura persisted, swirling with Orion as a small spiral galaxy.

Kline could offer no more than sympathy in his communication with the last man.

"Jim, I'm sorry. That was a good try." He paused. "The Platform cannot come down. We can't have any of this come back in. Do you understand what I'm telling you? We will have to go with their other option. It's all that's left."

Erhardt sat motionless at his controls within the Shuttle cabin, watching the tumbling structure in the distance. He only partially understood.

"Yes, yes. I realize what you mean. But, Jesus, what am I supposed to do? I can't sit here indefinitely, waiting for this miserable stuff to find a way inside."

Greg Sanders interrupted over the voice net from Sunnyvale: "Commander Erhardt. Director Sanders here, from DISA-SCEPTER Control. You won't have to wait."

He placed a call directly to President Lansing. The situation, he explained, was now hopeless. Permission was requested to activate the neutron laser. Lansing answered him more forcefully than expected, as if the President finally grasped the enormity of the decisions they would now make. They discussed the unavoidable actions which had to be taken—and their consequences. Permission to arm the weapon was granted.

As Sanders prepared the final commands to condition SCEPTER's energy column, the President placed a call of his own, over the direct relay to Moscow. The dialogue with the Kremlin was of no use. There was not the slightest trace of understanding on that side. The American President was advised to expect a limited retaliatory strike somewhere within the United States. It would happen within the next two hours.

From the control center at Sunnyvale final commands were sent up to SCEPTER. The neutron laser focused its line of sight on the blue-haloed Orion Platform, then full power was channeled into the beam. Erhardt was warned not to look—but could not take his eyes off the scene.

It was dazzling in brilliance. The resulting burst sent a wave of small particle debris showering against the Shuttle, rocking the ship. The light blinded its only survivor. What had moments before been Orion was now transformed into a glowing sphere.

Sanders' operations chief, in charge of sending the commands to SCEPTER, looked up at the DISA director, the expression on his face questioning the second set of signals he was given to transmit.

Sanders displayed not a shade of emotion.

"They are straight from the President. These are his decisions now."

The commands were sent. SCEPTER turned twenty degrees, trimmed its attitude precisely, then fired a second burst of particle-beam energy directly into the Shuttle, turning it instantly into a second ball of illuminated dust. The energy transformations produced two brilliant nebula.

SCEPTER's onboard sensors studied the phenomena, measuring and recording every last detail. Greg Sanders' eyes roamed from screen to screen, sharing SCEPTER's vision of the spectacular event, fascinated by the power he had just unleashed. At one corner of his console one display began a wild oscillation. It was seconds before he noticed the indicator alarm above his monitor glowing bright red. His attention went immediately to the display panel.

The biology sensors now revealed the resumption of intense biological activity—first one hundred, then one thousand, then one million times greater than even the initial readings from the opened payload. Sanders could only stare numbly at the figures flashing on the panel before him, growing at a rate his mind could no longer grasp. He looked again at the television monitor, the image being captured in real time by SCEPTER's onboard cameras.

As he watched, the two spherical forms which once contained Earth life became transfigured, reassembling into a single, overpowering blue radiance. They began an exponential expansion. Growing beyond all limits. Feeding off the energy. Merging together into one pulsating blue star-burst of pathogenic biology.

Only then did he comprehend the terrible, final truth. The mass was alive, and coming in. There was now absolutely nothing that could be done to prevent it.

Chapter Twenty-five

It was too late for President Lansing to find Daren Gray. The Pan Am 777 had landed at Christchurch hours before, and an inconspicuous group led by the young American was making its way by bus to a remote ranching community far up into the hill country.

Only two weeks had passed since a scarred, bandaged Mark Wilson discharged himself from Palo Alto–Stanford Hospital to retrieve copies of the anthrax DNA blueprints from his apartment in Mountain View. With some small programming assistance from Laine Jeremy, those were fed to the Stanford IBM 3034—along with the massive data catalogues supplied by Cornell. The catalogues contained billions of biological and environmental conditions from every conceivable region on Earth. It was not until the day SCEPTER trained its particle beam on Cosmos 1244 that the search converged to a positive result.

Stanford's computer found certain species of sheep native to New Zealand had produced an effective antibody forty years earlier against a local epidemic of one obscure form of anthrax. The immunity would be passed naturally through all subsequent generations. Its molecular structure dovetailed perfectly with that of anthrax-r, forming a genetic hybrid, a neutral bacterium. But the reaction was possible only within the unique biological environment of that isolated island nation. Most of their population would in fact be carriers of the antibody, and already immune. The process of extracting a serum from the island's sheep was straightforward.

Gray knew nothing of this activity until their escape to northern California. The call to Mark Wilson provided him with the details. The actions to take from that point became clear.

The nature of his news had gotten him the direct, personal attention of the President. He explained over the phone how a serum could be derived quickly, but would be effective only in New Zealand. There had been a suggestion that perhaps certain prominent people, scientists, officials, the nation's leaders, might take the precaution.

But Lansing refused to be put into the position of making those godlike decisions. He maintained their hopes rested with the astronauts of the USSA mission. Beyond that it was a matter for fate to resolve. As Gray heard what he suspected were tracers being connected to the line, he ended their conversation. The responsibility for what he then did was taken without hesitation or regret.

Mark Wilson was sent immediately to Christchurch, to produce the serum and locate a place for them to stay. A select group of primarily Stanford people—researchers, educators, and their close circle of friends—were asked to join them in a unique adventure—the possibility of beginning a new civilization. The twenty-five who had taken Gray seriously were onboard the Pan Am flight that morning.

On the bus carrying them into the foothills leading to Coleridge, Gray gave Laine's hand a gentle squeeze. News of the space disaster, as well as of the Soviet strike against Atlanta, had reached airport television, so they knew there was little time. A few days at the most. The hills ahead were green and inviting. Gray was reminded of the Sierra in late fall—the forests waiting for winter snows to turn everything white. He smiled. Their search could not have found a better location to begin again. And the Aquarian civilization would not repeat the errors of its predecessor.

ABOUT THE AUTHOR

Scott Asnin has been professionally involved with space mission design for fourteen years, with the Boeing Company, TRW Systems, and the Martin Marietta Corporation. During the 1970s, as a member of an advanced planetary programs group, his technical papers were presented to aerospace conferences at Vail, Colorado; Palo Alto, California; and Nassau, Bahamas, and were published in the *Journal of Spacecraft and Rockets*. Mr. Asnin is the recipient of numerous company awards for his treatises on spaceflight. His writings have dealt with missions to flyby Venus into Mercury orbit, a Venus orbiter capable of mapping that planet's surface by peering through its dense cloud cover with radar, and the concept of using unmanned spacecraft to retrieve a sample of the Martian surface for Earth-based analysis. He has also developed mission designs for Lunar Orbiter, Apollo, comet rendezvous, outer-planet Grand Tours, the Viking Mars Lander, and, more recently, a last-minute proposal to save Skylab using a Shuttle-carried space tug. He is a 1966 graduate of Iowa State University with a degree in aerospace engineering.

Characterizing himself as a contemporary mountain man, he spends his leisure time cross-country skiing, hiking in the Rockies, motorcycle touring, listening to jazz, and dabbling with poetry and essays. He lives in a mountain home which he designed and built in the hills west of Boulder, Colorado.